HOMETO

HOMETOWN HEARTS

The Sheriff of Heartbreak County

KATHLEEN CREIGHTON

◆ **HARLEQUIN**® HOMETOWN HEARTS

ISBN-13: 978-0-373-21458-7

The Sheriff of Heartbreak County

Printed in U.S.A.

Kathleen Creighton has roots deep in California soil but has relocated to South Carolina. As a child, she enjoyed listening to old-timers' tales, and her fascination with the past only deepened as she grew older. Today, she is interested in everything—art, music, gardening, zoology, anthropology and history—but people are at the top of her list. She also has a lifelong passion for writing, and now combines all her loves in romance novels.

For Gary, who brought the butterfly that sits on my shoulder.

Prologue

On Florida's Gulf Coast...

The telephone was ringing. Joy opened her eyes and saw that it was morning. Beside her, Scott stirred, swore and stretched out an arm to pick up the bedside extension. He growled, "Cavanaugh," then lay back to listen, responding from time to time with monosyllables, while Joy lay on her side and watched him, drinking in the newness and unimaginable sweetness of the miracle of him. Happiness lay on her like sunshine. Yancy was safe. And Scott loved her.

She thought, maybe my karma's finally changed.

Scott cradled the phone, lay back on the pillows and reached his arm around her to pull her close. "That was Agent Harvey," he said.

"About Yancy?" Joy craned to look up at him. "Have they finished questioning her? When can I see her?"

"Joy…" He enfolded her in his arms, and her heart began to thump against his chest.

"What's wrong? Scott? When can I see her?"

His sigh lifted her like a boat on a swell. "Sweetheart… I'm sorry. I'm afraid that's not going to be possible."

"Why? What—"

"Yancy's going into the federal witness protection program," he said softly. "Immediately. She's a witness to the murder of the DelReys' housekeeper and her husband. Plus, it seems Junior was really in love with her, and planned to marry her. He told her enough about the family business that she's never going to be safe as long as any of the DelReys or their organization are running around loose. She's got no choice, sweetheart. I'm sorry."

"I can't…" Joy swallowed, pain rushing into her chest and throat. "I can't even…say goodbye?"

Scott shook his head, bumping her head with his chin. His voice was rusty with sympathy and compassion. "I'm afraid not. She's already gone. They did it last night, right after she left you. It's done."

She was silent, weeping without shaking, without sobs. Scott held her, saying nothing, simply giving her his love…his strength.

Chapter One

Ten years later, in Montana...

The body lay as it had fallen, arms outflung, eyes staring into the wide Montana sky fabled in story and song. Except for the hole in the center of his forehead the expression on the victim's face was one familiar to all who knew him, an arrogant smirk that held no traces of fear or surprise.

Clearly, Jason Holbrook had not expected to die.

Not today, anyway, and for sure not like this, thought Roan Harley, duly elected sheriff of Hart County. Gunned down in his own driveway on a cool spring day like a mean and dangerous dog, which, come to think of it—and the sheriff knew he wasn't alone in this opinion—described the victim pretty well.

"Tom," he said gently to the deputy breathing heavily over his right shoulder, "if you're gonna puke, I'd sure appreciate it if you'd find someplace away from the crime scene."

"No, I'm good," Deputy Tom Daggett said, a little too quickly and breathlessly for the declaration to be entirely reassuring. He glanced over at Roan, blushing right up to the band of his Stetson. "It's just… I've never seen anybody shot dead before. Not like this. It's…different, you know?" There was an audible swallow.

Roan did know. To be truthful, he hadn't seen anybody shot dead before either, except for crime-scene photos in forensics classes he'd taken in college and a few refresher courses after getting elected sheriff. And his deputy had it right—all the car wrecks, hunting accidents and bar fights in the world didn't do much to prepare a man for violent cold-blooded murder.

"In that case," he said to Deputy Daggett, "hunker on down here. Tell me what you see."

Frowning earnestly, the younger man squatted on his heels beside the body. "Okay, uh… you got two—" he coughed self-consciously. "I mean, the victim appears to have been shot twice—once in the head, and then here, in the chest. Right in the heart, looks like. From the, uh, condition of the, uh…the size of the exit wound in the back of the head…maybe a .38?"

"More likely a .45," the sheriff said, nodding his approval. "Okay, so what do you think happened here, Tom?"

The deputy tilted the brim of his Stetson back and looked around, squinting in the bright morning sunshine. "I don't know, seems pretty straightforward. Looks like the shooter was waiting for him when he came home. Ol' Jase gets out of his truck, starts for the house, and bam." He shook his head, his enthusiasm returning with his confidence, now he was over the worst of it. "The guy must have been right there in front of him— shot him in the chest first, then made good and sure with the head shot. Doubt Jase even saw it comin'."

Roan shook his head. "Oh, he saw it, all right. Just didn't believe it. And the head shot was first." He stood up and waited for the deputy to do the same. "Look here—see this?"

He pointed to some spatters on the door of the brand-new white Chevy truck parked just beyond the body. "That's brain matter. So he was standing up when the bullet went through his skull. Then it went through the driver's-side window, right here, see? Slug's probably still in there, inside the cab. We're gonna want to find that." He glanced over at Deputy Daggett, who was looking a little green around the gills again, but controlling it manfully. "I'm thinking the shooter stood in front of him, face-to-face, like this—" he demonstrated, arm outstretched "—and shot him. From about three feet away."

The deputy looked doubtful. "He'd have to be a helluva shot, wouldn't he, to drill him dead center in the forehead like that with a high-caliber handgun?"

"Yeah, or a lucky one." *With a cool head and a steady hand.*

Roan turned back to the body on the ground, his jaw tightening as he gazed down at what was left of Jason Edward Holbrook. Considering everything, he wondered why he wasn't taking this more personally. He ought to feel *something* for the death of the man who was very likely his half-brother.

But, except for a profound sense of outrage

and insult that such a thing could have happened in his jurisdiction, on his watch, he didn't feel a thing. Not a damn thing.

"Then," he went on grimly, "the shooter stood over him and fired a second shot into his heart at point-blank range—see this here? That's powder residue. Also, considering the back of the victim's skull was blown off, the shooter had to know he was already stone-dead, but he put that second shot in him anyway."

The deputy gave a low whistle. "Takes a whole lotta mad to do something like that."

Again Roan shook his head. "Not mad," he corrected. "Hate. This wasn't any crime of passion, not in the usual sense of that word. Whoever did this hated Jason's guts, pure and simple."

"Well," Tom said, obviously pretty well recovered now from his former queasiness and sounding downright cheerful, "that's not gonna narrow it down much." Then, belatedly recalling the unwritten rule against speaking ill of the dead, he threw Roan an abashed look and, blushing again, muttered an apology.

An unfortunate characteristic for a deputy sheriff, that blush, Roan thought. For the kid's sake, he hoped he'd grow out of it eventually—maybe by the time he started shaving regularly.

Tom Daggett was right, though, about there being no dearth of people who might have entertained the notion of taking a shot at Jason Holbrook, one time or another. But for some reason, nothing he could put a finger on, just a gut feeling, Roan didn't think this was going to be some jealous husband or boyfriend. Something about the killing…facing him like that…and then that second shot at point-blank range…this was payback, was what it was. *Vengeance.*

And more than that: Whoever had meted it out to Jason Holbrook had wanted him to know beyond any shadow of a doubt who was killing him and what he was dying for.

Holding off the shiver that wanted to run down his spine, Sheriff Harley took his sunglasses out of his shirt pocket and slipped them on, then let his gaze sweep the area, taking in the long graveled driveway that slanted down through the pine trees from the paved road to the huge two-story log house Jason's dad had had built against the mountainside in the style of a Swiss chalet. He turned back to Daggett. "No sign of a weapon?"

Tom shook his head. "Didn't see one in the

immediate vicinity. Thought I oughta wait for you before I started looking."

"Good call. Stay away from the truck, too. And the body, it goes without saying—at least until the coroner gets here. Where's the school-bus driver that called it in?"

"She had a load of kids to deliver. I told her somebody'd be over there at the school later on to get her statement. Uh… Sheriff?" Roan nodded for him to proceed, and Daggett did, looking uncomfortable. "You planning on calling in the state guys on this?"

"Already did," Roan said. "They're on their way."

Then for a while he and the deputy just stood there, neither of them saying anything, both of them trying not to look at the body of Jason Holbrook cooling in a puddle of his blood, staring up at the blue Montana sky. It was a bright, beautiful spring morning, but Roan felt like a big black cloud was parked right over his head, the heaviness of it pressing down on him and the first rumblings of thunder already growling in the distance.

"Sheriff?" Tom looked over at him, uneasy again, thumbs in his hip pockets, kind of scuffing at the dirt with the toe of his boot. "You gonna break the news to the senator?"

Reflexively, Roan folded his arms on his chest. He'd been giving that some thought himself. "That's not something you want to hear over the phone," he said, shaking off guilt, wondering if he was being a little too eager to pass the buck. Talking to Senator Holbrook wasn't something he enjoyed doing even at the best of times. Which these sure as hell weren't. "I'll call the Washington PD, get them to send somebody to tell him in person."

Tom let out a breath like a tire going flat as he took off his hat and ran a hand back over his short blond hair. "Well, hell. No matter how he finds out, when he does, I expect the you-know-what's goin' to hit the fan."

Roan favored his deputy with a lopsided grin. "I expect you're right about that. Be nice if we had a suspect in hand by the time it does, don't you think? You got any bright ideas where to start looking for one?"

Trying not to look thrilled to be asked, Tom hooked his thumbs in his belt while he gave it some thought. Then he puffed out his chest and squinted at the pine-studded horizon. "I'm thinkin' Buster's Last Stand— you know, over on the highway?—might be a good place to start. That's where Jase normally spends...uh, spent his evenings. Somebody in there might know if he ticked off anybody in particular last night. Worse than usual, I mean."

Roan clapped him on the back. "Good call. Probably too early right now—best to wait for the evening crowd to assemble before we hit there though." He nodded toward the highway where a van had just turned off onto the lane and was barreling toward them at highway speed, crunching gravel and sending up a cloud of dust. "Here's the coroner. I'm gonna want you to stay and keep an eye on things for me, Tom. Pick up all the info you can from Doc Salazar and the major-case detectives when they get here, and don't let that bunch from Billings intimidate you, you hear? I want a full report—don't leave out any details. Once everything's squared away here, get on over to the school and get the bus driver's statement." He heaved in a breath and squared his shoulders. "Meanwhile, I'll head back to the shop and get the ball rolling on notifying next of kin. After that…"

Well, he didn't like to think what his life was going to be like after that and for the foreseeable future, but he figured he ought to do what he could to prepare for the inevitable flood of media and law-enforcement out-of-towners. He imagined it was going to be a while before Hartsville settled back down to its quiet and peaceful small-town ways.

One thing, Roan thought as he went to greet the county's coroner and deputy medical examiner, he sure didn't envy the person whose unhappy duty it was going to be to inform Montana's senior senator of the violent death of his only son.

His only acknowledged son, anyway.

Fridays were always busy at Queenie's "We Pamper You Like Royalty" Beauty Salon and Boutique. Tucked between Betty's Art Gallery and Framing and the law offices of Andrews & Klein on Second Street, half a block off Main and just a block down from the courthouse, it was a handy place for any of the downtown crowd with interesting plans for the weekend to drop in on their lunch hour for a wash and set. Its new proprietor, Mary Owen, generally stayed late on Fridays to accommodate the high-school girls gussying up for date night. And, of course, Miss Ada Major, the clerk of the court, who'd had a standing five o'clock Friday-evening appointment for a wash and set since roughly the Reagan administration.

Honoring Miss Ada's Friday five o'clock was, in fact, one of the conditions Queenie Schultz, the shop's former owner, had made Mary agree to when she'd sold the business to her six months ago—that, and a promise to do up Miss Ada's hair real nice for her funeral, in the event the lady ever did decide to depart this mortal coil. To be truthful, that second condition had made Mary shudder a bit, and of course Queenie, being down in Phoenix, Arizona, enjoying the heat and sunshine, probably wasn't ever going to know whether Mary actually stuck to that part of the bargain or not. But it wasn't Mary's nature to break a promise, and besides, at the rate Miss Ada was going, it didn't look like the issue was going to come up any time soon.

If there was anything Mary Owen had learned in her thirty-seven years it was that life was full of surprises, so there wasn't much point in looking too far ahead or worrying about things that hadn't happened yet. She knew from hard experience how things could change in the blink of an eye.

"How are you doing today, Miss Ada?" Mary asked as she settled the tall, dignified lady into the chair and gently snapped a drape around her sinewy neck.

"Why, just fine, dear, thank you for asking." The circles of rose-pink blush on Miss Ada's cheeks crinkled with her smile. Keen hazel eyes highlighted in tissue-papery cobalt blue met Mary's in the mirror—then went wide with horrified sympathy. "Well, my goodness me, what on earth did you do, hon?"

Mary's teeth scraped over the tender bulge on her lower lip—a reflex she couldn't help—but her voice was smooth as she replied, "Oh, it's nothing, just me being stupid and clumsy. I forgot to leave the porch light on last night, and I tripped going up the front steps in the dark. Are we doing color today, Miss Ada?"

Miss Ada interrupted her little gasps and cries of commiseration and glanced at her own reflection in the mirror just long enough to murmur, "No, no, dear, I think another week, don't you?" Her gaze flew upward past her determinedly auburn curls to home in once more on the vivid marks on Mary's face. "Did you put some ice on those bruises? And I know you don't wear makeup, but you know, a little dab of pancake and some face powder would do wonders."

"Oh, like I said, it's nothing, really," Mary said cheerfully as she tilted the chair back and settled Miss Ada's neck on the lip of the wash basin. "Just a little embarrassing. So…have you been having a good week? Anything exciting going on over at the courthouse?"

Keeping her blue lids firmly closed, Miss Ada gave a hoot of laughter. "Oh, well, today there's nobody talking about anything but what happened to Clifford Holbrook's boy. You heard about that, I suppose?" She sighed heavily, then went on without waiting for Mary's answer, her forehead wrinkling in distress. "It is a shame—a terrible thing. My heart just goes out to Clifford. He always was a good boy—I was tempted to vote for him in the last election, even if he is a Republican— but that son of his—that Jason…it's hard to know, isn't it, how a child from such a nice family can turn out so wrong?"

"Yes, ma'am." Mary murmured the all-purpose response she'd learned in a former life from a dear Southern friend, warming her fingers in the stream of water and ignoring the deeper chill inside her. "How's that, Miss Ada? Is that gonna be too hot?"

"No, no, dear, it's fine. Well, I suppose Clifford did the best he could, with his wife being in such delicate health most of the time. But that boy always was a bully." She sniffed, then added, "Still and all, nobody deserves to die like that. Shot dead right in his own driveway. Makes you wonder if any of us is safe anywhere nowadays." She gave a genteel shudder.

"Yes, ma'am." Mary watched her fingers massage moisturizing shampoo over Miss Ada's scalp.

"A good thing we've got a decent sheriff in this county," Miss Ada said with a sniff, her festively painted features settling into stern and uncompromising lines. "Roan Harley—now there's a fine young man. A real fine man." She opened her eyes and aimed them upward. "Have you met our sheriff yet, Mary?"

"No, ma'am, I don't believe I have—except to see him driving by, maybe." She wrapped a towel loosely around the old lady's head and raised the chair to its upright position.

Miss Ada pulled one knotted, blue-veined hand from under the drape to touch away a drop of water that had taken the liberty of trickling down her forehead, then gave one of her little hoots of laughter as she met Mary's eyes in the mirror. "Well, I suppose that is a good thing, isn't it? Not that I expect *you'd* have any reason to fear the law."

"Yes, ma'am," Mary agreed as she began to divide Miss Ada's sparse wet hair into quadrants, twisting each segment loosely and securing it with a clip.

Miss Ada's face seemed to droop with sadness as her eyes shifted focus to something only she could see, and she spoke more to herself than to Mary. "Oh my, that poor man has had more than his share of trials and tragedies to bear, yes he has…."

"Ma'am?" Mary said politely, only half listening, her mind already numbing with the tedium of winding thin strands of Miss Ada's hair onto the old-fashioned rollers she favored.

The old lady's eyes snapped back to Mary's, light kindling in them now as she prepared to enjoy the kind of harmless gossip people are wont to indulge in with their hairdressers. "The boy didn't exactly have a happy beginning, you know. No, he didn't. His mother—Susan Roth, her name was, a perfectly lovely girl—never married, and to be unwed and pregnant in a small Western town…well. You can imagine. You had to admire her, though, she held her head up. Never let her son feel ashamed, either. She worked hard to support herself and the boy—I have an idea the father, whoever he was, might've helped out some—and she managed to put money away for Roan's college. He applied for scholarships and won several—he was a very bright young man. He was going to become a lawyer—that was his mother's fondest wish. But then she got sick and died suddenly."

Normally it was Mary's habit to let this sort of gossip flow in one ear and out the other, but for some reason she was finding this particular story hard to ignore. She made murmurs of sympathy, and Miss Ada sighed.

"Yes…it was sad. Roan came home to bury his mother and never did go back to the university. Instead, he stayed on, married his childhood sweetheart, enrolled in the state law-enforcement academy—I believe he'd had a minor in criminology, or forensics, or some such thing, in college. Anyway, he became a deputy, and when Jim Stottlemyer retired, ran for sheriff and got himself elected first try. Youngest sheriff in the history of the county, and I must say, it was the legal profession's loss and Hart County's gain. Roan's been a fine sheriff." She paused for another sigh. "It should have been one of those and-they-lived-happily-ever-after stories, but it wasn't. No, indeed. Roan Harley's troubles were just beginning."

"Really? What happened?" Mary turned

the chair in order to reach the other side of Miss Ada's head, and Miss Ada's eyes met hers directly instead of in the mirror. Mary was startled to see a sheen in them that could only be tears.

"I'm sorry, dear," the elderly clerk of court said with a half-hearted smile. "Oh my. It's been four years, but it's still hard to talk about it. Seems like it happened just yesterday, yes it does. It was such a terrible tragedy, the kind of thing a small community like this never does get over." She paused, lifted a hand and absently patted the neat row of curlers that marched down one side of her head.

"Well, now… I told you Roan married his childhood sweetheart. Erin Stuart—she'd been a classmate of Roan's, all the way back to kindergarten, I believe. And her dad, Boyd Stuart, he'd befriended the boy, too, knowing he was growing up fatherless. Roan looked up to Boyd and respected him as he would a father, and Boyd…well, you could tell he loved Roan like a son. In fact, Boyd was so tickled when Roan married Erin, he signed over the deed to his ranch to the newlyweds and moved into the ranch foreman's cottage." Miss Ada chuckled, then took a quick breath as if it were a shot of whisky she was tossing back to fortify herself before going on.

"Well then, two years later Erin and Roan had a little girl. They named her Susan Grace, after their late mothers—Erin's mother, Grace—she was a Pascoe, from over in Lewiston—had passed away, too, when Erin was still in high school. For the next three years—that was when Roan ran for and was elected sheriff—the family was so happy. Truly blessed." She paused, and when she went on her voice had a quiver in it.

"Then...one night while Roan was out of town on a case, there was a fire. It woke up Boyd down in the cottage, and he came running... Oh, he tried his best, but he was only able to save the little girl. His own daughter, Erin, died in the fire. Boyd and the child were both seriously burned."

"My God," Mary whispered. She felt cold clear through, and a little queasy—and how in the world had she let this county sheriff's unhappy story slip past her radar and take dead aim at her heart? She'd taken care to keep her feelings sandbagged and fortified against just such an assault. She couldn't afford the luxury of caring. Now more than ever.

Miss Ada's tear-bright eyes flicked upward and softened when they found Mary so obviously touched by the story. "Yes...yes. Poor Roan, he was just devastated, as you can imagine. He tried to pick up the pieces after the tragedy, I think for his little girl's sake as much as anything, but I do believe he carries scars from that fire still, just as surely as Susie Grace and Boyd do. The only difference is, Roan's scars don't show." She heaved another sigh. "I don't imagine it helps, either, that he's never been able to find out who did it—who killed his wife and maimed his child."

Mary's hands stilled, a curler half rolled. She fought to control a shudder of horror. "You mean...it wasn't an accident?"

"Oh, no, dear," Miss Ada said softly. "The fire was deliberately set, no doubt about it. It haunts Roan, I think, that the crime remains unsolved to this day."

"I'm sure it does. It must be awful for him," Mary murmured. But it was only words, and once again safely distanced from feeling. Her defenses had slipped momentarily, but they were back in place, now.

"It was terrible for everyone," Miss Ada said firmly, reaching up to pat the tissue paper band Mary was fastening around her hairline to protect her skin from the dryer's heat. "The worst time this town's had since the mines closed, I do believe. And now this." She threw Mary a look as she accepted the hand she was offering to help her out of the chair. Her eyes were fierce again, and her voice brisk—it was the tone and the look that had kept jurors in line for so many years. "I am sure of one thing: Roan won't let it happen again. Whoever it was shot Jason Holbrook, the sheriff will find him. I know he will."

"Yes, ma'am," Mary murmured. She was confident that, with the dryer humming away, even Miss Ada's keen senses couldn't have caught the tremor that had just rippled through her.

Dave Salazar, Hart County's coroner, was also both a licensed physician and deputy medical examiner for the State of Montana, and, as such, fully qualified to conduct autopsies, which he did, on the relatively few occasions one was called for, in a basement room at the county hospital. That was where Roan caught up with the two detectives from the state's Special Cases Unit.

Kurt Ruger was short-legged, barrel-chested and looked like a college football player, with a brushy blond crewcut, prominent brow ridge and sharp, rather small and close-set blue eyes. His partner, Roger Fry, appeared to have been picked to balance the team in just about every way, being tall, lanky, dark-haired and balding, with benign brown eyes behind rimless glasses perched on the end of an oversized nose. He reminded Roan of an economics professor he'd once had.

After murmured introductions and handshakes all around, both SCU men sidestepped to make room for one more in the cramped space against the observation window, well out of the way of any stray odors or splatters.

Roan had seen his share of autopsies and had pretty well gotten over being squeamish about the process. He folded his arms on his chest and stepped closer to the partially draped nude body on the stainless-steel table, startling the coroner, who'd been so engrossed in his examination of the body he was oblivious to everything else, including the arrival of one more observer.

The doctor glanced at him in mild surprise. "Hey, Sheriff."

"What you got for us, Doc?"

"Haven't started the autopsy yet, but I

found a couple of things that are kind of interesting." He nodded his head, swathed in a green surgical cap, toward the two SCU detectives. "Like I was saying to these two gentlemen, I wanted to wait until you were all here—no sense in going through everything twice." Roan nodded, and the doctor reached up to adjust the overhead lamp, then pointed with a gloved finger. The two SCU detectives moved in closer.

"See this here? Laceration on his lower lip?" He delicately inserted a fingertip into the victim's mouth and turned the lip downward to expose the puffed and discolored inside. "That's a bite mark. Not self-inflicted—the curve's wrong. Definitely human, definitely ante-mortem, I'd say two hours, at least."

Roan frowned. "You mean..."

"Unless Jason Holbrook had a secret nobody knew about, there's only one way I can think of that could have happened. And that is, he forced himself on some gal, and she bit him."

One of the detectives let slip a snort of laughter, hastily stifled. Roan said dryly, "Yeah, that sounds about like Jase. You said a couple of things. What else?"

The doctor turned away from the table and

gestured for the others to follow as he moved to some articles of clothing spread out on a stainless-steel countertop. He paused in front of the light gray Western-style shirt that was liberally soaked with blood, shifting to allow Roan and the SCU guys to move in close. He pointed, careful not to touch. "Okay, this is interesting—there's some blood here on the left sleeve—see that? Now...look at the way he went down. Fell backward, arms went straight out, right? Never came in contact with either of his wounds."

One of the state detectives—Kurt Ruger—cleared his throat and frowned. "Spatter, maybe?"

The doctor shook his head. "It's a smear, not a spatter. And it's on the back side of the sleeve. Again, the way he fell, there's no way spatter would've hit there. No...look here. Think about it. What do you do when you get hit in the nose or mouth, and you're bleeding? You wipe with your sleeve, right?" He demonstrated. "That puts a smear right about where this one is."

"Okay, so he got his lip bit and wiped the blood on his sleeve." Roger Fry sounded as if he wanted to add, "So what?"

Roan waited. He knew Doc better than the

two newcomers did, well enough to know he wasn't finished.

Salazar took a breath, threw the three lawmen an expectant look, and backed up a step. "Okay. Now look at his other sleeve. The right one. You got more blood smears here, see? But on the *inside* this time. Now, you try wiping your mouth with that part of your sleeve." Again he demonstrated. "It's awkward—unnatural. You'd have to really twist your arm to put a blood stain where this one is. Anyway, I thought that seemed odd, so... I tested it." He paused, eyes gleaming. "Just a preliminary, so far, but I'll tell you this, it doesn't match Jason's blood type. And something else. It's female."

Roan felt a chill go down his spine, but he kept his arms folded and said mildly, "You got a scenario in mind, Doc?"

The coroner nodded. "If I may... Detective... Ruger, is it? Mind if I borrow you for just a second?"

The muscular blond cop half grinned and lifted a wary eyebrow in his partner's direction, but allowed himself to be maneuvered into an awkward sort of embrace with the slightly built ME, who narrated as he demonstrated.

"Okay, I've just been bitten by this lady, right? What's my first reaction gonna be? If I'm the sort of guy to force myself on a woman to begin with, I'm probably gonna strike back." The doctor doubled up a fist and grazed Ruger's square chin with it, as Ruger obligingly offered a falsetto squeal of pain. "So, I smack you a good one," Salazar went on. "Your mouth is bleeding, too, now. But that's not enough for me, I'm good and riled up, not to mention intoxicated—"

"Is that theory, Doc, or fact?"

Salazar jerked Roan a look over his shoulder. "Fact—blood alcohol level was way up there. Anyway, now I'm *really* gonna get rough with this lady. Something like this…" Turning his demo partner around, he placed his right arm across the detective's broad chest. "Now, she's gonna be struggling, trying to get loose, so I tighten my hold, pull my arm higher, up to her neck…like this, see? And my sleeve brushes across her mouth— or anyway, the blood from it." He let go of Ruger and held up his right arm, pointing to the wrist in triumph. "Voila! Right there, and that's just where you see that smear on the victim's sleeve." The ME subsided, looking expectantly from one member of his audience to another.

Roan and the two SCU detectives looked back at him, not saying anything for a moment or two, none of them smiling. Then Fry pushed his glasses up the bridge of his nose, gave a small cough and said what they were all thinking.

"So, are we thinking rape, here?"

Roan dragged a hand over his face and let out a breath. Ruger glanced at him, eyebrows raised. "Hey, if the victim raped somebody—or tried to—and got shot in the process, that makes it self-defense, maybe." He shrugged and looked doubtful. "I don't know if the senator is going to buy that, though."

A vision of that crime scene flashed into Roan's head in full living color: Jason Holbrook stretched our flat on his back in his driveway beside his brand new Chevy truck, a third eye, bloody and black, in the middle of his forehead. He shook his head, but didn't say anything. Too soon, he told himself, to be jumping to any conclusions.

He knew one thing, though. Whoever had shot Jason Holbrook, man or woman, it hadn't been self-defense, not in the legal sense, anyway. It had been more like an execution.

"Strange, though," Salazar continued in a musing tone, peering interestedly down at the body, "she puts her 'take that' shot here, in his heart. Most women…uh, payback for rape… I'd think they'd aim farther south…" He pointed delicately at the part of the body modestly concealed beneath the drape and lifted his sharp black eyes to Roan. "Know what I mean?"

Chapter Two

It was half past eight when Roan walked into Buster's Last Stand Saloon, which put it right about the time family dinner hour would be finishing up. He'd learned this was the best time to catch the regular crowd of Friday-night drinkers, just when they were starting to get their tongues loosened up but before they'd quit making any kind of sense at all.

He and the two SCU detectives had agreed Roan should be the one to question the victim's last-known associates, since it stood to reason locals were more likely to open up to one of their own. Ruger and Fry had drawn straws to see who'd get the honor of driving to the airport in Billings to meet the senator's plane. Ruger lost, so that left Fry to accompany the victim's clothing and vehicle to the state crime lab in Helena.

The state detectives were nice enough guys, Roan allowed, easy to get along with and willing to let him take the lead in the case. No doubt they did know their stuff. Still, he was just as glad to have them out of his way, even though he'd been the one to call them in on the case in the first place. Which, to be honest, he'd done mainly because he knew the first thing Clifford Holbrook would want to know when his feet hit the tarmac in Billings was whether Roan had called in the big guns from state yet. Roan didn't take it personally; the senator'd most likely be wanting to call in the FBI, the CIA and Homeland Security, too, if he could think of an excuse to do it.

However, Roan figured he was smart enough to know and man enough to admit when he was in over his head, and also confident enough to know when he wasn't. In this case, the victim's father might be a national figure, but the crime looked to be down-home local. The fact was, someone in this town— *his* town—had shot Jason Holbrook, most likely someone Roan knew well, somebody he'd spoken to, looked in the eye, maybe even gone to school with, played baseball with… or danced with, he thought, remembering that female blood evidence on the vic's shirt sleeve.

Why do I keep calling him the vic? His name was Jason. Jason Holbrook. The guy was a bully and a sonofabitch—maybe even a rapist—but he was also my brother.

Buster Dalton, the owner of the Last Stand Saloon, was where he could be found most nights after the dinner hour—behind the bar, riding herd on his regular drinking customers. When there wasn't a rodeo in town, Buster ran a fairly tight ship, and since he topped out at six four and 350 pounds—and looked even bigger because the bar was elevated two steps up from the rest of the room—there weren't many that ever got drunk enough or stupid enough to argue with him when he decided they'd had enough for the night. Buster was first and foremost a good businessman who believed in looking out for his customers' welfare, his philosophy being one of Live and Let Live—and Come Back to Spend More Money Here Another Night.

He greeted Roan with a cordial "Howdy,

Sheriff," which was echoed by most of those already occupying stools at the polished antique pine wood bar. The saloon keeper plunked Roan's "usual"—a mug of black coffee—down on a paper napkin on the well-scuffed surface, and after a glance along the bar to see if his regulars were likely to be needing refills any time soon, folded his beefy arms, placed them on the bar and leaned on them.

"Figured you'd be in tonight," he said in a low, rumbling voice he probably thought passed for a whisper. "Helluva thing about ol' Jase, ain't it?"

Roan didn't answer as he laid down a dollar bill for the coffee and slid onto a stool. Buster leaned in closer.

"Don't guess I oughta be sayin' this, given the circumstances, but hell—can't say I'm surprised. Lotta folks'd say Jase had been askin' for it for years. Sooner or later, somebody was bound to oblige him."

Roan didn't smile. He sipped coffee, then swiveled a casual half turn on the stool, gave the saloon keeper a sideways glance then looked away. "You got anybody particular in mind?"

Buster gave a snort, the breeze of it stirring

his thick gray walrus mustache. "You could start with the Hart County phone book."

This time Roan let his mouth tilt sideways in a grin. He drank more coffee. "Let's narrow it down a bit. How 'bout…say, last night? Was he in here?"

"Oh, hell yeah—like always." Buster shook his head. "Man, this place ain't gonna seem the same…."

"He get into it with anybody? More than usual," Roan added with another crooked smile, beating Buster to the punch.

Which the barkeeper acknowledged with a grunt, then straightened up, looking uncomfortable. In response to some signal from the other end of the bar Roan hadn't noticed, he busied himself filling a couple of beer glasses with draft, expertly raising the head to just the right level. When he'd delivered them to the customers and deposited payment in the huge silver antique cash register that rose like an altar behind the bar, he came back over to Roan, folded his arms and hunkered down again with a heavy sigh.

"Well, gosh darn," he muttered, "I sure do hate to put anybody on the hot seat…"

"Why don't you let me worry about that?" Roan said mildly.

Buster gave him an unhappy look, smoothed down his mustache with a meaty hand, then immediately undid the effects of that by exhaling like a locomotive blowing off steam. "Hell. Okay, well, I did notice he was hitting pretty hard on that little ol' gal from the beauty shop. The one that bought out Queenie when she retired and moved down to Phoenix last winter," he elaborated, when Roan responded with a slight shake of his head.

"Don't know her."

"Doesn't surprise me. She hasn't been here long—six months...maybe a little more, but definitely an out-of-towner. And, she's kinda quiet—seems like a real nice girl, not the type to show up on *your* radar screen, if you know what I mean." He frowned as he straightened up once more, looking thoughtful. "Funny thing is, you wouldn't think she'd show up on Jase's radar, either. Kind of a mousy little thing, not bad to look at, you know, just...not exactly a head-turner. Her name's Mary," he added almost as an afterthought. "That's kind of what she looks like, too. The way you'd expect somebody named Mary to look. Definitely not ol' Jase's usual type, but for some reason, he was going at her pretty good last night." He shook his head. "Not that she was buyin'. She made it pretty clear she didn't want any part of what he was sellin'."

"She got a boyfriend? A husband?" Like… a very jealous one? Roan thought. Jealous enough to murder.

Buster shook his head. "Not that I've ever seen or heard of. If you saw her, you'd understand why—she's…like I said. Quiet. Nice, but kind of shy. Stand-offish."

"If she's such a nice, sweet, shy girl, what was she doing in here?" Roan half grinned and let his eyes crinkle at the corners to show he hadn't meant any offense by it.

Buster snorted and gave him half a grin back to show he hadn't taken any. "Not drinkin', I'll tell you that. Don't think I've ever seen her order so much as a glass of wine or that weasel whiz they call lite beer. Naw, truth is, she likes ol' Pedro's cooking." He jerked a nod in the general direction of the kitchen. "I guess Queenie told her before she left he was the best cook in town, and the poor thing never had the sense to learn better." He guffawed a little at his own joke; everybody knew The Last Stand *did* have the best food in town, in spite of its seedy looks and rowdy reputation.

"Anyhow, she stops in most nights on her way home from the shop and picks up something to take home for her dinner. Told me she hates to cook." He shrugged. "You just missed her, in fact. She left here just a couple minutes before you walked in."

"This lady got a last name?" Roan asked casually as he slid off the stool. "An address?"

"She's renting Queenie's place over on Custer. Don't know her last name." Buster threw another quick glance at his regular customers, then draped a dishtowel over one massive shoulder and lumbered down the two steps and around the end of the bar. He followed Roan out to the saloon's big double-doored entry, which was well-lit by the dozen or so neon beer signs crowded in amongst the Plains Indian paintings and artifacts on its knotty pine walls. The worn wood floor was crowded, too, with a couple of coat and hat racks, an assortment of gumball, candy and toy vending machines, and racks offering a variety of free advertising publications.

"Look, Sheriff," the saloon keeper said, nodding at the dove-colored Stetson Roan had just taken from the rack, "I know what you're thinkin', but if that gal had anything to do with shootin' Jase, I'll eat that hat a'yours. Right here and now."

Roan threw him a mild glance as he settled the hat on his head. "You know I've got to ask." He tilted his hat brim toward the door of the saloon, through which he could hear the thumping accompaniment to an old Dwight Yoakum classic somebody had just programmed into the antique jukebox. "Chances are looking good you people in here are the last to see Jason alive. And you did say he was hitting on this woman pretty hard."

"I never said she might not've had cause to kill him," Buster muttered, looking uncomfortable again. "Just that I can't believe she would." Recognizing there was more the man wanted to say and wise enough not to push him, Roan waited him out. Finally the saloon keeper blurted it out in a muttered undertone. "Look—the fact is, I know something did happen between those two last night—Jase and Mary. He followed her out to the parking lot—you know, after she brushed him off? He had a smile on his face and a bad look in his eye—she'd given him the brush in front of a whole barroom full of regulars, and Jase wasn't happy about it, you could see that. I thought about going out to make sure she got to her car okay. Only I got busy right then—somebody got to pushing and shoving at the bar, a glass got broke…you know how it is." He dabbed his face with the bar towel on his shoulder and scowled at the Plains Indian dreamcatcher hanging on the wall next to a neon Coors sign.

"Anyway, a few minutes later—maybe five or ten, like I said, I was busy—Jase comes back in. He's dabbing at his lip—I could see it was bleeding—and I mean he was *ticked*. Couple of the guys started raggin' him—well, hell, it was pretty obvious what'd happened. Jase was riled up, pushing chairs around, cussin' and generally making an ass of himself. Then he knocked back what was left of his drink—he'd already had plenty, I was ready to cut him off anyways—and he slammed down some money for his tab, and out he went." He paused…let out a breath. "Never did come back. That's the last any of us saw him, I guess."

"Except for the one that shot him," Roan said, and got an angry look in return.

"Like I said, I can't believe—"

"Like *I* said, I have to follow it up. You know that." Roan laid a calming hand on the big man's shoulder. "I appreciate you telling me about this." Buster muttered something unintelligible but was obviously unhappy, and Roan clapped him good-naturedly on the back. "Hey, come on, you know I'm gonna be fair. If this lady's as innocent as you say she is, she's got nothing to worry about. But I am going to need to talk to her. *Tonight*." The easy smile on his lips tightened into grimmer lines. "Be seein' you, Buster. You take it easy, now."

The sheriff touched the brim of his Stetson and plunged through the door and into the twilight.

"You can stare at me all you like, but that's all you're getting," Mary said firmly to the beast watching her avidly from his perch atop the kitchen counter. "The rest is mine. You're getting too fat anyway."

The animal, a huge and amazingly ugly orange tabby tomcat, blinked at her in slow motion and went right on staring. He'd come with the house, and allowing him to remain there, as well as providing him with food and other feline comforts, had been another of the conditions under which Queenie Schultz had consented to leave her home and business in Mary's custody. So, she tolerated the creature, and since he had no name that she knew of and because he reminded her—with a bittersweet ache of longing for a place and time lost to her now—of Audrey Hepburn's cat in *Breakfast at Tiffany's*, that's what she called him. Cat.

For his part, the animal seemed to have accepted the alien presence in his domain, although he did insist on staring at her with unnerving intensity, as if he expected her to turn back into Queenie at any moment, in a puff of magical smoke.

Mary picked up the last triangle of her smoked turkey club on whole wheat bread and was about to sink her teeth into it when Cat startled her by coming abruptly to life. He leaped down from the countertop to land with a heavy *thud* on the linoleum floor, then vanished into the nether regions of the house. An instant later, there came a knock on the front door.

Her heart leaped, then plummeted, a fair imitation of the maneuver Cat had just demonstrated. *Who on earth?* Her eyes went automatically to the oversized purse on the table that sat in the dimly lit living room just to the right of the front door. In all the months she'd lived in Hartsville, she'd never had anyone knock on her door before. And at this time of night?

But then a strange sort of calm settled over her. Because, of course, she knew.

She laid the uneaten sandwich carefully on its plate, picked up the pair of dark-rimmed glasses lying on the table and arranged them on her face. She touched the tender place on her jaw and skimmed her teeth across the swelling on her lower lip. Then she drew a deep breath, rose and walked to the door.

She paused to open the wide mouth of the purse and shift it slightly so as to put it within easier reach of her right hand, before taking a deep breath and calling out, "Who is it?"

"Sheriff Roan Harley, ma'am. I'd like to talk to you, if you wouldn't mind." The voice was deep and growly, pleasant and even soft in pitch, but there was no mistaking the iron authority in it.

Mary closed her eyes briefly, then reached once more for the purse, this time picking it up, then bending over to tuck it under the table. She unlocked the door and opened it a cautious crack, leaving the screen door latched. And a moment later was clutching it for support as she felt herself tumbling headlong into a memory she thought she'd put away and forgotten long ago.

I thought Diego DelRey was the most handsome man I'd ever seen. Tall, dark and exotic, he was standing in the middle of that vast hotel lobby in a shaft of sunlight from the leaded-glass skylight, smiling at me through the cascading waters from a Moorish fountain.

"Throw a penny in the fountain and make a wish," he said in a voice softly accented and exotic, sensual and dangerous as a tiger's purr. "Tell me what it is and I'll make it come true."

And I thought, as I smiled back at him, Oh, but I think you already have.

Why do I remember this now? This man is nothing at all like Diego DelRey. If he reminds me of anyone it's the Marlboro Man.

Still clutching the latched screen door, she said politely, "May I please see your I.D.?"

The man standing on the front porch seemed surprised by the request, as if it wasn't one he was accustomed to getting. While he fumbled to pull the folder containing his badge from his shirt pocket with one hand—the other was full of a big light-colored cowboy hat—Mary had time for more analytical thoughts.

He was tall. She was tall herself, but he was taller by half a head, with hard, sinewy flesh arranged sparingly but well over big bones. His hair, sculpted in classic cowboy fashion by the press of the hat brim, gleamed like tarnished gold in the overhead porch light. His features were strong— maybe too strong to be called handsome, with high cheekbones and a square-cut jaw—but his mouth looked as though it might smile easily and well. There were depressions in his cheeks that lacked the benign cuteness of dimples, but rather lent his face a rakish kind of charm that seemed somehow at odds with the somberness of his profession. And even though it was coming on night and his eyes were in shadow, they seemed to squint a little, as if from a lifetime spent gazing at sunshot horizons.

He stepped forward into the light and handed over his identification. She took her time studying it, then deliberately met his eyes for a long unflinching moment as she gave it back to him. His eyes, a cool glittery blue, returned her appraisal for a time that seemed just a little too long.

He won't miss much, she thought. *No, there's no resemblance to Diego at all. But... maybe it's that supreme and unshakable self-assurance that's the same.*

A shiver found its way past her defenses

and scurried away down her spine as she stepped back and held the door open, wordlessly inviting him in.

"Sorry to bother you so late, ma'am," he said in his soft, rumbly voice, and shifted his feet as he moved past her, as if he would have liked to wipe them on a doormat that wasn't there.

In the better light, she amended her thoughts about his eyes. They seemed tired, she thought. *Or sad.* Remembering Miss Ada's tale of this man's personal tragedies made her tone warmer than it might have been.

"That's all right, I just got home myself, actually." She closed the door and turned with a gesture, directing her visitor through the shadowy living room toward the lighted rectangle of the kitchen doorway.

And as she did that, she was aware of each of her movements as if a camera's eye was scrutinizing her face and body in the finest detail. She was conscious of every expression, every muscle and nerve, in a way she hadn't been even in those long-ago times she'd spent in front of a real camera.

And she was conscious, too, and even ashamed, of the room they were passing through. She tried not to see the comfortable but drab brown tweed sofa and worn beige fake leather rocking chair, or the faded green braided rug that could only have come from a long-extinct mail-order catalog. Even the attempts at decoration made her cringe: The mass-produced and overly sentimental prints of cats and dogs—or worse, houses with impossibly lovely gardens and lighted windows—that hung on the walls, the bowl of artificial daisies that shared the coffee table with a book of Life magazine photographs and a ceramic rooster, the basket of pine cones and the stuffed blue calico cat on the hearth in front of the unused fireplace. Nothing wrong with any of it, and the homey little knickknacks were pretty enough, she supposed, but so...alien to her. It felt like a set, and she walked through it like an actor on a stage.

But this is who I am, now. Shabby...ordinary. I should be used to it by now. And I must not forget it...ever.

"I was just having a bite to eat," she said, touching her mouse-brown hair in a self-conscious way that was only partly artifice. "If you, um...wouldn't mind talking in the kitchen? I'm sorry things are such a mess… as I said, I just got home."

She's nervous, Roan thought. He didn't make too much of that, nervous being a pretty usual way for people to be around officers of the law, he'd found, even the ones who had no reason to be. *Especially* the ones who had no reason to be.

Like Buster had said, the woman fidgeting her way from table to sink to fridge as she cleared away the remains of her evening meal definitely wasn't the head-turner type. Not the kind of woman to stand out in a crowd in spite of how tall she was. Not the type to stir a man's juices to lust, either, not at first glance anyway. Though that may have been due in part to the fact that whatever figure she did have was all covered up by the loose-fitting pink nylon smock she wore.

All together, he decided, she wasn't bad-looking or what he might call homely, just… plain. As in, ordinary. Her hair was kind of a neutral brown, neither curly nor straight, without much body or shine to it and no particular style either, just sort of twisted up on the back of her head. Which struck him as kind of odd for somebody who made her living fixing up other people's hair. Her eyes were unremarkable, too, a flat greenish-gray in color, like old moss—though it was hard to tell much more about them, hidden as they were behind a pair of dark-rimmed glasses even he knew were both too big for her face and years out of style.

"Can I get you something to drink?" she asked as she brushed some imaginary crumbs off the tabletop. "Some...coffee?"

"Oh, no ma'am, thanks, I just had a cup over at the Last Stand." He laid his hat on the tabletop she'd just cleared off and pretended not to notice the way she'd twitched when he mentioned the saloon. "I'll try not to take up too much of your time. I just need to ask you a few questions...."

"Oh—of course." She leaned her hip against the countertop and folded her arms in a way he didn't have to be a student of body language to know was defensive.

He regarded her for a moment, watching her throat move as she swallowed, not intending to make her more nervous than she already was, but simply pondering the best way to proceed with this woman. He felt a little bit like a hunter stalking a doe, part of him not wanting to spook her, but a part of him secretly hoping she'd wake up to the danger she was in and get herself out of his gunsights while there was still time.

He quelled that notion and drawled with deceptive friendliness, "You can start by telling me your last name. All the folks over at the Last Stand know you by is Mary."

A smile flicked over her lips and died. She cleared her throat, and one hand rose as if to touch her mouth before halting abruptly and diving back into the bend of her folded arms. "It's, um, Owen. Mary… Owen."

But he'd already noted the puffy swelling on her lower lip she'd remembered too late not to call his attention to. And the purple bruises on her jaw—he'd noticed them, too.

"Mary Owen…" He repeated it as he took a notebook and pencil from his shirt pocket and jotted it down. Then he looked up and casually asked, "Do you know Jason Holbrook, Mary?"

No twitch this time. She was expecting that.

She met his eyes calmly, poise restored, the nervousness apparently conquered. And during the long pause while she gazed at him without replying, something odd happened to him, something he couldn't recall ever having happened before, at least not under those circumstances, questioning a suspect in the investigation of a crime. For no reason he could think of his pulse quickened and a strange little weight came to sit in the middle of his chest, one that made him feel as if he needed to catch a breath. A breath that was mysteriously hard to come by.

"I've met him, yes." Then she added with a note of quiet reproach, "But sheriff, you know that, or you wouldn't be here. I also know he was found shot dead this morning." She paused again, and her mouth twitched briefly with a small, bitter smile. "This is a very small town."

He acknowledged that with a nod and a wintery smile of his own. He glanced down, shifted the position of his hat on the table, then returned his gaze to her. "So...you mind telling me when the last time was you saw him?"

Her lips tightened again, impatiently, this time. "I'm sure you know that, too. I saw him last night, at the Last Stand. He...spoke to me while I was waiting to pick up my to-go order."

"The way I heard it, he did a lot more than speak to you," Roan drawled, and now for some reason he was noticing her skin, wondering why he hadn't noticed before how clear and pale it was, almost translucent, not like most of the women he knew, whose skin, once they passed infancy, got to showing the effects of sun and wind and cold dry weather pretty quickly.

Noticing, too, the way hers changed color with her emotions, the same way his Susie Grace's did. And when she shook her head and looked away, he didn't miss the faint pink blush that washed across her cheeks.

"He came on to me. It wasn't the first time. It wasn't a big deal." But she swallowed. He didn't miss that, either.

"What about when he followed you out to the parking lot?"

Her eyes snapped back to him, the pink in her cheeks deepening to crimson as he watched, and he felt a stab of inappropriate delight that a woman her age could still blush.

"You mean you don't know that, too?" Her voice was low, barely above a whisper, but he could almost see her body vibrating with emotions fiercely contained, and behind the unattractive glasses she wore, her eyes had come alive. They seemed to shimmer now with green-gold fire. "Didn't your witnesses tell you?"

He leaned toward her, making his voice as

soft as hers, just sort of friendly. "No, but I think I can guess what happened. I've known Jason Holbrook for a long time, so I know what a— pardon me, ma'am— what a sonofabitch he can be. And Jason had a laceration on his lip the coroner says is a bite mark. Buster, over at the Last Stand, says when Jase came back after seeing you outside, his mouth was bleeding and he was cussin' mad. It doesn't take a genius to figure things out, does it, Miss Mary?" He ducked his head, cajoling her with kind eyes and a wry smile. "So tell me—the truth, now—are you the one that bit him?"

She looked away, made a sound, cleared her throat and finally spat it out—and that was what she reminded him of—a cat spitting. "He…grabbed me as I was getting into my car." Her folded arms tightened, and revulsion thickened her voice. "He…kissed me. He wouldn't stop when I tried to push him away. So, yes… I bit him." Again her eyes lashed back at him, as if to say she wasn't one bit sorry about doing it, either. And this time he knew the green-gold fire in those eyes was defiance.

Ignoring another of those strange disturbances in his midsection, Roan leveled a gaze at her and waited. It had been his experience at times like this that silence was more apt to provoke further revelations than questions. It didn't work in Miss Mary Owen's case, though. She stared back at him and didn't give an inch.

He leaned toward her once more, stooping down a little the way he normally did when he spoke to women—a habit he'd developed when he'd first shot up to where he was a good bit taller than most of the girls he knew. When he remembered *this* woman was darn near as tall as he was, he straightened up again. "And was that absolutely the *last* time you saw him?"

She didn't answer, but the fire died out of her eyes as he watched, leaving them that dull and lifeless gray.

He persisted, his voice gentle again...persuading. "Mary? Did you see Jason after that? Did he come back a little later on...follow you home, maybe?"

She looked away, still not answering, though he could see her throat working. He stepped closer to her and reached toward but didn't quite touch the bruise on her jaw. He felt a stab of almost physical pain when she flinched. It was either the pain or the surprise of it that made his voice harden. "Did Jason do this to you?"

She edged away from him and turned... picked up a perfectly clean dish from the countertop and put it in the sink. "No— nobody *did* it. I—it was just a stupid accident. I tripped on the steps—the porch light was burned out, and I...fell."

That told him one thing: the lady was a terrible liar.

"A man's dead, Mary. And lying to me isn't going to do anything but get you in a whole lot of trouble." He paused, waited again. And as he waited he thought about moving in on her, crowding her space, closing her in against that sink where she stood with her back to him, using the kind of subtle intimidation tactics he'd have used with any other suspect. But then he got a clear picture in his mind of that swollen lip and the bruise on her face, and of Jason doing the exact same thing but with a whole different purpose in mind, and he went cold and sick with shame at the thought.

He folded his arms across his chest and hitched in a breath. "Something else the coroner found, Mary. Jason had some blood on his shirt sleeve that wasn't his. Appears it was a woman's blood. And I'm guessing if I take a sample of your DNA—and I will have to ask you to let me do that—I'm about as certain as I can be it's going to match that blood."

Still she didn't say anything…didn't move a muscle. He could hear the tension humming inside her, like an overload of electricity. He could see the wisps of brown hair that lay on the back of her neck, escapees from the nondescript arrangement that was neither bun nor ponytail but something halfway between and that had already seen her through a hard day's work.

He thought how vulnerable that part of her seemed. And that at the same time, oddly graceful, too.

"Mary?" Barely whispering… "Did Jason Holbrook rape you?"

Again her body jerked as if he'd struck her. She turned slowly, and he saw her face, not vulnerable, now, but white and still, like something carved in marble. Her voice was hard, too, and brittle with contempt. "No. He was too drunk. He tried. When he couldn't, he…hit me instead."

Roan swore colorfully, but only inside his mind. Aloud, he prompted in the same quiet, implacable way, "And then?"

"Then?" She shrugged, and he saw her scrape her teeth carefully across her swollen lower lip. "He left." As she turned back to the sink she drew a breath, and it was the only thing that betrayed her body's trembling.

He waited a moment, steeling himself. Then asked the question he hated to have to ask: "Mary, do you own a gun?"

Chapter Three

He waited patiently in the silence while she puttered around the sink, doing what looked to him were totally unnecessary cleaning chores, and it occurred to him only then how out of place this woman looked in that particular kitchen. He hadn't known its former owner, Queenie Schultz, all that well, except to say hello to when he'd dropped off Erin or picked her up from her monthly trip to the beauty shop, but he sure did remember her big-toothed smile and big brassy laugh, and the pinkish-tinted platinum blond hair she wore teased up and lacquered into a bouffant the size of a basketball. That, and her short but big-busted shape she liked to squeeze into smocks that were just a wee bit too small, so she always put him in mind of a little strutting pigeon.

Her he could see in this kitchen, with its pink and yellow flowered wallpaper, ruffled curtains, potted sweet potato vine on the windowsill and potholders shaped like kitty-cat faces. Miss Mary Owen didn't fit, like the one kid who hadn't gotten the word it was supposed to be dress-up day, and he wondered if that might account for some of her awkwardness.

He felt a strange desire to reassure her...put her at ease. He'd almost forgotten the question he'd asked, when she gave him the answer he didn't want to hear.

"Yes, I do own a gun." She threw him a quick defiant look over one shoulder. "I have a license for it, too, in case you're wondering." Then she turned and leaned against the sink and folded her arms with an air of weary acceptance as if answering his questions was an unpleasant task she'd decided to get over with as quickly as possible. "I got it several years ago. For protection, since I live alone, and I often work late."

"Mind if I ask what kind it is?"

"It's a Ladysmith," she replied without hesitation. "Thirty-eight caliber."

Again, it wasn't the answer he'd hoped for. He lifted his eyebrows. "That's a lot of gun for a woman. Know how to use it?"

Her lips flirted with a smile that made him aware of how he'd sounded—like a bad John Wayne imitation. "Yes, Sheriff, I do. I practice at a firing range at least once a month."

"So you're a pretty good shot?"

Watching him, she hitched one shoulder in a wary shrug. "I usually hit what I'm aiming at."

"How long's it been since you went shooting?"

Behind the ugly glasses he saw her eyes kindle again as she countered softly, "I went this last weekend."

Convenient alibi, Roan thought, *in case a weapon turns out to have been fired recently.*

"Where's the gun now? Mind if I take a look at it?" He asked it in a friendly way, smiling. "Take it with me, run a few tests on it?"

The smile she gave him back was a lot less friendly than his. "Don't you need a warrant for that?"

"I do if you make me get one," Roan said, still showing his teeth, "or, you could agree to give me the gun of your own free will. Save us both some unpleasantness."

While he waited for her reply, it struck him that it was an odd sort of conversation to be having with a murder suspect. More like a verbal fencing match than an interrogation— rapid and light in tone, almost playful, but with an underlying tenseness, each of them concentrating with laser-like focus on the other, both of them wary...poised to thrust or parry for real at an instant's notice.

Excitement raced through him as she lifted her chin and threw at him in direct challenge, "I could...but you'd have to tell me why you want it."

The tension rose again to a screaming pitch while he pondered his options...while he wondered what kind of a lawman he was to be playing this kind of game with a suspect in a murder investigation. Finally, he drawled, "Oh, I think you know why."

She sighed and her lips curled, but not with a smile this time. "You think I shot Jason Holbrook with it."

"Did you?"

"No." It was a quiet but vehement explosion.

Roan narrowed his eyes. He wasn't conscious of movement, but the distance between himself and the woman seemed to shrink. "But didn't you say you got the gun for protection because you work late…protection, I'm assuming, against just the sort of thing that happened to you last night?"

She stared at him and didn't answer…didn't confirm it, or deny it, either. But he could see shadows of what might have been fear or pain, or maybe both, flit across her eyes.

"So, if you *didn't* use the gun last night when Jason attacked you," he went on, scratching his chin in a puzzled way, "my question would be, why not? It would make sense to me if you had shot him—might even be considered self-defense." He knew damn well it hadn't been, but handed it to her like a gift, just to see what she'd do with it.

Again she didn't bite, just looked at him with eyes green and deep as the sea and quietly said, "Do I need a lawyer?"

He folded his arms and gave her an ambiguous little nod. "Not if your gun checks out."

She let out a breath, then pushed abruptly away from the sink…stalked across the darkened living room with a long and pantherlike stride. And as he picked up his hat and hurriedly followed, Roan was conscious once more of the woman's unexpected grace. And something else. Something he couldn't put his finger on, but that stirred up a prickly feeling on the back of his neck. Something about that walk...

When he caught up with her she was pulling out her purse from underneath a small table beside the front door. His stomach lurched when she opened it and took out a slim, lethal-looking handgun, but she merely handed it over to him, butt first.

"I'd like it back as soon as possible," she said, and this time there was no mistaking the flicker of fear in her eyes.

So... I guess maybe she wasn't lying when she said she needed this thing for protection, Roan thought as he carefully wrapped the weapon in his handkerchief. The lady was definitely afraid of something—or someone. Not for the first time, he wondered where she'd come from and what she was doing here, a couple of hundred miles from nowhere, and if it was the usual domestic abuse thing she was running from, or something more sinister.

One thing for sure, he was going to be running a check on Miss Mary Owen the minute he got back to the shop. Maybe he'd call in from his vehicle, get the ball rolling even before that.

"I guess you'll be wanting something with my DNA."

He looked up and found her gazing at him, head held high and bruised jaw set at a proud angle, eyes fathomless now, behind the glasses. Since he was juggling his hat and the gun, about all Roan could do was nod. He was doing that, getting ready to say the usual things he'd say to a viable suspect he wasn't quite ready to arrest yet, when he came close to dropping everything in his hands and just about jumped out of his skin.

Something brushed across the back of his legs.

He did a clumsy sort of pivot, swearing under his breath, adrenaline hitting him like a blast of buckshot. Then, with an embarrassed snort, he bent and scooped up the big orange tomcat busily doing figure eights around his ankles. "Jeez, cat," he muttered, "you damn near scared me out of my growth." The animal's only reply was a raspy purr as he butted his big head up underneath Roan's chin hard enough to make him see stars.

He lifted his eyebrows and shifted his gaze

back to Mary Owen. "This monster belong to you?"

But she seemed to be in some sort of trance, staring at the cat as if it had just sprung full-grown from his chest, like an alien birth. Roan had to repeat her name twice before she twitched her eyes back to his and words came gasping out of her already open mouth.

"No—I mean, yes—but…he's Queenie's—he came with the house. But he's never let me get near him, much less pick him up. What on earth did you *do?*"

"Cats are funny about who they decide to like," Roan said, and the cat's purring was so loud and ratchety he had to raise his voice to make himself heard over it. He chuckled as he gave the cat a good scratch along the edge of his jaw and the purring rose to a snarl of pure ecstasy. "He's sure a big ol' boy—seems friendly enough now. Here, maybe he'll—"

He was about to hand the cat over to her when the beast lunged out of his grasp and, hissing and spitting, vaulted off Mary's un-prepared arms and hit the floor with a heavy *thud*. From there he surged upward in one fluid leap to the back of the sofa where he crouched, eyes round and glowing, fur rippling, tail twitching, growls coming from low in his chest.

"Well, now you see what I mean," Mary said as she gazed dispassionately at the bleeding scratches on her forearm. She reached into the pocket of her smock, pulled out a crumpled tissue, pressed it against the scratches and handed it to him. "That should do it for DNA. If not, you know where to find me."

She groped for the doorknob, her jerky movements telling him she didn't have it together as well as she wanted him to believe. "If there's nothing else, Sheriff…" She hitched in a breath as she pulled the door open and held it, gazing at him and waiting.

It was too dark for him to see the color of her eyes, but he'd have bet they'd gone that fiery greeny-gold again.

Thinking about that, remembering those eyes and that curiously electric fire, he felt a stirring on his skin, as if something had flown close enough over it to disturb the fine hairs there.

And then he thought of an old horse trainer he'd once known, a member of the Blackfoot tribe, who'd told him about spirit power, and how he must listen to the messages given him in dreams by the spirit animals, which might be a bird or a wolf, or even a buffalo. And that he must obey them, because one day when he needed help he could call on the spirit animal and be answered. Why he should remember this now he couldn't imagine, but that stirring across his skin did seem to him like a warning of some kind...call it instinct, call it a gut feeling, but *something* was telling him that something about this lady wasn't right.

"Ma'am," he said, and gave her a nod as he stepped through the doorway. He'd barely drawn his first breath of the chilly spring night air when he heard the door close and a dead bolt lock slide home behind him.

Back at the four-wheel-drive SUV that served as his patrol car, he got a couple of evidence bags out of the back and stowed the gun and the tissue with Mary Owen's blood on it, then unhooked his cell phone from his belt and climbed behind the wheel. He'd already hit the quick-dial button he used most when it came to him—the thing that had been bothering him about the woman he'd just left, the thing he hadn't been able to put his finger on, the thing that just wasn't *right*.

It was her walk. More specifically, the way she'd walked when she'd left him standing in the kitchen and crossed through the living room on her way to the front door to get her gun. That one time when she'd been too upset, too ticked off to remember the role she was supposed to be playing.

Like a panther.

How was it that mousy Miss Mary should have a walk that was long-legged, strong, confident and graceful...the walk, not of a shy homely mouse, but of a beautiful woman?

Yes...a tall, graceful woman with a panther's walk and eyes that sparked with green-gold fire. It struck him, then, that Miss Mary Owen was anything but mousy. That she was, in fact, a very beautiful woman, though she seemed to be trying her level best to hide the fact. And he and everybody else in town had evidently been too damn blind to see beyond her disguise.

Everybody...except for Jason Holbrook, who was now dead. *Coincidence?*

Sitting there in his SUV on a quiet street in the town he'd lived in most all his life, Roan felt the Spirit Messenger stir once more across his skin.

Inside the house that wasn't and never would be her home, the woman who called herself Mary Owen leaned back against the door and closed her eyes. As she waited for the sound of the sheriff's car starting up and driving away, she felt the fear creep over her... the hollow sense of dread that meant her life had just taken a hard left turn and was about to go careening off in an unexpected direction.

It wasn't a new feeling. She'd felt it for the first time almost twenty years ago, that fear, the day she'd run away to New York City to pursue a modeling career, never to return. Not exactly an original move for an unhappy young girl in a drab and miserable existance; a few decades earlier, she might have fled to Hollywood with dreams of becoming a movie star.

A life of glamour, excitement and beauty... what young girl didn't dream of such things? How many found the courage to risk everything, leave the security of the only life they'd ever known to follow the dream? Darn few, Mary thought, with a valiant lift of her head. Darn few. She didn't regret leaving home, even if the dream she'd sought so long ago still fluttered like a rare and lovely butterfly, tantalizingly beyond reach.

Not that she'd be all that sorry to leave this town, she thought, at least no more sorry than all the other times she'd had to pull up stakes and start over again someplace new. It had begun to seem natural to her always to be the new face in town. The shy, retiring stranger who keeps to herself and never lets anybody get too close....

Hartsville, Montana—Heartbreak, she'd heard the oldtimers call it, the ones who remembered way back to when the mines went bust. She'd come to the town purely by chance. It had merely been the place she'd wound up in last winter when she'd pulled off the interstate in the middle of a snowstorm because a warning light had come on in her car and she'd needed to find a service station right quick. Waiting in the coffee shop across the highway from the Gas-n-Go Kwik Service for a new alternator to be installed in her elderly Ford Taurus, Mary had found herself in friendly conversation with Queenie Schultz, owner-operator of the town's only beauty parlor. She'd learned that Queenie's sister down in Phoenix had been after her to move down there, and that Queenie had about had her fill of the cold and the snow, but couldn't bring herself to run off and leave her faithful customers with nobody to do their color and sets.

Mary hadn't expected to spend the rest of her life in Hartsville. But not even six months? That was a record, even for her.

She opened her eyes and found the cat still crouched on the back of the sofa, watching her with an expression of profound disdain. The silence in the room crawled over her skin and pricked her scalp like a premonition.

Why hasn't his car started up yet? Why hasn't he gone away?

She crept to the front window, fingered back the brown plaid drape and its heavy insulated lining and peered out. The sheriff's SUV was still parked in front of the house—across the bottom of the driveway, in fact. To keep her from escaping, she wondered? Her skin prickled again, and she shivered. *What is he doing out there?*

"Daddy!"

Roan felt his heart lift, the way it always did when he heard his daughter's voice… which at the same time, oddly, also made his heart ache.

In the darkness and privacy of his patrol vehicle, his mouth formed a grin. "Hey, peanut, how ya doin'? You and Grampa Boyd eatin' supper?"

"Yeah… Grampa made hot dogs and beans…*again*." Roan chuckled; he could almost *hear* those eyes rolling. "We were gonna make cornbread, but Grampa said we should save that for when you're home, 'cause we *know* how much you like cornbread. Dad…"

"Yeah, peanut?" Roan pressed his thumb and forefinger against his forehead and rubbed, bracing for Susie Grace's inevitable disappointment.

"Grampa said you have to work because something bad happened and a man got killed and you have to find the person that did it. But when *are* you comin' home?"

He let out a gusty breath. "I'm gonna be pretty late, Susie-G. Most likely it'll be past your bedtime, so don't you try and wait up for me, now. You go to bed when Grampa Boyd tells you, you hear me?"

He heard a noisy exhalation that was a pretty good imitation of his own. "Okay. But, Daddy?"

"Yeah?"

"If I'm asleep when you get home, would you come and kiss me good night and tuck me in anyway?"

"Don't I always?"

"Yeah, but promise me anyway."

Roan gave an exaggerated sigh. "I *promise*."

"Okay, then. G'night, Daddy. I love you bunches and *bunches*."

"Love you the same back atcha. G'night, now. Be good."

With the cell phone dead in his hand and the silence of night settling in, Roan realized his face was aching—most likely because he was still wearing that grin. He scrubbed a hand over his face to ease the muscles and was reaching for the ignition key when his radio crackled to life.

He thumbed it on and ID'd himself. "Yeah, Donna—what's up?"

"Sheriff, uh…what's your ETA back here at the shop?" The night dispatcher sounded uncharacteristically restrained.

"Let me guess," said Roan with a new and decidedly sardonic grin stretching his face muscles. "There's a United States Senator sitting in my office right now, spittin' bullets."

"Uh…that sums it up pretty well, only he's not sittin'. More like…pacing. Think…a big old mountain lion in a cage."

He chuckled and reached for the ignition. "I'm on my way."

As the SUV's lights came on he looked

up at the house once more, in time to see the window curtain twitch back into place.

At least, the sheriff thought as he drove away from the dark, quiet house and its puzzling, enigmatic and oddly disturbing occupant, *I can tell the victim's father we have a possible suspect.*

He wondered why that thought didn't make him happier.

Mary let the draperies fall back into place, laughing silently at her own foolishness. He'd only been checking in, or calling in, or whatever it was policemen did when they'd been absent from their radios for a time. She was being paranoid, worrying for nothing. Sheriff Harley had her gun, and if he was as competent and as good and decent a man as Miss Ada said he was, it shouldn't take him long to conclude that she'd had nothing whatsoever to do with the murder of Jason Holbrook.

But I could have. Maybe I would have....

Revulsion rippled across her skin, and she fought down a wave of nausea as for a terrible moment it all came rushing back—the smell of his breath, hot and thick with beer and tobacco and lust...the pressure of his arm across her throat, and the rising curtain of blackness and terror that threatened to suffocate her...the sharpness of his belt buckle cutting into the small of her back...the sound of his breathing, intent and determined...the sense of stark disbelief that curtained her mind from the thought that shrieked from some distant place: *Oh God, I'm being raped.*

And perhaps most shockingly, she recalled the violence and brutality of her release, and the strange mixture of rage and relief that had shaken her then, to the very depths of her soul. *Not raped...violated nonetheless.* She had not been a well-loved child, nor had she lived a protected life up to then, but she had never been spat upon before. She had never been struck in the face. Even Diego had never struck her in the face.

She could still taste the sickness that had risen into her throat after Jason had left her, in spite of all her efforts to prevent it.

Oh, I wish I could have killed him.

Would she have, she wondered now, if she had been able to reach the gun in her purse, the one she'd bought and practiced with so faithfully, then left sitting on the table beside the front door when she'd stepped onto the porch to check on the burned-out light bulb...only to realize a moment later, with a horrifying clutch of fear in her belly, that the bulb had been deliberately removed…and to know, with a cold sick sense of irony, that all her vigilance and preparation had been for nothing?

For nothing. Because in the end, the boogieman had found her anyway. Not the boogieman she'd been expecting, true, but bad enough. Definitely bad enough.

But the sheriff had taken her gun, and the forensics would prove she hadn't shot Jason, no matter how much she might have wanted to. She had nothing to worry about.

Well, maybe not *nothing.* The sheriff had struck her as a man to be reckoned with, a man who wouldn't be easily fooled.

Once again a little frisson stirred through her body as she recalled the cool blue glitter of those farseeing eyes, and it was followed by the surprised realization that, like the first time it had happened, when she'd first seen Roan Harley standing on her front porch, this wasn't exactly an unpleasant sensation.

"What are you looking at me like that for?" Mary said to Cat, who was still crouched on the back of the sofa, staring at her with what she could have sworn was a sneer of contempt. "Just because *you* took a fancy to him.

You're a *cat*—what do *you* know? The man's dangerous, I'm telling you."

The cat gave her one of his slow-motion blinks and turned his face away.

Mary shrugged. What had she expected? She was, as she had been for ten long years, utterly and completely alone.

Taking a purposeful breath, she crossed the living room to the door that opened onto a short hallway and thus to the house's two bedrooms and only bathroom. She went into the bathroom, turned on the light and closed the door.

With only the briefest glance at her image in the medicine cabinet mirror above the sink, she pulled the clip from her hair, letting it fall to her shoulders, not in the vibrant tumble of curls that was its true nature but in limp straight strands. She scrubbed her scalp vigorously with her fingers for a few moments, then opened the cabinet below the sink and took out several plastic bottles with applicator tips, a small glass bowl and a number of odds and ends she'd become all too familiar with during the past ten years.

Slipping disposable gloves onto her hands, she squeezed dollops from the plastic bottles into the glass bowl and mixed them thoroughly. Then, using a small soft brush, she began to dab the resulting jelly-like gunk onto the strip of flaming red at the roots of her dirt-brown hair.

Roan entered the sheriff's station through the front door, removing his Stetson as he nodded at the dispatcher ensconced in her cubbyhole behind a pane of bulletproof glass. At that hour, the business day and visiting hours at the detention center being long over, the lobby was empty. There were no washed-out women balancing babies on their hips waiting to visit their no-account husbands in the lock-up, no parolees keeping appointments with their parole officers, no unhappy teenagers and grim-faced parents waiting to pay traffic fines. The silence had a suspenseful, waiting quality, like a held breath.

The blast of the buzzer announcing the unlocking of the door to the inner sanctum sounded raucously, making him wince as it always did. The combination sheriff's station and county detention center was a relatively new facility, having been one of the first major promises Roan had made good on after getting himself elected sheriff. Considering that the one it replaced could have been taken straight off the set of a Hollywood Western movie, the effect had been to boost the county's law-enforcement capabilities from the nineteenth to the twenty-first century in one giant leap, vaulting over the twentieth in the process. The facility had been all state-of-the-art at the time, with the latest security safeguards considered necessary in this age of terrorism. Roan had no objections to the protection, even if any terrorists to be found in the environs of Hart County, Montana, were likely to be of the homegrown drunk-and-disorderly-cowboy or disgruntled-hunter variety. He did wish that buzzer could have been toned down a bit, though.

As the outer door closed behind him he paused to stick his head through the open top half of the dispatcher's doorway and said in an undertone, "He still here?"

Donna gave him a grim look and tilted her head toward the back of the building. "Down there in your office."

Roan nodded, slapped his hat against his thigh and continued on down the hallway. He didn't hesitate at the door to his office; the way he saw it, postponing the moment wasn't going to make it any easier. He took a firm grip on the doorknob and turned it.

Chapter Four

The man standing with his back to the door pretending to study the large topographical map of Hart County and its environs hanging on the wall behind the desk jerked around when Roan walked in, then pushed past the corner of the desk and came toward him.

He was a tall man, similar to Roan in both height and build, but now he seemed to have folded in on himself, so that his buff-colored Western-style suede jacket hung from his broad shoulders like a coat on a rack. His normally strong-sculpted features appeared shrunken, too, and his skin, yellowed and darkened to the color of old parchment, draped across them in ill-fitting folds and hollows. Only his eyes seemed as sharp and intense as Roan remembered, their ice-blue glare glittering out of shadowed sockets like the eyes of a starving wolf homed in on his prey.

He's aged twenty years, Roan thought. But he wasn't all that surprised. He'd seen the look before, on his father-in-law, Boyd Stuart's face, right after Erin had died—the look of a man fixing to bury his child.

"Good to see you, Senator," he said as he clasped the big, rawboned hand. "Just wish it didn't have to be for this. Can't tell you how sorry I am." He meant it sincerely. He hadn't had much use for Jason Holbrook, but he wouldn't wish the pain of losing a child on any man.

Holbrook gripped Roan's hand tightly in both of his—a politician's handshake—then released it. "Hell of a thing," he muttered as he swiped a hand over hair that was still luxuriant but more silver now than gold. "Just a hell of a thing." He coughed loudly and abruptly, then narrowed his wolf's stare at Roan. "Tell me you're gonna find whoever did this. Tell me you're gonna get the son of a bitch that shot my boy."

Roan met the older man's gaze with an

almost identical one and quietly replied, "I mean to. I believe I will." He laid his Stetson on the top of his desk as he rounded its corner and pulled out his chair.

Senator Holbrook was pacing again. He paused to frown distractedly at nothing. "You've called in the state boys—that's good. That's good. That detective that picked me up at the airport—seems like a good man. Seems to know his stuff."

Roan nodded and sat. "I think he does. Name's Kurt Ruger. Partner's name is Roger Fry—he's not here right now. I sent him with the forensics evidence to the lab in Helena. They're both good men."

Holbrook aimed the scowl at him again. "Sure that's going to be enough manpower? I can have the FBI in here by tomorrow morning. In fact, if this was in some way directed at me…"

The chair creaked as Roan leaned back in it, deliberately adopting a casual attitude, masking the tension he felt with calm eyes and even tone. "At this point there's nothing about the shooting that would indicate a national security connection. In fact, we're pretty certain this was local."

"Local…as in…"

"Personal."

"Ah." The senator's mouth tightened. Then he rubbed a hand hard across his eyes, as though the fire in them burned even him. "I see," he said heavily, and hauled in a breath. "Well…okay then, I don't want to step on your toes, Roan. Just trying to help. You let me know if you need anything, now, you hear me? Anything at all. Just find this guy."

"Oh," Roan said softly, "I'll do that."

Instead of leaving then, the senator jerked out one of the chairs that faced Roan's desk and perched himself on the edge of the seat, then leaned forward with shoulders hunched and hands clasped. "Okay, so tell me what you've got so far. Any leads? Any suspects?"

Getting down to brass tacks, thought Roan. The fact that he'd anticipated this didn't make it any more welcome. He shifted warily. "Now, Cliff, you know I can't—"

Holbrook silenced him with an impatient gesture and grimace. "Don't give me that, Roan. You think I can't get access to anything you or those state boys have got? Take me one phone call. I hope you're not gonna make me do that. Lord, son, this is family."

Family. Roan let out a breath, hating the jolt that had kicked inside him at the word. He doubted the senator, given his current frame of mind, even realized the implications of what he'd said. No sense making anything of it.

He shrugged. "We've got some ideas. Pretty good idea what happened, anyway. For starters, it looks like Jason most likely knew the person that shot him."

The senator's eyes narrowed. "That's why you're saying it was personal."

Roan nodded. "He was shot at fairly close range, no sign of any struggle—in fact, it looks like Jase may not have known he was in serious danger, not until it was too late."

Holbrook let out a groaning breath and leaned back in his chair, shaking his head.

"And," Roan added reluctantly, "some of the forensic evidence suggests there may have been a woman involved."

The senator's grunt didn't sound surprised by that information; the man knew his son as well as anybody did. He put a hand over his eyes and said tiredly as he rubbed, "So... you're looking at, what, a jealous boyfriend? Husband?"

It was the moment and the question Roan had been dreading, but he didn't see how he could avoid answering it. He couldn't explain his reluctance, or the pulse tapping in his belly, as if he were about to betray a personal confidence. From a woman he'd just met, and a suspect to boot. *Weird*.

"Could be. Seems he had an altercation with a woman outside Buster's last night." He cleared his throat, but the words still came hard. "This woman seems to be the last person to have seen Jason alive."

Holbrook's head jerked up and his eyes sparked like coals coming to life. "So? Why isn't she in here? Why aren't you questioning her?" He paused, then did a double take and said incredulously, "Are you telling me a *woman* might have done this?"

Roan made a gesture of impatience that rocked his chair, making it squeak again. "I'm not saying that, no. At this point, anything's possible." He reined himself in, leaned forward and placed his clasped hands on his desktop. "Cliff, I've just come from questioning the woman. She's voluntarily turned over her gun and a DNA sample, both of which will be on their way to the lab first thing in the morning. Meanwhile, we're running a check on her—appears she's new in town, hasn't lived here more than a few months." He paused, hating, for the senator's sake, what he had to say now. Whatever else Jason Holbrook may have been, it didn't change the fact that he was this man's child. He coughed, then spat it out. "There's something you need to know. There's a good possibility Jason may have assaulted this woman. May even have raped her."

"Lord." Holbrook ran a hand over his eyes. Then he looked up at Roan and his eyes hardened, became splinters of cold steel. His voice, hushed to begin with, rose with anger to a muted roar. "Are you saying this was... what, some kind of *self-defense?*"

"No, I'm not saying that at all. I don't think it was, not in the legal sense. I'm just—"

The senator's clenched fist thumped the desktop. "She—or somebody—shot my *son,* dammit." He pushed himself upright, leaning on that closed fist, until he loomed above Roan like a thunderhead. His voice grated harshly between clenched teeth. "Jason wasn't any saint. Hell, I know that. But he was my *son.* I want whoever did this to pay for it. If this woman shot my boy—no matter what he did, she had no right to take his life. I want her arrested, prosecuted and locked up, you understand me?" He straightened, and his rugged face spasmed with grief as he turned to go. Then he paused, and his voice quivered slightly as he added, "You do this for me, son. I'm countin' on you."

Roan sat still while a storm raged inside him, gripping the arms of his chair to hold himself steady against the battering of the anger and too many other emotions he couldn't name. Through a shimmering haze he watched the other man walk toward the door, the man he'd looked up to as a boy and young man and secretly believed—or perhaps wished—was his own biological father, seeing him suddenly stooped and old. He heard himself ask, in a hard, cracking voice, "Where are you staying? You realize your house is still being processed as a crime scene?"

Cliff Holbrook hesitated, then turned to look back at him. He seemed dazed. Almost...lost.

Vulnerable. Roan didn't want to think it. Couldn't help it.

"Tell you the truth, I...hadn't really thought," the senator said, smiling slightly.

Roan sure as hell didn't want to feel sympathy for the man, not right now anyway. But he couldn't help that, either. "Why don't you go on out to the ranch?" he heard himself say in a voice like a washed-out gravel road.

"You're welcome to stay as long as you need to. I'll call Boyd, tell him you're coming."

There was a moment...a flicker of something in the other man's eyes, there too briefly to read...a softening, perhaps, or even...regret? Then Senator Clifford Holbrook seemed to gather himself and grow taller...stronger... harder. "Thank you," he said crisply, more like himself again, "but I'll make do with the local motel until my house is released. I want to make this understood right now, Roan—" he jabbed the air with a forefinger and his voice took on the timbre and conviction of a man making a campaign speech "—I am not leaving this town until the person who murdered my son is behind bars. Count on that."

Roan watched the door thump shut behind the senator, then blew out a breath and leaned back in his chair, fingers laced behind his head. Half of him felt small and disappointed and rejected and wanted to kick something because of it. The other half wanted to laugh at himself for being so stupid. When was he going to stop thinking anything between him and Clifford Holbrook was ever going to change?

Time to go home, he thought, but a glance at his watch gave him a jolt of surprise and sent a squirt of guilt through him, too. Way past time. Susie Grace would be sound asleep by now, and Boyd most likely, too, snoring on the sofa in front of the television, which would be playing away on Mute, tuned to the History Channel. There'd be dinner left for Roan in the kitchen, but he didn't relish the idea of eating microwaved leftovers alone, or going home to a cold silent house, for that matter, tiptoeing like a thief into his daughter's room to kiss her good night, his belly sore with knowing he'd disappointed her again.

Then he thought about the man who'd just left his office to go alone into an empty motel room, knowing the son whose room he'd once tiptoed into for a goodnight kiss was lying cold and dead on a table at the morgue.

I've got a job to do, Roan thought.

He swiveled his chair around and punched the button that would bring his sleeping computer to life. Say what you would about the Internet, at least it never closed. If nothing else, he could still do some checking up on the lady named Mary Owen.

Mary lay shivering in a tumble of clammy sheets and watched daylight slowly wash color into the featureless gray of her bedroom. She'd been awake for hours, tossing and turning, afraid to go back to sleep, knowing she'd dream of Diego again. Not the Diego of last night's unexpectedly awakened memory, smiling and sexy-eyed, handsome as sin. The Diego DelRey who waited for her in the shadowy darkness of her nightmares was the *other* Diego, the one who'd looked at her that last time with eyes that were filled with hate. The one who had stabbed the air with a finger like a dagger and vowed in words only she could hear that he would find her one day. Find her and make her pay.

Why is this happening to me now? Diego isn't coming to kill me. He'll never find me. I thought I was over the fear.

Was it because, for the first time in many years, she was without the comfort of a weapon? Or…was it something else entirely? *He violated my space…got under my skin… inside my head. Made me vulnerable.*

She wasn't thinking of the man who'd tried to rape her.

She lay still, concentrating on breathing evenly and deeply, and once more closed her eyes. *I won't be afraid,* she thought. *I have nothing to be afraid of now.*

Little by little she felt the tension ease from her muscles, and her body take on the heaviness of impending sleep. Cautiously, she released her mind, letting it drift through memories of happier times, like a boat floating down a river past pleasant scenes on its banks: the apartment in New York, the dear, dear face of her roommate, Joy. Diego again, leaning toward her across a table, his eyes flickering in the light of a guttering candle, the air soft with humidity and fragrant with the scent of tropical flowers...his hands so warm, holding hers, the sudden lovely coolness of the ring he placed on her finger.

"Marry me," I remember he said to me in his husky, sexy voice, "and I will make all your dreams come true." And I looked into his eyes, filled with so much love for me...and how could I not believe him?

But now...those eyes faded into shadows and another pair came to take their place, not the dark and smoky Latino eyes of Diego Del-Rey, not even the ones from later on, hard, now, with hate. These eyes were an intense and glittering blue, and squinted a little, as if from a lifetime of gazing at sunshot horizons. They seemed to look straight into

Mary's soul, down into the deepest darkest places where all her secrets slept.

She opened her eyes, shaking, as fear swept through her like a cold Montana wind.

Deputy Tom Daggett knocked on Roan's office door at seven forty-five Saturday morning.

"Yeah?" Roan grunted, trying to look as if he hadn't just been asleep with his head on a pile of expense reports.

Tom looked wary, but came on in anyway. "Sorry to bother you, Sheriff—thought you'd want to know. Just got a call from the crime lab in Helena. That evidence we sent over—too soon for DNA on that second blood sample, but the slug we dug outa the dashboard of Jase's truck?" He paused, flushed with the import of the news he bore. "It's from a Colt 45 revolver."

"A Colt 45. No kidding." Roan scrubbed a hand over his stubbly jaw and glowered at his deputy, who he considered had no business being this fresh and enthusiastic so early in the morning. His own mouth tasted like the bottom of a chicken coop, and even the station's off-duty-room coffee was sounding good to him right now. "A damn six-shooter," he muttered on an exhalation. The dispenser of so many doses of frontier justice. It seemed fitting, somehow.

And not a Ladysmith. Which should have made him feel better, but for some reason didn't.

He leaned back in his chair, making it squawk, and dug the keys to his patrol vehicle out of his pocket. "There's a couple of evidence bags in the back of my car," he said as he lobbed the keys at Tom. "They need to get over to Helena right away. Like...yesterday. Lori can do it—I hate to keep using those state detectives for errand boys. Then I want you to get over to the courthouse—they ought to be opening up about now. Get on over there and look up the deed to that beauty shop Queenie Schultz sold when she left town last winter. Find out everything you can about the person who bought it. Her name's Mary Owen. I want to know what address she gave Queenie and how she paid for that shop. Then I want her bank records, her social security number, her birth certificate, passport and driver's license numbers. I want you to find out where she parks her car and get me the license plate and VIN off it. I want to know where that woman lived before she came here, where she went to school, what she did for a living, who she was married to, what childhood vaccinations she got. Anything and everything. You got that?"

"Uh...yeah, but...it's Saturday, Sheriff. Courthouse is closed." Tom looked as if he was beginning to regret being the one to bring the sheriff up to speed on the latest developments. "Anyway, don't you need a warrant for some of that stuff?"

"Yeah, you do, for pretty near all of it," Roan admitted grumpily. Frustration gnawed at him. He didn't like being thwarted when he had a mystery to solve. "Okay, since it's Saturday...here's what you do: call up Miss Ada and ask her to get hold of the circuit court judge. Hurry up if you want to catch him before he goes off fishing."

"Me, sir?"

Roan heaved a cranky sigh. "Just tell Miss Ada we need the judge *today.* I'll take it from there. Okay?"

Tom muttered something Roan couldn't hear, which was probably a good thing. He went out, closing the office door behind him.

Alone again, Roan leaned back in his chair and had himself a good stretch, which didn't do a lot to relieve the crick in his neck or the stiffness in his legs, either one. He put his hands flat on his desktop and was about to unfold himself and go find a bathroom and a cup of that lousy coffee, in that order, when the door to his office opened once again, without a warning knock this time.

He heard a gravelly voice he knew well say, "Little bit, what'd I tell you—"

And the eyes he'd rather have looking back at him than any others in this world were peeking around the edge of the door, those blue eyes, sparkling with mischief, lighting up the morning like the sun coming up over the top of a hill. A little girl's eyes...and so much like her mother's he felt a stab of pain every time he looked into them.

"Hey, peanut," he said, his voice going soft and husky, "where'd you come from?"

There was a throaty giggle, and the rest of his daughter's face slid into view around the edge of the door, wearing an off-kilter smile of delight. And the spasm of pain and guilt and rage that hit Roan then wasn't just a stab; it was a knife thrust deep in his guts and then twisted. But it was a pain he was used to, so he was good at hiding it behind a warm and welcoming smile.

"We wanted to surprise you," Susie Grace

said as she danced across the room and into Roan's arms and gave him a loud smacking kiss.

"Uh-*huh*," he grunted, swiveling away from his desk to make room for her in his lap. "Well, you sure did that." His eyes lifted over her head to the man who'd followed her into his office. "Boyd… What're you guys up to so early?"

"We brought you some breakfast," Susie Grace announced. "Grampa made bacon-and-egg samwiches."

"Figured you could use some coffee, too." Boyd hefted the old-fashioned, black-painted metal lunch-box he was carrying, the kind that holds a thermos bottle in the lid. Being the sort of man who never liked throwing things away, he had a lot of that sort of antique junk around his place. "If you don't mind the good stuff, instead of that swill you got here."

A Montana cattleman by birth, ancestry and tradition, Boyd still perked his coffee in a big enameled pot, which sat and simmered on the back of the cookstove throughout most of the day and by evening, Roan happened to know, the contents came to resemble something a man could waterproof his boots with.

This early in the morning, though, Boyd's coffee sounded like pure heaven, especially after a night like he'd just had. With a growl of gratitude, he shifted Susie Grace to one knee while he opened up the lunch-box, took out the thermos bottle and poured himself some in the red plastic lid. He closed his eyes and savored the smell of his first cup of coffee and the sweet warm weight of the child in his lap and decided this day might not turn out to be so bad after all.

While Roan slurped down some coffee, Susie Grace got busy unwrapping one of the two fat foil packages from the lunch-box. "You have to eat, Dad," she told him sternly. "If you're going to work so long you have to keep your strength up."

"Grampa tell you that?" Roan winked at Boyd.

Keeping her eyes lowered, watching her scar-stiffened hands painstakingly unfold the sandwich wrappings, Susie Grace lifted her chin a notch, giving Roan a glimpse of the shiny puckered skin that covered most of her neck and the right side of her face. "No, *I* told myself. I have a mind of my own, you know."

Boyd snorted and Roan came near losing the swallow of coffee he'd just taken. "Yeah, you do," he said, chuckling, while Boyd rolled his eyes toward the ceiling.

Tom Daggett tapped on the open door and leaned into the room. "How you doin', Mr. Stuart? Hey there, Susie Grace. When you've got a minute, Sheriff?"

Roan gave him a nod, then swiveled around and nudged the little girl in his lap. She hopped off obligingly, but with a pitiful sigh for effect. "I know...you have to go to work."

"I do, peanut. Sorry. What've you guys got planned for today?"

Susie Grace's eyes danced and her mouth formed its quirky lopsided smile. "We're goin' *fishin'*. Grampa says I'm old enough now, he's gonna teach me how to fly cast. Only I can't wade in the creek, 'cause the current's too strong."

"Not to mention you'd freeze your fanny off," Boyd said in his crotchety way, making an impatient come-here gesture with his gnarled and burn-scarred hand. "Come on, now, little bit, let's get out of your daddy's way and let him do his job." The hand was gentle as it ruffled his granddaughter's hair, then settled protectively onto her shoulder. "Guess we'll see you later, Roan."

Roan said, "I'm gonna expect some fried trout for supper tonight."

Boyd snorted and Susie Grace threw Roan a cheeky grin over her shoulder. "Then you hafta come home or you won't get any."

Roan laughed. "Well, I guess I will, then." He kept the smile on his face and gave a goodbye wave as he said, "Have fun," and Susie Grace waved back and blew him a kiss. Then he sat with a heavy ache at the bottom of his throat and watched the old cattleman and the seven-year-old child go out the door together, the one bent over and rump-sprung from too many years spent on the back of a horse, the other skip-hopping and holding on to his hand, her flame-red pigtails bouncing. All the family Roan had left in the world, and both of them wearing the scars that were a constant reminder to him of the dear one he'd lost, and of how near he'd come to losing the two of them as well.

"That Susie Grace sure is growin' up fast," Tom said as he came on into the room.

"Yeah, kids have a way of doing that." Roan picked up a bacon-and-egg sandwich and bit into it, adding as he chewed, "What you got for me, Tom?"

"That evidence you mentioned? Lori's on

her way to Helena with it right now—just drove out of the parking lot. And, uh… I thought you'd want to know, Jason's dad— Senator Holbrook—he just pulled up out front." The deputy shifted uncomfortably. "How much do you want me to tell him, Sheriff? About the investigation, I mean. I know the usual procedure, but him being a United States Senator, and all…"

Roan looked at what was left of the sandwich, then put it down, having lost his appetite. "Might as well give him everything we've got," he said, frowning into the plastic thermos lid, now empty. "He'll just get it anyway—" he looked up at his deputy and grinned without humor "—him being a United States Senator, and all. You get hold of the judge yet?"

"Miss Ada's workin' on it. Said to meet her over at the courthouse and she'll put me in touch with the judge. I'm about to head over there now."

"You say the senator's coming in the front?"

"Yes, sir."

Roan picked up his sandwich again and made a face at it. "In that case, you might want to go out the back."

Of course, he knew the inevitable couldn't

be avoided forever. By mid-afternoon, with both state detectives, Ruger and Fry, and Roan's deputy, Lori Thrasher, back from Helena, and Tom having reported in from the courthouse, Roan knew the inevitable had arrived. He was going to have to bring Senator Cliff Holbrook up to date on the investigation into his son's murder. More specifically, the investigation into the background of the only viable suspect in the case so far, namely, the woman who called herself Mary Owen.

The senator's response was about what Roan expected.

"What do you mean, she doesn't exist?"

Tom and Lori both winced, and Roger Fry shifted restlessly and looked over at his partner. All four lawmen looked as though they'd rather be anywhere but where they were.

Roan folded his arms and carefully leaned back in his chair, just far enough so it wouldn't squeak. "Well," he drawled, "that's maybe overstating things a bit. Mary Owen *did* exist, but unfortunately she died in 1971." He paused, then added, "At the ripe old age of eighty-three."

"The *hell* you say!"

"The woman *we* know as Mary Owen,"

Roan went on calmly, ignoring the senator's exclamation, "moved here from Coeur d'Alene last winter. Before that she lived in Cheney, that's in Washington state. She's moved around a lot, our Mary, but we've been able to trace her back about…what, Tom? Ten years? That's when she showed up in St. George, Utah. Before that, nothing. Nada. According to all the records we've got, prior to ten years ago this woman did not exist. Anywhere."

He spoke calmly, but there was a slow burn in his belly. He had a bad feeling about where this was headed. What he felt like was a passenger on a fast train heading straight off a cliff, knowing there wasn't a damn thing he could do to stop it.

"Well, what are you waiting for?" The senator's voice was a low, tense growl. "You said this woman was the last person to see my son alive, that she might have had reason to want to hurt him. Now you're telling me she's got a shady past? Why haven't you got her in here? Why aren't you questioning her?"

"No, now, I never said she had a shady past. What I said was, she had *no* past. That means she's got secrets, maybe even something to hide. It doesn't make her a killer. Her fingerprints aren't in the system."

"You said she had a gun." The senator had that wolf-look in his eyes again—burning cold and hungry. He had his prey in his sights and wasn't about to let her go.

"Which isn't the murder weapon," Roger Fry pointed out, after a deferential cough.

Holbrook threw him a look and made a dismissive gesture. "Of course it isn't—I'm sure that's why she gave it up so easily. Look, if the lady's got one gun, she can have others. You haven't found the gun—you said it was a Colt 45, right?—the one that shot Jason. Have you?"

Tom Daggett jerked to attention. "No, sir, that's right. Not yet, we haven't."

"She could easily have gotten rid of it—hell, it could be anywhere out there." The senator made a wide, furious sweep with his arm, then gripped the arms of his chair and leaned toward Roan. "Look—her blood was on Jason's shirt, wasn't it?"

"Appears to be," Roan said, with a glance at Detective Fry. "We won't know that for certain until the DNA results come back. But look, she's admitted Jason assaulted her that night. That's not in question."

"And she went and got her gun and came back and *shot* him." Holbrook thumped the chair arm. "She had motive, means and opportunity, for God's sake. What more do you need?"

"Evidence?" suggested Roan, and earned himself a steely, narrow-eyed glare.

"I want that woman brought in for questioning," the senator went on in a soft and dangerous voice. "If you're not willing to do it, Roan, I'm sure these fellas here'll be glad to."

Detective Fry coughed and looked down at his feet. Roan wasn't sure he knew what hackles were, but if it was another word for temper, he could definitely feel his rising.

However, he showed no outward signs of annoyance as he rocked gently in his chair and said with meticulous courtesy, "Sir, I have every intention of questioning Miss Owen further, particularly in light of what we've found out—or rather, what we haven't found out—today. However, I'd prefer not to drag the lady out of her shop in the middle of a Saturday afternoon and leave a bunch of this town's female citizens with their hair all gunked up with chemicals." He peered pointedly at his watch. "I figure she ought to be closing up in…oh, about fifteen minutes, which is when I expect to be there. If that's okay with you?"

Roan brought his eyes back to Cliff Holbrook, and he wasn't surprised to see the older man's complexion had darkened considerably. It had grown unnaturally silent in the room, as though the other four people in it had faded into the woodwork, leaving him and the senator to face each other alone.

"I want to go with you when you pick her up," Holbrook growled, head lowered and eyes burning—more angry bull, now, than wolf.

Roan shook his head and said firmly, "Sorry, Senator, I can't let you do that." He rose and reached for his hat. "This is my job. I'll deal with Miss Mary Owen."

"Alone?" Holbrook's voice sounded hoarse and strained. "Shouldn't you at least take some backup?"

Roan gave him a crooked smile. "Cliff, this isn't Ma Barker we're dealing with. Besides," he added with pointed looks at his deputies, "these folks here have plenty else to do. Tom, Lori, don't you have a murder weapon to find?" As the two deputies snapped to attention, he nodded at Ruger and Fry. "And if you gentlemen wouldn't mind, I think maybe a trip to Coeur d'Alene might be in order."

He got their nods of agreement, settled his

hat on his head and nodded at the senator, then briskly took his leave. Nobody was more surprised than Roan when Clifford Holbrook sat in his chair and let him go without another word of argument.

Chapter Five

Mary was sweeping up after her last client when the light seemed to dim around her, as though a cloud had passed in front of the sun. Then the glass front door to her shop slapped open and Sheriff Roan Harley stepped inside, politely removing his hat as he closed the door behind him.

Her heart thumped like an alarmed rabbit and fear fisted in her stomach, but she gave no outward sign of that as she called out, "Be with you in a minute," and went on carefully coaxing snowdrifts of crisp gray-white hair into a dustpan.

Oh, but even without looking she could feel

his presence, jarring and alien, too much raw-boned masculinity for such a cozy, pink, feminine place. And she could feel him watching her. When she straightened, dustpan in one hand and broom in the other, awareness bloomed warm in her cheeks, and she touched an unsteady hand to smooth back the strands of hair that dangled limply around her face.

Don't be a fool...don't let him get to you... he can't hurt you. She sang the words silently to herself like a calming lullaby while she tilted the dustpan into the nearest wastebasket and propped the broom against the wall beside the work station. Then, jamming her hands into the pockets of her smock to stop their fidgeting, she turned resolutely to confront her visitor.

And once again, as it had the night before when she'd first seen the sheriff of Hart County through her latched screen door, she was conscious of a strange sense...not of déjà vu, exactly, but more as if she were seeing a double exposure...the vibrant flesh-and-blood man standing before her, and the memory of a much different man, one from a life she'd put behind her long ago.

Right now, today, *this* man, the real man, was turned sideways to her, leaning on one elbow against the glass display case that served as a reception counter, turning his hat around and around in his hands and watching her through the arrangement of white artificial tulips in a Blue Willow bowl.

Against that image, blurring it like rain cascading down a windowpane, the memory: *Dark, sultry Latino eyes laughed at me behind a single red rose, taunting me...daring me...seducing me into dancing the tango....*

Then the sheriff straightened and she moved toward him and the memory shimmered into nothingness.

"Miss Owen," he said in his soft, grumbly voice, nodding his head toward her in an awkwardly formal way that was oddly attractive in so self-assured and masculine a man.

"Sheriff," she said, returning the nod. And for some reason she found herself gazing, not at his face with its probably uncharacteristic shadowing of beard stubble, but at his thick sunshot hair, with the imprint of a hatband molded into it. Her fingers tingled with the urge to plunge into it...burrow through it... fluff out and smooth away that telltale cowboy's furrow. The hairdresser in her, she told herself. Except that hairdressers weren't supposed to think of how that hair would feel, were they? *Warm silk...vibrant and alive....*

She forced her lips into the shape of a smile, and the twinge of pain that action caused was an acute reminder of why this man was here. She touched her lip and asked, "Did you come to give me back my gun?" Knowing he hadn't. Her heart was beating as if she'd been running hard uphill, beating so fast it made her chest hurt.

He didn't return her smile. "'Fraid we're going to be needing it a while longer." His sky-blue eyes studied her narrowly, and there was a hardness in them that hadn't been there before. "I'm going to need to ask you a few more questions, too, if you wouldn't mind coming down to the station with me."

"Would it make any difference if I *do* mind?" Mary asked, tilting her head slightly, still holding on to the smile. Surprised at how little emotion she felt, now that this moment— the moment she'd been dreading—had finally arrived.

The sheriff kept his face impassive. He stood tall and arrow-straight now, a commanding presence, but completely relaxed, with his feet a little apart and his hat held casually in both hands. "No, ma'am," he said, "I don't believe it would. I guess it's up to you whether you want to make it easy or hard on yourself."

"Are you arresting me?" And how was she able to ask it so calmly, while deep in the pockets of her smock her tightly clenched fists felt like chunks of ice?

He made a small dismissive gesture with his hat. "Ma'am, like I told you, I'd just like to ask you a few questions."

"I can't imagine what I could tell you that your deputy hasn't found out already, over at the courthouse," Mary said pointedly.

The sheriff acknowledged that with a hint of an ironic smile. "News travels fast."

"It's a small town," Mary said. "And Miss Ada's a good customer—and friend—of mine." Anger was beginning to seep through her veil of calm. Anger and a bitter sense of irony. *After all I've been through, everything I've sacrificed, to have it all undone by some small-town back-country sheriff with a great big murder to solve.* "I've given you my gun and my blood—what else can you possibly want?"

"Well, for starters," the sheriff drawled as he folded his arms on his chest and seemed to take root and grow immoveable as a ponderosa pine, "I'd sure like to know your real name."

The world darkened. A rushing sound filled the inside of her head. Her voice caught, and then she said, "My...my name? I don't know what on earth you mean." But there was no real conviction in it. She'd waited just that critical heartbeat too long.

She heard a soft hissing sound—an exhalation. The sheriff's eyes narrowed and his features hardened...darkened...became the face of a man nobody in his right mind would care to cross. "Oh, sure you do," he said in his soft, growly voice, and Mary marveled that a voice she'd thought so pleasing, even sexy, could sound so dangerous now. "We both know you're not Mary Owen. For one thing, she's dead—been dead for thirty-some years. So that brings me back to my question: *Who the hell are you?*"

Mary did the only thing she could think to do. She drew her hands from the pockets of the smock, nudged her glasses more firmly onto her nose as if girding herself for battle, then folded her arms tightly across her waist and slowly shook her head. She made a small, throat-clearing sound and said, "Don't I have a right to remain silent?"

The sheriff's chin jerked up a notch. For a moment or two he didn't answer, and the space between them pulsed with the shimmering, vibrating silence. A muscle twitched in the side of his jaw—the only sign of any annoyance he might have felt. "If I place you under arrest," he said finally.

Then once more the silence waited, growing denser...harder to break. Mary's throat and mouth were too dry to form words and swallowing didn't help. In the end she had to whisper them. "Then I guess you'll have to do that. Because I have nothing more to say to you."

The sheriff made that hissing sound again, and slowly shook his head. "Miss Mary," he said as he settled his hat on his head, "you have no idea how sorry I am to hear you say that."

Roan closed the door to the interrogation room carefully behind him, resisting an unprofessional urge to slam it. Frustration tension gripped his neck and shoulders as he nodded brusquely at the man standing with folded arms in front of the observation window, then continued on down the hallway to his office without saying a word.

After a moment, Senator Holbrook pivoted and followed, his steps hurried and heavy with anger. He fired point-blank as he pushed through the door behind Roan, almost on his heels. "You didn't arrest her?"

"No," Roan snapped back without turning as he rounded his desk and jerked back his chair, "I did not."

Gripping the back of the chair closest to the desk, Holbrook leaned on his white-knuckled hands, hardened his already iron jaws and demanded tightly, "Why the hell not?"

Instead of answering immediately, Roan stared down at his own hands and pictured his daughter's face—for him the equivalent of counting to ten. The fact that the man standing before him huffing and snorting like an angry bull was a United States Senator didn't have much bearing on Roan's efforts to cut him some slack, but the fact that he was the murder victim's father sure did. All Roan needed to keep his own temper under control was to remember what it had felt like to be in this man's shoes.

"The fact that she's not willing to talk to us, aggravating as that may be, does not mean she's guilty," he said patiently, bringing his eyes up to meet Holbrook's narrow and glittering glare. "I'd really like to have some evidence she is before I arrest her, and right now we don't have any hard evidence connecting her with Jason's murder. We know the gun she gave us isn't the murder weapon, and we didn't find any others when we searched her place. Her blood on Jason's sleeve only proves he assaulted her, it doesn't—"

"It proves she had motive to kill him, dammit! I said it before: she had motive and opportunity. She was the last person to see my son alive—"

"That we know of," said Roan.

"—and she knows how to shoot a gun," the senator forged on as if Roan hadn't spoken, stabbing the air like a stump speaker at a political rally. "You said she told you she's a good shot, and if she has one gun she could just as well have had two. You didn't find it because she got rid of it, obviously—hell, she'd have to be a dang fool to hang on to it after she'd shot somebody with it! She's not who she claims to be, so that already makes her a liar. And she's for damn sure a flight risk, given what little history you have for her. You let her walk out of here now, and what makes you think she's gonna still be around when that evidence you're looking for does turn up? Dammit, Roan, if you won't arrest that woman, I'll find somebody who will. Hell, I'll get those state guys to do it. If I have to."

Roan closed his eyes and rubbed the lids with the fingers and thumb of one hand, and it occurred to him to wonder if Cliff Holbrook's red-rimmed eyes felt as tired and sore as his did; he imagined neither one of them had gotten much sleep last night. And exhausted though they both might have been, he had to admit the senator was right about one thing: The woman calling herself Mary Owen was one hell of a flight risk.

Projected against the backs of his eyelids he saw an image of her as he'd seen her last, sitting unnaturally still and upright in a straight-backed chair in the center of his interrogation room. And neither the ugly dark-rimmed glasses veiling her dull gray eyes nor the strings of dirt-brown hair drooping into the collar of her pink nylon smock could disguise the elegance of bone structure, the symmetry of features, the translucence of skin she tried so hard to hide. Now that he knew it was there he wondered how he ever could have missed it.

Another image took the place of that one:

a man he knew well, lying on his back with his arms flung wide, sightless eyes staring up at the sky and an ugly dark hole squarely in the center of his forehead. And try as he would, Roan could not make those two images come together in his mind.

It just didn't jell. Not that he had a whole lot of experience to judge by, but it didn't feel right.

On the other hand, there was no getting around the fact that the woman had been living under a false identity for the past ten years. And she was definitely a flight risk. And if there was one thing Roan was certain of right now, it was that he didn't want Mary Owen—or whoever she was—to slip away from him before he got some answers to his questions.

He let out a breath and the words he didn't want to say came with it. "All right, dammit, I'll arrest her." But he still didn't think it was going to solve his case. It just seemed like the only course open to him right then. His belly knotted and burned as he snatched his phone from its cradle, and it occurred to him that the way things were going, this case, the senator, that woman, were going to give him ulcers.

"What are you doing now?" Holbrook demanded as Roan stabbed at the numbers on the phone.

Roan shot him a look, wishing he had the gumption to say the words that had popped into his mind. *None of your damn business, Senator.* Instead, he calmly explained, with only a slight touch of sarcasm, "I'm calling a lawyer. I doubt the woman knows anybody in town to call, and since she's choosing to exercise her Constitutional rights, we can't deal with her without one."

"Do you understand these rights as I've explained them to you?"

Mary focused her eyes on the pair of hands that were loosely clasped together on the wooden tabletop just across from her. She nodded.

"Would you mind answering out loud for the recorder, please?"

That voice. Why had she ever thought it warm-sounding and pleasant? It reminded her now of the purr of a tiger.

"Oh," she said, "I'm sorry." She cleared her throat lightly. "Yes. Of course I understand." *No, I don't understand. Dear God, why is this happening to me?*

"All right, that's it then, until your attorney gets here." The sheriff turned off the recorder.

Mary's eyes followed him as he picked it up and rose from his chair. "May I—" She paused to take a breath; the rapid tapping of her heartbeat against her breastbone made it hard to speak, harder to keep her voice steady. "May I make a phone call?" The sheriff looked down at her, frowning in a rather remote, distracted way, and she felt her temper kindle. "I do get one phone call, don't I?"

He snorted softly. "You can have more than one, far as I'm concerned. But like I told you, your lawyer's already on his way. You might even know him—he's a neighbor of yours. Harry Klein—Andrews & Klein? They're right next door to your shop."

She waved that aside with a gesture. "That's not—I'd like to call someone else. If I'm allowed."

There was a long pause while the keen blue eyes studied her, their gaze no longer remote. Then, "Sure. Fine. I'll have Lori bring you a phone. Do you need a phone book?"

She shook her head, then added self-consciously, "No. Thank you."

He nodded and went out. Mary sat still, refusing to look toward the mirror she knew wasn't really a mirror, listening to the relentless thumping of her heart, trying to summon enough moisture in her mouth to relieve her papery throat. *I should have asked for a glass of water. Or he should have offered me one,* she thought with a flash of resentment. *But then I'd probably have to ask to use the restroom.* And she felt a cold quivering deep in her stomach as the realization hit her: *This is what it's like to be arrested. You have to ask permission to do* everything.

A young deputy with dark hair and a suggestion of Native American heritage in her cheekbones came in carrying a cordless phone. She placed it on the table and turned to go, then paused, looked back and asked, "Want anything? A soda? Glass of water?"

The unsolicited kindness caught Mary unawares, and she found herself fighting an unexpected urge to cry. And once again memory came, not déjà vu, just the past overtaking the present.

Oh God—I hate these memories! But the room was so much like this one, although I hadn't been arrested then, only placed in "protective custody." I felt numb though, like I do now. It seemed like a bad dream, and I was too exhausted to make myself wake up.

I can still hear the FBI agent's voice. "You do realize that you must not contact anyone from your past life, ever?" His face...so grave it scared me. "If you do, we won't be able to protect you. I need you to understand that." He waited for my nod. "Do you have immediate family members you'd like included in the program with you?"

I thought...but there was nobody. "Just... my friend, Joy," I said, "and she's not..." There was an aching tightness in my throat. I whispered, "Will I have a chance to say goodbye?"

He shook his head and leaned toward me. His eyes seemed to bore into mine. "I'm sorry. There's a U.S. Marshal waiting outside that door right now. His name's Stillwell. He'll explain in more detail, but basically he's going to take you to a safe house tonight, and you'll stay there until we get everything squared away. Once we have all the red tape taken care of, marshals will escort you to a remote location where you'll stay until it's time for you to testify, at which time you'll be brought back to Jacksonville under the tightest security for the duration of the trial. When it's all over, you'll be taken to your final destination and set up with your new identity. Okay? Do you understand everything so far?"

Do I understand? I wanted to shout at the man, scream at him, No! No, I don't understand! How did this happen? All I wanted was to meet a handsome prince and live happily ever after, and now you tell me my life is over! How could this have happened to me?

But I only whispered—I think I whispered, "Yes."

The FBI agent said brusquely, "It's a lot to take in, I know." *I remember that he reached over and placed his hand on mine and gave it a squeeze. Then he stood up and as he did he looked back at me and I saw that his eyes were kind.* "Can I get you something to drink?" *he asked me.* "Coffee? Some water?"

That terrible aching tightness gripped my throat, just as it's doing now, and just as I am now, I was fighting to hold back tears. How strange, I thought then, after everything I'd been through, the horrors I'd seen, the fear and disillusionment and despair I'd felt, to be undone by a small unexpected kindness....

"Yes, thank you. I'd love some water," Mary murmured, and the young female deputy nodded and went out.

Mary counted slow deep breaths until the

deputy came back in with a bottle of water. She thanked her and unscrewed the top of the bottle and drank thirstily while the deputy went away again. Only then, left alone and feeling much more in control, did Mary pick up the phone the deputy had left on the table. She shifted her chair around so that her back was turned toward the wall mirror and the unseen watchers behind it, then closed her eyes, huffed out one more breath, and with cold stiff fingers punched in a number she was surprised she still remembered.

After only one ring an androgynous voice droned, "U.S. Marshal's Office, Special Services."

"Deputy Marshal Stillwell, please. That's in Witness Protection." Oh, how her heart was pounding! She pressed her hand against her chest, which didn't help at all. The hand that was holding the phone began to tremble, and she couldn't stop that, either.

After what seemed like a very long pause, but was probably no more than a minute, the voice was back. "Marshal Stillwell is no longer with the service, ma'am. Would you like to speak with someone else?"

"I—are you *sure?* James Stillwell?"

"Yes, ma'am, James Stillwell retired from the service two years ago."

"But he was my—" She stopped, unable to think. She felt a curious sensation of being adrift, or of falling, like someone who'd grabbed hold of her one lifeline only to discover there was nobody holding onto the other end.

"Ma'am, if you'll give me your I.D. number, I'll see if I can find out who's handling your case. It might take a while." The voice had begun to sound testy and harassed. "We're short-handed around here right now. Maybe you'd like to call back a little later?"

"Yes...all right...thank you," Mary whispered. Her throat ached terribly, and it wasn't just her hand that was shaking now. She didn't remember disconnecting the phone call; her mind seemed capable of processing only one thought: *Oh God, I'm going to jail...for murder. How can this be happening? What's going to happen to me now?*

On Sunday morning right after breakfast, Boyd announced his intention to ride up to the high pastures to see if the feed was high enough yet to turn the cattle out. Naturally, Susie Grace wanted to go along, so Roan decided they might as well all go and make a day of it.

After the events of the last couple of days, he figured he needed a break, though he suspected it was going to take more than a pretty spring day and a horseback ride with his daughter and father-in-law to cleanse his mind of the images of Mary Owen the way he'd seen her last. Looking...not like any murderer he'd ever seen before—not that he'd seen so many, but no murder suspect he'd ever encountered or imagined over the course of his career had ever seemed so...*bewildered,* he guessed was the best way to describe it. The expression on her face, the look in her eyes... The way those changeable eyes of hers had clung to his as she was being led away to lock-up, neither the flat gray-green that so effectively hid whatever she might be thinking nor that surprising golden shimmer of anger, but the deep slate of storm clouds, and the message in them plain and troubling as thunder: *Help me.* A plea her hopeless expression acknowledged was not likely to be answered that day.

The day had started out cool, but by the time they reached the saddleback ridge the sun was hot on their shoulders. They paused there on the pretext of shedding their jackets, but in truth it was to do as they always did, turn and survey the vista spread out around them, which Roan considered to be 360 degrees of pure heaven on earth. From where they stood, on the crest of a wide-open space knee-deep to their horses in lupin and paintbrush, the world rolled away on one side in gentle waves of foothills carpeted with new green, speckled with buttercups and tiny blue forget-me-nots and dotted with clumps of juniper and sage, down, down, down to the ranch far below, looking like a child's play toy with its cluster of red-and-white painted barns, stables, corrals and feed-storage silos, the main house barely visible in its copse of pines and cottonwoods, and beyond and a little way up a wooded draw, the foreman's cottage where Boyd lived now, and beyond that, the sweep of hazy blue and purple mountains stretching all the way north to Glacier Park and Canada. On the other side, the high country began just beyond the thickets of pine and aspen that bordered the meadows, where snow lay in shady places until mid-summer, bald eagles nested and in the autumn the slopes rang with the shrill challenges of bull elk in rut. And above it all, the never-ending sky. It made a man feel small and unimportant, that sky, and damn lucky just to be alive underneath it.

"Been a good rain year. Feed's lookin' good," Boyd said, squinting into the sunlight and nodding to himself as he leaned on his saddlehorn. And Roan knew the old rancher was feeling much the same way he was.

He clicked to his horse, a bay gelding named Springer for the habit he'd had when he was younger of shying at every little thing, tugging his nose out of the grass and clover he'd been sneaking mouthfuls of during the respite. Beside him, Boyd, mounted on Foxy, his favorite Appaloosa mare, did the same, and they went on at a walk, scaring up clouds of little yellow butterflies and an occasional meadowlark, which would fly, scolding, almost from underneath the horses' hooves. Susie Grace, impatient with their leisurely pace, kicked up Tootsie, the little red-gold mare she'd picked for her own because, she said, it had hair the same color as hers, and went loping on ahead. To Roan she looked frighteningly small and precarious perched on top of that horse with her blue cowboy boots sticking straight out in their stirrups and her pigtails flapping under the brim of her blue cowboy hat.

He hollered at her to take it easy and was about to take off in pursuit when Boyd looked over at him and said, "Let her be. She'd ain't gonna fall offa that horse, and you know it. The kid rides like an Indian. Comes by it naturally—her mama was the same way. Erin used to scare her mother to death."

His tone was easygoing, but when Roan glanced over he saw that the rancher's face wore the same bleak and aged look it always got when he spoke of his daughter. He shifted his gaze back to the little girl and her red-gold horse galloping blithely through a sea of wildflowers, her hat now blown off her head and bouncing against her back, caught by the cord around her neck. The sun struck red-gold fire into her hair the same way it had once done her mother's, and Roan caught his breath, waiting for the stab of grief and pain to follow.

It came...it would always come, but now it mostly came when he summoned it, rather than keeping him company every waking moment of every damn day and then haunting his dreams at night. Sometimes he even thought if he could just find the bastard who'd set the fire that killed her he might be able to move on. He knew he needed to; the years since Erin's death had been damned lonely for him, and besides, a little girl needed a mother. He knew human beings weren't supposed to be alone, and that it was supposed to be possible for them to fall in love more than once in a lifetime, in theory, at least. Maybe, he thought, it was coming time to put that theory to the test.

Though...with Clifford Holbrook's ravaged face fresh in his mind and the sadness he'd gotten used to seeing in Boyd's, he thought it must be different for a parent losing a child. He didn't think the pain of that ever did go away. He tried to imagine how it would be for him if Susie... But his mind refused to go there, and he shifted in his saddle, cold to his core in spite of the noonday sun beating down on his shoulders.

"Heard you arrested somebody for the Holbrook kid's murder," Boyd said, as though his mind had been following the same trail.

Roan threw him a look, half-surprised, half-ironic. "News travels fast."

"It's a small town, what'd you expect?" Boyd let his horse plod on a few paces, then hitched a shoulder in an off-hand way. "Little bit and I stopped in at the one-stop on the way back from fishin' last evenin' to pick up some lemons and breadcrumbs to go with them trout we caught. Ran into that deputy of yours—what's her name? Lori? Said you'd arrested the gal that took over the beauty shop when Queenie moved south last winter." He glanced over at Roan, eyes squinted almost shut in the shadows of his hat brim. "You really think she did it? That little gal?"

"Wouldn't have arrested her if I didn't," Roan said in an even tone. He didn't exactly feel comfortable discussing his case with a civilian, even if he was family. And he was even less comfortable with the nagging doubts that question kept stirring up in his own mind.

Boyd lifted up in the stirrups and resettled his bony backside more comfortably in the saddle, a sure sign his arthritis was hurting him. "I don't know, just can't hardly believe she'd be capable of doin' somethin' like that."

"You know her? Mary Owen? How'd you manage that? You've never been inside a beauty parlor in your life."

Boyd snorted. "The hell I haven't. Used to take my wife for her permanent wave every so often—Grace was a good customer of Queenie's right up until just before she died." He threw Roan another look, quick and oddly furtive. "Don't really know the new gal, except to see her around, you know. Seems kinda meek and mild, though, like she wouldn't hurt a fly. Sure don't seem like the type to commit murder."

"There isn't any 'type' when it comes to murder," Roan said grimly. "Anybody'll kill if you give 'em enough cause. Even meek, mild people you'd think would never hurt a fly."

"Well, I guess you'd know," Boyd said.

After an oddly unhappy little silence, by some unspoken accord both men nudged their horses to an easy gallop, heading down the gentle slope to where Susie Grace waited for them at the edge of the grove of aspens.

Chapter Six

The Hart County courthouse was a much grander ediface than the size of the town and county it served would seem to warrant, having been built during Hartsville's boom-town days when the mines were still going strong. A massive and sturdy granite block with two-story concrete pillars flanking the arched front portico, it dwarfed all the other buildings in the downtown area. The citizens of Hart County were enormously proud of it.

The first floor housed all the offices of county government except for the sheriff's station and detention center, and emergency services. The courtroom, jury rooms and judge's chambers were all on the second floor, reached either by a grand curving staircase or the stuffy creaking elevator that had been put in after the Citizens with Disabilities Act went into effect. In contrast to the rest of the building the courtroom itself was almost stark, having been renovated during an era when simplicity was in vogue, with floors, paneling, judge's bench, jury box, witness stand and spectators' pews all done in some pale golden-brown wood, unembellished and naturally finished. It reminded Roan of the inside of a church, one of the more austere Protestant varieties. Which was maybe why he always felt an impulse to whisper when he was in it.

It obviously didn't have that effect on Senator Holbrook, who hadn't stopped fuming and cussing like a bullwhacker since the moment the judge brought his gavel down. He kept it up while he and Roan waited for the other spectators to file out of the courtroom, and was still going at it as they made their way down the curving staircase together.

"What the hell was the judge thinking, granting that woman bail?" Holbrook's hoarse attempt at a whisper echoed down the courthouse's wide ground-floor corridor, causing heads to turn.

Roan, walking beside him, felt the tension and energy pulsing through the man's body, and it reminded him of the geysers down in Yellowstone, the way they'd hiss and fume and rumble just before they blew.

"You might want to keep your voice down," he said mildly, nodding toward the crowd of reporters and photographers gathered on the courthouse steps just outside the double glass doors. The senator's heated indictment of the circuit court judge had included some adjectives of the type usually bleeped by the media, just clumsily enough so it was impossible to mistake the true meaning. Roan imagined getting caught using language like that wouldn't do a politician's public image much good.

Holbrook evidently didn't share Roan's concerns, because his comment on the media's presence in Hartsville was more of the same—though he did deliver it with slightly lowered volume. At the bottom of the stairs he made an abrupt left turn and began to pace furiously back down the corridor away from the entrance, dragging a distraught hand through his hair.

"My God, they're like a flock of turkey buzzards, aren't they? Like they're waiting for your horse to die. Where do they come from? How do they get wind of things like this so fast?"

Roan considered a man who made his living in national politics ought to be used to dealing with the news media, but when he made a comment to that effect, the senator waved it angrily aside.

"That's politics. This is personal. There's a line there, and if those vultures can't see it they sure as hell ought to."

From what Roan knew of the media, he thought the line between personal and politics had gotten blurred a long time ago, but he knew better than to say so.

Instead, leaning one elbow on the newelpost at the bottom of the staircase and fiddling with his Stetson in an easygoing way, he drawled, "They're just doing their job. Can't fault 'em for being good at it. Like you can't fault Harry Klein for being good at his. All he did was point out the reasons why his client ought to be granted bail, namely, no criminal record, no previous history of violent behavior, local business woman..." He paused when the senator frowned at him—not that he was surprised by the look; he hadn't tried all that hard to tone down the sarcasm. He met the steely stare with one of his own. "The judge was doing his job when he granted it."

Holbrook made an impatient gesture and resumed his pacing. "I don't give a damn about her previous history. That woman shot my son. If she gets away—"

"That's not gonna happen," Roan said evenly. The adult part of him was controlling his temper and hanging on to his patience for the sake of another man's grief, but somewhere deep down inside him that little boy he liked to pretend wasn't there was still nursing the secret hurt of being denied the acknowledgment and approval of his father. Pitiful, he knew, but not much he could do about it. "For one thing, Judge Conner set the bail high enough I doubt she'll be able to make it, at least not right away. By the time she does we should have some results back from the crime lab. With physical evidence to back us up we might be able to get the judge to reconsider."

Holbrook scrubbed a hand over his face, and Roan could see him making an effort to rein himself in. "What about this protected witness thing? Any chance they might whisk her away again, right out from under our noses?"

"Well, that might be what she was hoping for when she called 'em," Roan said with a dark half smile. "If she was, she's gonna be disappointed. The U.S. Marshal's Office doesn't intervene for protected witnesses in local criminal matters. They'll cooperate with us on this—if they ever find her case worker and her file."

"Doesn't mean she won't try to disappear on her own," the senator growled.

"If she does," Roan said, still being patient, "we're going to be there to stop her. But she's going to have to come up with that bail money first, and I don't think—" He broke off because it was obvious Holbrook wasn't listening to him. The man was staring past him toward the courthouse doors like a wolf who'd just spotted a rabbit, and Roan could almost see the fur on the back of his neck bristling.

"What the hell? Isn't that—"

Roan pivoted in time to watch his murder suspect, wearing the dowdy blue-denim skirt and faded pink blouse she'd had on in court earlier, whisk through the double glass doors and disappear into the maw of the hungry media mob waiting outside.

"That's her—that's Owen. How the hell—"

Sputtering, Holbrook turned to glare at Roan. "What the hell just happened?"

"Looks like she made bail after all," Roan muttered grimly. Seeing the woman—even that brief glimpse—had given him one helluva jolt, and set his heart beating in a way he couldn't account for, though he sure did try. Adrenaline, he told himself. The gut instinct to give chase when somebody's running. And she was running. He knew it with a certainty that clutched at his belly and shivered through every muscle and nerve in his body.

"Evidently," he said in a grating voice, "the woman has resources we didn't know about. Or somebody put it up for her."

"Put it up for her?" The senator looked around him in a half-bewildered, half-furious kind of way. "Goddammit, who'd do a thing like that?"

"I did, Clifford, and I would appreciate it if you would not swear in this courthouse, please."

At the sound of that firm and rasping voice, Holbrook jerked and spun around like a man who'd just taken a haymaker punch to the chin. Roan pretty much did too, and he wondered if it was possible a United States Senator could be feeling the same way he was right then—like a tardy schoolboy caught in the hallway after the bell had rung. Together, both open-mouthed and speechless, they watched Ada Major, the court clerk, march toward them with her pocketbook under one arm, corseted and painted to within an inch of her life.

Roan was the first to find his voice. "Miss Ada," he said, nodding a greeting.

"Sheriff," said Miss Ada, returning the nod with her customary dignity. She turned back to the senator and clamped one bony blue-veined hand over his. "Clifford, I want you to know how sorry I am about your boy. Truly sorry. I know the sheriff here is going to find out who did this awful thing—" she paused to fix Roan with a tight-lipped glare "—even if he has gotten off to an unfortunate start. Arresting Mary Owen…" She tsked and gave her head a shake, making her starched auburn curls bob only slightly.

"Ada," the senator said in a wondering croak, "why in the world did you put up that woman's bail? You let my son's killer just… walk out of here?"

The lady made a very unladylike noise. "Oh bosh. That girl never killed anyone. She certainly doesn't belong in jail. Besides—" Miss Ada's eyes twinkled; she gave her curls a girlish pat "—if Mary's in jail, who'll do my wash and set come Friday?"

"Miss Ada—"

"Roan." The lady transferred her cool hard grip from the senator's hand to Roan's. "I've been working in this courthouse since before you were born—and you, Clifford, were a muddy-faced schoolboy. I've seen a good many criminals come and go. I like to think I've developed some instincts over the years, and they are telling me that girl is no criminal."

"You don't need to be a criminal to commit murder, Miss Ada," Roan said, thinking about the conversation he'd had with Boyd just yesterday. "Sometimes you just have to be desperate."

Miss Ada's eyes narrowed shrewdly. "Ah, but this wasn't a desperate kind of murder, was it? From all I hear, whoever shot Jason Holbrook did so with a good deal of malice aforethought. If you can find so much as an ounce of malice in Mary, I'll eat my Aunt Fanny's wig!"

Roan didn't know what to say to that, so he just shook his head. The fact that in his heart he half agreed didn't help his mood any.

"Well," said Miss Ada briskly, "I'd best get back to work. Clifford, it's nice to have you come visit. Though it's a pity it took a death to bring you home. Sheriff…" With a curt nod for each of them, she went clicking on down the corridor.

"My God," Holbrook said as he watched the lady disappear into the clerk of court's office, "I tried my first case in that woman's courtroom, fresh out of law school. She hasn't changed a bit, has she?"

"Nope," said Roan, "and not likely to. She'll be wearing that blue eyeshadow and red hair when they put her in her coffin." Since he didn't think it would be a good idea for the father of his murder victim to see him grinning, he ducked his head and spent an extra second or two setting his hat in place.

It only took those moments for the little spell of amusement to pass and that powerful sense of urgency and exasperation grab hold of him again. Mary Owen might not be Miss Ada's idea of a murder suspect, but at the moment she was the only one he had and he'd be damned if he was going to give her a chance to slip through his fingers.

He started for the doors, then paused and

turned back, frowning. "Senator, can I get somebody to drive you home?"

"No, you go on." Holbrook gave a gusty and resigned exhalation. "I think I'm going to stay here a bit...settle myself down some before I face all that." He nodded toward the mob beyond the glass doors and glared fiercely at Roan, his face pinched and grim. "Go—just...whatever you do, don't let that woman get away."

Roan nodded and touched his hat brim with a forefinger. His step was rapid and purposeful as he strode down the corridor and pushed through the double doors, his narrowed eyes following the tall figure of Mary Owen as she pushed her way through the crowd of reporters and photographers...head down, one hand up in a desperate attempt to shield her face from the pitiless eyes of the television cameras.

The media horde had caught Mary unprepared. She hadn't even thought about the possibility of—*Oh God, television cameras!*

But she *should* have known, she realized, now that it was too late. Here was the son of a national political figure murdered in the classic tradition of the Old West...a young female suspect and some lurid sexual innuendos thrown in—all the ingredients of a media circus.

If only she'd waited for her lawyer—maybe he could have shielded her, whisked her out of the courthouse another way. But after Miss Ada had paid her bail and she'd been told she was free to go, all she'd been able to think about was escape. Like an animal let loose from a trap, she'd bolted blindly, her only thought to run...as far as possible away from here!

But now it appeared she'd escaped from the trap only to stumble into the midst of a pack of ravening wolves. The heat from their bodies was suffocating as they crowded around her, pushing, jostling, grabbing, thrusting... their words, their questions, their shouts all running together in a chorus of hungry-sounding yips and howls, deafening to her ears and terrifying to her soul. *Oh God—not now. Please not now—I hate remembering.*

It was hot that day. The Florida humidity made my clothes stick to me, but I felt cold clear through to my bones, cold as I do right now. I trembled with the cold as the microphones stabbed at me and the lights from the television cameras blinded my eyes. The questions came from everywhere at once, a jumble of noise, but here and there one jumped out at me....

"Miss Lavigne, how does it feel to be the woman who brought down the biggest drug and arms cartel in the western hemisphere?"

"Mary! Mary Owen—did Jason Holbrook attack you?"

"Do you expect the DelRey family to seek revenge because of your testimony?"

"Miss Owen! Will you be pleading self-defense?"

"Are you afraid for your life, Miss La-vigne?"

I ducked my head and tried to hide my face with my hands then, too. And just when I felt the panic closing in, there were the marshals, one on each side of me, and their linked arms made a shield of safety across my back.

Panic. Oh God, please...

Then...miraculously, just as on that distant day, she felt a strong arm slip across her back, and a hard sinewy body come close against her side. Only one body, but it had the same solid strength. And, as on that day, it made her feel warm...and *safe.*

She knew at once who it was. Something in her, some instinct she didn't wonder at or question, seemed to know his smell...clean clothes and leather...aftershave and peppermints. Before she could even look up at him, she heard the voice that was already familiar to her, the growly, easygoing drawl that carried the unmistakable ring of authority.

"Okay, folks...gonna ask you to step aside and let her pass. There's nothing for you here. I believe Senator Holbrook is plannin' on makin' a statement, though, if you all would care to hang around for another minute or two. Now if you'll excuse us...that's it...move aside...thank you kindly...'preciate it...."

And all the while, that strong arm across her back was guiding Mary through the gap in the crowd that seemed to open magically before her, and the shouting, demanding voices receded gradually, fading to a distant babble, like a flock of grackles moving away through a forest.

When she was able to breathe again, and speak without gasping, she looked up into the impassive face of her rescuer and murmured, "That was...kind of you."

"No problem." The sheriff's voice was a softer growl now, pitched just for her, and light...almost cheerful. "I'd hate for you to get trampled on before you get your day in court."

They were in the clear, hurrying along the walkway that meandered across the courthouse grounds between newly planted beds of snapdragons and sweet-smelling stocks. She was surprised at how cold it had become; it had been such a lovely warm spring day on Saturday, the day she'd been arrested. But while she'd been locked away the weather had changed, the way it can in Montana in the springtime, and today a mean little wind was swirling through the forests of satellite dishes that had sprouted from the sparse spring grass, bringing with it the smell of the snow that was already dusting the slopes of the Bitterroots.

"Thank you," she said, gulping a breath. "I'll be fine. I don't think they're going to follow me anymore, not right now. You really don't need to come with me any farther."

"Oh, I think I do," the sheriff drawled. "You're pretty shaky."

She couldn't argue with that—she *was* shaking, but only because she was cold, she told herself. The lawyer, Mr. Klein, hadn't thought to bring her a sweater when he'd brought clothes for her to wear to the arraignment.

Arraignment. Another shudder rippled through her, and because the sheriff was so close to her, once again he couldn't help but feel it. She'd been too panic-stricken to notice before, but her skin tingled oddly where he touched her—oddly, because it wasn't an unpleasant sensation. She had to remind herself this was the *sheriff,* the man who'd arrested her, the man who believed her capable of shooting someone in cold blood.

She could feel his eyes resting on her, their expression lost in the shadows beneath the brim of his hat. *They don't miss much, those eyes.*

New panic seized her, a gut-level sense of danger that made her muscles clench and spasm with the overwhelming need to flee.

I'm in danger...got to run, got to hide, got to save myself... Must get away from him... How can I? Can't make him suspicious... Oh God... I've got to get away!

And again...the same thoughts, same feelings, same panic... But a different time, different place, different images.

I remember... I'd gone looking for Diego. Something strange was happening or about to happen on the island, there had been so much activity and tension in the house all day, and a kind of indefinable electricity. At the same time I felt a heaviness in my spirit, as if a thunderstorm was brewing.

Because I couldn't find Diego, I went looking for Anita, the housekeeper, to ask her if she knew if the family was planning a trip or a party or some such thing that would account for the unusual frenzy. She was from Diego's native country and didn't speak much English, but I would much rather go to her with my questions than one of the DelReys or their security guards. I was still, to tell the truth, a little afraid of them.

I went to the kitchen. Anita wasn't there, but I heard voices, men's voices, coming from the large storeroom off the kitchen. The storage room was a necessity since the estate was on an island and all food and supplies had to be brought in by boat or helicopter. Maybe, I thought, a new shipment of supplies had just arrived and the men were bringing them in. The door was open and the light was on, but I couldn't see who was inside. Anita must be there, I thought, directing the unloading.

I didn't call out. Why didn't I call out? Thank God I didn't call out.

For some reason I went quietly closer... tiptoeing. And I saw them—Anita and her husband Eduardo, who took care of the gar-dens—lying on the floor of the storage room, lying so still I knew they must be either un-conscious or dead.

I stood frozen, I remember, my heart bang-ing inside my chest. The rumble of voices in the storage room grew louder, and somehow I was moving, moving like a flash of lightning, not even feeling myself move and yet I was no longer standing in front of the storage-room door but was instead crouched down beside the cooking island with my hands pressed tightly over my mouth to hold back my whim-pers of fear.

Three men emerged from the storage room, talking quietly and urgently in Spanish. I rec-ognized the voice of Señor DelRey, Diego's father, the family patriarch. The other two were security guards—I didn't know their names. One of them locked the storage room door—my body jerked when I heard that loud click, and when it did my terror nearly over-whelmed me. What if they'd heard?

But they didn't hear, and they didn't see me. They passed by within three feet of me, still talking, and went out of the kitchen, and it was a long time before I was able to rise from my hiding place, shaking in every part of me, every bone in my body aching, and only one thought in my mind: I've got to leave this place...got to run....

But I was on an island, and there was no place to run to.

This town... Hartsville...such a small town. It seemed to her much like an island, in a way. Because once again, there was no place to run.

While Mary was struggling to sort through the chaos of memories in her mind, the sheriff said in a casually friendly way, like a neighbor she'd happened to run into shopping, "Where are you headed? You don't have a car here. How 'bout I give you a ride home?"

She jerked a look at him that made her frozen neck muscles creak. "No—that's...thank you, but I don't need a ride." She didn't try to say more; her shivering was making her teeth chatter, and she couldn't make it stop. Only her mind pleaded: *Go away, please, just go away and leave me alone!*

The sheriff gave her a sharp look; he wasn't actually touching her anymore, but her chattering teeth were hard to miss. "You're cold," he said. Then quickly, before she could object, he shrugged out of the leather jacket he was wearing and draped it around her shoulders.

His body's warmth and that strangely familiar smell embraced her, and she felt loneliness and longing rise like thickened honey in her throat. "You didn't need to do that," she muttered in a voice choked with it, and with a perverse and inexplicable anger. "I'm just going to the salon—it's right around the corner from here."

Again she felt those inquisitive eyes studying her as he effortlessly matched her quickened stride. "Going straight back to work? That's dedication."

She glanced at him, trying to decide whether he was mocking her or not, but the depression in his cheek that wasn't quite a dimple told her nothing. "Of course I'd respect my clients' appointments," she said evenly. "If I had any. But I wouldn't have clients today, anyway. I'm closed on Mondays."

"So, why go in? People bailed out of jail, my experience is, most of the time they want to head straight home…take a shower, put on their own clothes…have a beer, feed the cat…."

"The cat I live with has plenty of food, a litter box and a kitty door. Plus, he hates me anyway." She turned her face toward him, then lifted her hand to catch at a lock of hair that, jarred loose from its haphazard bun by the movement, chose that moment to unfurl across her cheek like a flag in the wind. "What business is it of yours where I go?" she demanded then, a freshet of anger making her incautious, and perhaps, illogical—a fact her unwelcome companion lost no time in pointing out.

"I'm the sheriff of this town," he said in a soft and dangerous voice, "and you've been charged with murdering one of its citizens." He lifted a hand to her cheek and, ignoring her quick, startled intake of breath, carefully slipped a finger under the misbehaving strand of hair and guided it behind her ear. "That makes everything you do my business, Miss Mary, from now until you come to trial."

Her heart seemed to leap into her throat and catch there. Her lips felt stiff and dry. She licked them, to no effect whatsoever, and mumbled, "What happened to 'innocent until proven guilty?'"

"Just want to make sure you stick around long enough for a jury to decide which one you are," the sheriff drawled, facing forward again.

"I'm out on bail," Mary said acidly. "Where do you think I'm going to go?"

"Oh, I don't know. People charged with murder have been known to jump bail. Especially when it's somebody else's life savings they're forfeiting."

She gave a little gasp, anger and shame making a hard knot in her chest. "I'd never do that to Miss Ada. Never!" *I would have left the deeds to Queenie's house and salon to pay her back!* Appalled at how near she'd come to blurting that out in her own defense, she managed to say in a choked voice, "Is that the kind of person you think I am? Not only am I a murderer, but someone who would... who'd do..."

As she struggled to find words adequate to describe so unpardonable an act, her steps slowed to a halt. She found herself staring, uncomprehending, at the back of Queenie's Beauty Salon and Boutique...at the crisscross of yellow crime-scene tape and the unfamiliar padlock on the door.

Chapter Seven

"See, that's the thing, Miss Mary," Roan said as he took a key out of his pocket and stuck it in the padlock. "I don't know what kind of person you are."

The lock sprang apart in his hands. He disposed of the crime-scene tape with a sweeping gesture, then pushed the door open and held it while he looked back at the woman standing there in the hard-baked dirt alley, huddled like a refugee inside his jacket. Her eyes were shimmering behind the lenses of those damned ugly glasses she wore, and he grabbed and held on to his anger like a desperate man. "Fact is," he continued, hardening his voice, "I don't even know *who* you are. Do I?"

She stood where she was, ignoring both his remark and the open door, and said in a voice tight with impotent fury, "You searched my *shop?*"

"Oh, yeah. That's what happens when you get charged with murder. You coming in, or not?"

She moved grudgingly through the doorway, throwing him a hot bitter look as she passed him. "My lawyer said you'd searched my house, so I guess I shouldn't be surprised. What did you expect to find? My bloody shoes? A smoking gun?"

"That'd be nice," Roan said affably, "but no, actually." He closed the door while she flipped a light switch and they moved together through a storage room that smelled of the permanent waves his mother used to get every spring and fall, past a tiny bathroom that held a toilet, a vanity and an assortment of mops and brooms. "I have a lot more respect for your intelligence than to expect anything like that. Fact is..." He paused to let her go ahead of him through a pink-curtained doorway. "I was hoping I might find something that'd tell me a little bit about you.

Like…you know, what your real name is… where you come from. What the hell you're doing in my town."

She was moving ahead of him through the salon, between rows of hair dryers and wash basins, slowly, as if in a daze. She hadn't turned on the lights, and even though the front of the shop was mostly glass, with the weather being gray and overcast like it was, the room had that ghost-town look closed places get when you're used to seeing them full of people and chattering voices and laughter.

She said without turning, in a soft, weary voice, "My name *is* Mary. And I didn't shoot Jason Holbrook. That's all that really matters, isn't it?"

"Maybe," he said just as softly, as he moved close behind her. "If I could believe it."

She turned her head quickly to one side as if she meant to reply, and the jerking movement made his jacket slip off her shoulders. He caught it before it fell and settled it around them again.

Then, somehow, without any thought or guidance from him, his hands came to rest there, too, as if that was where they belonged. Before he could think of all the reasons why he shouldn't be touching her, or, God knew, even talking to her, he found himself curving his fingers around her shoulders and turning her to face him.

"Dammit, Mary," he said in a low, guttural voice that wasn't familiar to him, "I almost do believe you. But the problem with one lie is, it poisons everything you say. I know you lied about who you are, so how am I supposed to know if you're telling the truth when you say you didn't kill Jason?"

She gazed at him for a moment, her eyes that opaque gray color he was beginning to hate because it reminded him of shuttered windows...and felt like a door slammed in his face. Then she turned her face from him in a hopeless way that made him want to shake her. "I shouldn't even be talking to you. If my lawyer..."

He was frustrated enough that he did give her a little bit of a shake, just enough to bring her eyes back to him. "For God's sake, Mary, forget the lawyers. I know the damn protocol. Just...give me a reason to believe you. That's all I'm asking."

Instead of answering, she slipped off his jacket and handed it to him—though he supposed that was a kind of answer, just not the one he was hoping for. Then she moved away from him, rubbing her arms as she gazed distractedly around her at the clutter left by the searchers.

Roan drew a breath, reining in and gentling himself down the way he'd seen Boyd do with a riled-up horse. Even so, he couldn't keep his exasperation out of his voice.

"Look—all I care about is getting the person who did this thing. But I have to tell you—and the reason you're being charged with it—at this point the right person looks like you. Do you understand that? There might not be much in the way of physical evidence against you, but that isn't gonna matter. This is a small town and this is a personal killing. Jason was a jackass, especially where women are concerned, but the fact is, there isn't another person around here who had a big enough beef with him to go and shoot him over it."

He paced a few slow steps to the windows and stood looking out at the street, which was mostly empty here in spite of all the hullabaloo going on just a block away at the courthouse. He watched a couple of scrub jays courting one another in a yellow-flowered shrub across the way, apparently oblivious to the unspringlike weather, and felt a certain edginess in his spirit. He was dragging a restless hand through his hair when he remembered it was a favorite habit of the senator's and made himself stop.

"Mary," he said with a sigh, "to a certain extent, my hands are tied here. The father of the man you're accused of killing is a United States Senator, a powerful man with a lot of pull. If I hadn't arrested you, he'd have found somebody else to do it —the state lawmen, probably."

"Why are you telling me this?" Her voice came from behind him, faint and breathless.

He turned, and because he knew he had to, hardened his eyes and voice. "Because if you didn't kill Jason, then whoever did is still walking around somewhere in this town. *My* town. That idea doesn't sit too well with me." He shrugged into his jacket and said distantly, "Look, if you want to get whatever it is you came in here for, I'll run you home."

She jerked slightly and her arms came across her body in a defensive embrace. Almost whispering, she said, "You don't need to do that."

"Well, since your car's been impounded—" He stopped when she gasped softly. "Yeah," he drawled with a humorless smile, "so in case you were thinking of leaving town that way, I guess you're gonna have to come up with a plan B."

He watched her while she struggled with it, the tension in her body and the fire in her eyes the only outward signs of the battle he knew she must be fighting against emotions he could only imagine: anger, fear, frustration and despair. And then, as she turned slowly to survey the disarray left by the searchers, he saw her shoulders sag with defeat—or was it only a temporary retreat? Maybe even a feint to throw him off? How in the hell was he supposed to know what was going on inside her head when she shuttered her eyes like that?

Trembling deep inside, Mary picked up a pink smock that was lying over the back of a chrome-and-leather swivel chair and slipped it on. It was all she could do to make herself look at the sheriff in silent acquiescence. For a moment he looked back at her with a certain wariness in his eyes, as if he'd been caught off-guard by the sudden lull after the heat of battle. Then, and with a wry smile and a nod of mock gallantry, he waved her ahead of him.

When they reached the ruffled curtain that

divided the back rooms from the salon, he reached past her to pull it aside for her—more gallantry that could only be meant in a sarcastic way, given the fact that he was the man who'd arrested and charged her with murder. And if that was so, why did the brush of his arm against her shoulder make her shiver, and heat blossom in her belly at his nearness... his smell?

"You sure must like pink," he remarked as he twitched the curtain back into place.

"I *hate* pink," Mary said in a choked voice, and she was shocked to discover how close to the surface the anger was, and the tears. And the fear.

He threw her a startled look, no doubt wondering why anyone should become so passionate over something so *un*-passionate as the color pink. But he only said mildly, "Coulda fooled me."

"This is all Queenie's," she said, trying not to let her voice show how fast her heart was beating. "I've...never cared for pink."

He tilted his head back and looked at her from under his hat brim. "No kidding? Neither does my daughter. Thinks it's awful girls are expected to like pink."

There was a pause while they maneuvered

through the back door, the sheriff trying to play the gentleman and open it for her while Mary tried her best not to let her body brush against any part of his. Outside, she waited, hunched inside the thin nylon smock that was no barrier at all to the wicked little wind that skirled around her ankles and reached freshly under her skirt, while he snapped the padlock in place.

He turned back to her, hitching his jacket closer against that taunting wind, and went on in a conversational, almost friendly tone, "In her case it's maybe because she's a redhead. I seem to remember hearing somewhere that redheads don't like pink. Why is that? Think maybe because it clashes with their hair?"

"Or their skin tones," she said dully. And it was her turn, now, to watch him, and to wonder what might be behind the sudden transformation from steely-eyed lawman to easygoing companion. *Be careful, Mary... be careful. He's trying to lull you into saying too much.*

They started down the alley together, and after a moment, because the silence felt awkward to her, she said neutrally, "So, your daughter has red hair?"

"Got it from her mother." Glancing at him

she saw something flicker in his eyes, a brief darkness, like a bird's shadow. It was quickly gone, though, and he added with an air of surprise, "Come to think of it, she wasn't partial to pink, either."

Mary felt the keen blue eyes studying her, inviting her comment, but this time she had herself together enough to know better than to reply. *They don't miss much, those eyes....*

They went the back way through the alley to the parking lot behind the courthouse that was reserved for law-enforcement vehicles and the various officers of the court. Mary knew this place; it was where she'd been brought from the jail early this morning by two sheriff's deputies she'd never seen before. They'd put handcuffs on her and whisked her into the courthouse through a heavy steel door at the top of some concrete steps and into a barren little room where she was to meet with her lawyer, Mr. Klein, and change into the clothes he'd brought for her to wear before the judge. She could still feel the cold bite of those handcuffs...and the sick fear in the pit of her stomach.

Suppressing a shudder and making a conscious effort not to rub her wrists, she allowed the sheriff to guide her to an SUV with the department's logo on the side. He unlocked the door, opened it and waited for her to get in, then went around to the driver's side, taking off his hat as he opened the door, and tossing it onto the back seat.

Like we're going on a date, Mary thought, and almost smiled at the irony.

The sheriff spoke briefly and, to Mary, unintelligibly into his radio, then started up the SUV. His ice-blue gaze slid across her when he turned to look over his shoulder as he backed out of the parking space, and she couldn't hide her shiver.

"Cold?" he asked, and turned on the SUV's heater without waiting for her reply.

She turned her face quickly to look out the window, emotion catching her unawares. *Why are you doing this? Why are you being nice to me?* she wanted to ask—and then, to her dismay, she did.

"If you've told me the truth about killing my b—Jason," he said, narrowed eyes focused on the road ahead, "I've got no reason not to be nice to you. Do I?" She didn't answer, and after a moment he shook his head and let out a breath in an exasperated sigh.

"Ah... Mary. I don't know what I can do to get you to trust me."

She gave a sharp, disbelieving laugh. "*Trust you?* You must be joking. You arrested me for murder."

She saw the depressions in his cheeks deepen with his frown before they were partly obscured by a big, long-boned hand scrubbed impatiently across the lower part of his face. "Dammit, I told you, I didn't have a whole lot of choice." He threw her a brief, stinging look. "The truth is, I—ah hell." Scowling through the windshield again, he growled, "Look, I want the truth, that's all. If you didn't kill Jason, if you've got nothing to hide, then... then for God's sake tell me who you are. Tell me what your real name is...who you're being protected from."

Mary made an involuntary sound, then just gazed at him, heart pounding.

He turned his head to give her a sardonic little smile. "Oh, yeah, I've pretty much figured that part out. Look, dammit," he said, facing forward again, "if you're a federally protected witness, you know I'm gonna find that out sooner or later. The U.S. Marshal's Office isn't going to protect you from a charge of murder."

"Then why do you need me to tell you anything?" she said bitterly, watching houses and yards flash by, bravely clinging to their fresh spring finery in the face of winter's spiteful reprise. *Blackberry winter...that's what my mother used to call this weather.*

Thoughts of her mother were so unexpected, and so predictably painful, she wasn't even aware of where they were until the SUV came to an abrupt stop. For a moment she stared at the little white clapboard house without recognizing it as hers. Then she noticed that while she'd been in jail the big lilac bush beside the front porch had come into bloom, and that brought another flood of unwelcome memories.

"I want to help you," the sheriff said softly.

She couldn't help herself. She laughed— and was shocked when she felt warm fingers brush her cheek.

Her breath snagged delicately, like roughened skin in fine silk. She caught and held it with infinite care, terrified to let it go for not knowing what might come with it. It had been so long since anyone had touched her this way...gently, with that special kind of tenderness that happens between lovers... and how was that possible when this was the man responsible for her utter and complete humiliation?

She wondered what he saw when he looked at her...a beautiful woman, a pitiful victim or a vicious killer? What did her skin feel like to his work-roughened fingers, and did he feel her blood surging hot and wild beneath it?

"If you're innocent, why is that hard for you to believe? It's my job to protect the innocent, just as much as it is to catch bad guys."

His voice was like his fingers...warm, a little rough, but gentle and oddly stirring. His fingers caressed her cheek as he watched her...stroked a strand of her hair aside as if it were an obstruction to his view. Under their hypnotic spell she no longer felt the least bit cold...and yet she shivered. *Protect? Who can protect me, if the marshals won't?*

Loneliness and longing descended on her like a blanket, pervasive as the need for sleep; her eyelids grew heavy, and the muscles in her face and neck cramped with the fierceness of her struggle against the desire to rest her cheek on his hand.

"I can't help if you won't talk to me, Mary." *Talk to me....*

Could he help her? Against all common sense, was it possible this man *would* protect her—this man who, by all indications, appeared to be trying to put her in jail for the rest of her life? What was it about him that, against all common sense, made the urge to trust him so strong? Was it his eyes, that seemed to know so much? His voice, so soft and yet so powerful? His hands, so strong and yet so gentle?

While she struggled with it, tense and silent…on the verge of giving in, his hand left her cheek. He leaned across in front of her to open the door, muttering, "Oh, hell, I just hope to God Harvey Klein doesn't catch me talking to you like this."

Her skin felt tingly and cold where his hand had been. She wanted to put her hand up and rub the spot, almost as if he'd slapped rather than caressed her. Instead, in ignominious retreat, she cringed back from his arm and the too-intimate warmth of his body, grasped the door with both hands and held on to it for support as she slipped blindly from the car. With the pavement firm under her feet, she turned to slam the door, only to find the sheriff still leaning toward her, one arm across the back of the seat she'd just left. The other hand was holding out a key.

"You're gonna need this." He nodded toward the house. "It'll open both locks, here and the one at your shop."

She took the key and managed a stiff and grudging, "Thank you."

The steely blue eyes seemed to darken as they stabbed into hers, and his mouth curved into what she knew better than to think was a smile. "I'm going to be watching you, Miss Mary. Count on it. So do yourself a favor— don't try to leave town."

Then she did slam the door. As she hurried up the walkway, she heard the SUV roar to life and drive away, but she didn't look back. She *wouldn't* look back.

Alone on the porch she paused, shivering with anger and cold and hopelessness, bathed in the scent of lilacs that was almost too sweet to bear. She stood staring at the criss-cross of yellow police tape and the padlock on the front door, with the key to the padlock a nugget of warmth in her cold hand. Warm from *his* hand… And the thought of lifting it and inserting it into the lock, of opening the door and going alone into that stranger's house, made her very soul cry out with loneliness.

Caught up in her misery, she almost didn't notice it at first…the peculiar ratchety humming sound that seemed to come from nowhere…and all around her. And then… something soft, warm and heavy bumped her leg. As Mary stared down at the broad feline head covered with moth-eaten fur and sporting a pair of scarred and tattered ears, it nudged—incredibly—at her ankles. The strange snarling sound grew in volume. The mottled back arched and the raggedy tail quivered as the sinewy body twined and rubbed itself around her legs.

"Oh, Cat," she whispered. And a tear fell with a soft plop to make a tiny wet stain on the wood porch floor.

The days that followed were easier than Mary, in the long dark hours of that first sleepless night, had feared they'd be.

No sooner had she left the house the next morning, filled with dread but determined not to crawl into a hole and hide like a coward, than a sheriff's department SUV came cruising down the street and pulled up beside her. Her heart gave a drunken lurch and slammed into her ribs as the window slid down and a familiar rumbling voice drawled cheerfully, "Mornin'. Just happened to be passing this way, thought I'd give you a lift to your shop."

"Yeah, right," Mary muttered without pausing. She'd almost been looking forward to walking the half-dozen blocks in spite of the persistant wind and a hint of frost in the air... remembering a long-ago life in a faraway place where walking to work in all kinds of weather was the normal way of things. *New York, New York...* She'd had so much there... friends, an exciting career...and Joy, who'd been more like a sister than a friend. *Why wasn't it enough? Why wasn't I happy with what I had?*

Why am I letting myself remember all this now? I can't think about this now.

"Thanks," she said distantly as she strode briskly along, "but I'm fine."

The car rolled silently, keeping pace with her, and the growl from within was deeper and somewhat less cheerful. "Mary, get in the car."

She halted and turned, hugging her sweater around her and lifting her face to the wind, grateful for that wind now, hoping it might be blamed for the breathlessness of her voice and the flush she could feel burning her cheeks. "Am I being detained?" she inquired in a cool, polite tone. "Should I get in back? I assume that's where you put prisoners."

The sheriff made an exasperated sound.

"Don't be ridiculous. My department's impounded your car. I'm giving you a ride to work."

"All part of your service to the community."

"Right…keeping dangerous criminals off the street." He leaned his long body across the seat to yank the passenger-side door open, the way he'd done the night before. "Mary, don't make me come out there and get you." Though his tone was mild, she caught the glint of a dangerous light in his steel-blue eyes.

Her pitiful rebellion fizzled as quickly as it had flared, and she even felt an odd sense of relief as she got into the SUV, pulled the door shut and clicked her seatbelt into place. The thought flashed into her mind: *I'm safe now.*

"That's better," the sheriff said, sounding almost as if he were purring. He glanced at her as he put the SUV in gear. "Did you sleep well?"

Mary looked back at him and thought the gleam in his eyes seemed more amused now than dangerous. "Please don't try to pretend this is a just a friendly favor," she said evenly, though her heart was still beating hard and fast. "At least respect my intelligence enough for that."

A wry smile tilted his lips and deepened the dips in his cheeks as he transferred his narrowed gaze to the road ahead. "Fair enough," he said.

The SUV pulled into the street, and Mary rode to work in a tense and humming silence.

Throughout the rest of that day, as she was cutting someone's hair, dabbing on color, sweeping the floor, answering the phone or ringing up someone's check, and happened to look out the window or catch the street's reflection in a mirror, more often than not she'd notice a sheriff's department patrol vehicle cruising by. Her heart would quicken, her stomach clench and the sour taste of fear rise into her throat, but she would only return a serene gray gaze to whatever client she was working on at the time and murmur a reply to whatever had been said, as if nothing out of the ordinary had taken place.

I'll be watching you....

Her clients, too, seemed anxious to maintain the myth that nothing had changed at Queenie's "We Pamper You Like Royalty" Salon and Boutique...that the quiet and retiring lady wielding scissors and pouring noxious chemicals on their hair hadn't just been charged with committing a cold-blooded murder. Mary had dreaded going into the shop, had wondered whether she'd have any clients show up at all, but to her surprise, not a single person cancelled her appointment that first day. In fact, as the week progressed she seemed to have even more business than usual. She suspected Ada Major of having a hand in that; it was a small county, and virtually everyone in it had served on Miss Ada's juries at one time or another and could probably expect to do so again.

Mary thought she also had Miss Ada to thank for the fact that almost no one stared at her openly or whispered when her back was turned—although some did try too hard to be upbeat and cheery, and her older clients—those of Miss Ada's generation—did tend to give her motherly little pats of sympathy. Mary didn't mind. She was grateful to have people around, work to do, to keep her from thinking about what lay ahead.

The sun hadn't set when Roan turned his department SUV into the alley behind Queenie's Salon and Boutique, but at that time of year it was already well into the dinner hour and the last patrol car to drive by the front of the beauty shop had reported its owner appeared to be closing up, getting ready to leave for the day.

He pulled up beside the back door of the salon and turned off the motor and keyed his radio mike. "Donna, this is SD Mobile One, I'm gonna break for dinner. Call me if you need me."

"What do you mean, 'dinner,' Sheriff?" the dispatcher's scratchy voice came back. "Don't you think you oughta go home?"

Roan chuckled, signed off and settled down to wait.

Sitting alone in his car as the evening quiet nestled around him, he began to feel a peculiar sense of restless anticipation that had nothing to do with the possibility the woman he was waiting for might try to escape his jurisdiction. The way it felt to him was more like the first time he'd asked Erin out on a real date, when he'd knocked on her door and was standing there on her front porch where he'd stood a hundred times before, hearing Boyd's heavy footsteps coming across the hard pine floor. A hundred times before he'd stood there, but this time his heart was beating like a tom-tom, his belly was quivering, his palms were wet and his mouth was dry, and he'd kept telling himself, *Man, what's wrong with you? It's just Erin, we've known each other since we were babies!* Only he'd known good and well the way he felt inside was trying to tell him something he needed to listen to, which was that it wasn't *just Erin* anymore, and never would be again.

He knew it was one thing, though—feeling like that over a girl he'd known all his life and had known he was going to eventually marry for about half of it, and who was his best friend besides—and that it was something else entirely to be getting a quiver in his belly over a woman he'd just arrested and seen charged with murder, and who he was going to be expected to do his best to help convict.

He knew all that and it didn't change a damn thing, so he was feeling less than pleased with himself by the time the back door of the salon opened and the cause of his frustration appeared, looking like a mouse venturing out of her hole.

She hesitated when she saw him waiting there, looking for a moment as though she wanted to slip back into that hole and close the door. Then, darting a desperate look around as if searching for a new place to hide, or run to—or hoping there'd be somebody else there to rescue her—she came slowly toward the car. Roan rolled down his window and she halted, looking now like someone about to meet the hangman. She drew a shaky breath and said, "Okay, what now?"

Blame guilt, or his grouchy mood; he snarled back at her, "What do you mean, what now? I'm here to take you home, dammit."

And instantly her shoulders got hunched up and she seemed to flinch. "You don't need to do that."

He couldn't seem to stop himself from scowling at her. "Look, are we going to go through this again? I brought you here, I'll take you home. Get in."

Still she hesitated, and he said impatiently, "For God's sake, Red, you don't need to look at me like I'm the Big Bad Wolf. I'm just giving you a ride home."

He didn't know what to think when she went pale and jerked back as if he'd slapped her.

Chapter Eight

Her eyes, framed by those godawful glasses, reminded Roan of terrified wild critters cowering in the shadows. "What…what did you say?"

Watching her narrowly, he said, "Uh… Big Bad Wolf… Little Red Riding Hood? You know—"

"Oh—of course." A smile blossomed, misty with embarrassment and relief.

"What the hell did you think?" He still felt wary, and oddly shaken. But there was a new tingle of alertness running through him, too…a feeling there was something important in this little misunderstanding, if he only knew what it was.

She tried her best to divert him with a nervous laugh and a not very convincing gesture. "I thought—you reminded me of something, that's all."

Something? *Or...someone?* But he didn't see any point in pursuing the issue. Not then.

Gathering up his patience, which he seemed to have been losing his grip on a lot lately, he said in a weary voice, "Well, all right, Miss Mary, but do you think you could get in the damn car? I'm not gonna eat you, you know."

She threw him her vivid green glare and muttered, "You might not believe that either, if you could see your face." But she trotted around the SUV and opened the passenger-side door.

While she was doing that, Roan had a chance to look at himself in his rearview mirror. What he saw made him snort, then laugh silently. He was smiling when she slipped in beside him, fingering back a lock of limp brown hair that had escaped the confines of the ponytail she'd clipped haphazardly to the back of her head. Watching her, his smile grew broader.

"What now?" she demanded, instantly suspicious again. "Why are you smiling?"

What was he going to say? He couldn't tell her he was thinking how he'd like to take that damn clip and pitch it out the window, then slip his fingers into the silky softness of her hair...and that he was smiling the same way he would if he'd just set eyes on a meadow full of wildflowers, or a wild red sunset, or a nice piece of horseflesh running free. For no other reason than to acknowledge and thank God for the beauty of it.

And he didn't want to ask her why she was trying to hide how beautiful she was, either—not then...although he did file that question away for a future time and place, along with the others he'd collected. Because he was more and more certain the dowdiness she put on with those ugly glasses and oversized clothes wasn't ignorance or bad taste. Considering the woman made her living making other people beautiful, it was hard for him to believe she wouldn't know how to recognize it in herself.

Which meant...his pulse quickened as his mind tripped quickly along the path that thought opened up for him. *Say she's a protected witness, but a new identity, a new lo-*

cation, aren't enough. Say she's recognizable whoever or whatever she is. If she's trying to hide it, could it mean it's the fact she's beautiful that makes her recognizable?

He put on an expression of mock bewilderment and adopted a wounded tone that wouldn't fool Susie Grace. "Hey, a minute ago you didn't like my face because I wasn't smiling, now you don't like it because I am? I just can't win with you, can I?"

She didn't answer that, but busied herself fastening her seatbelt, then turned her head and studied him thoughtfully while he started up the SUV and checked his rearview mirrors. When they were headed down the alley, she shifted to face forward and said conversationally, "Don't you have anything better to do than chauffeur a murder suspect around town? Like…a department to run? Criminals to catch?"

"See, that's the good thing about being the boss," he said cheerfully. "You get to delegate. Happens I've got a whole bunch of good people working for me. Amazes me, sometimes, how much they can get done so long as I stay out of their way." His eyes slid past her as he made the turn onto Main Street, and he added softly and without a trace of humor,

"The fact is, Miss Mary, right now you're my number-one priority."

I wonder why he calls me that—Miss Mary, she thought.

I wonder why I don't mind that he does.

There was a knot of tension sitting at the very top of her chest, and she rubbed it absently as she watched the quaint Old-West-style storefronts on Main Street flash by. She noticed that many of them were wearing new coats of paint now that spring had come, and some had flower boxes sitting out in front, planted with pansies and snapdragons and daffodils that nodded in the wind. A lot of them had hung American flags, too.

I wonder why he looks at me the way he does sometimes...as if he really does see right through this charade of mine...as if he knows who I really am.

I wonder how he can know who I am when even I don't, and why it bothers me so much that he does.

I wonder why I wonder about him so much....

"What do you do when you're not working?"

Her heart gave a nervous lurch and her breath hitched, and she'd already flicked him a startled glance before she caught herself and murmured, "What do you mean?"

Watching the street ahead, he casually lifted one shoulder. "What do you like to do in your spare time? Read? Garden? Build birdhouses? Go out with friends?"

Warning instincts shivered over her skin. *What is he doing? Is he trying to trick me?* "Why are you asking?" she said lightly, on guard now.

The glance he gave her seemed more amused than exasperated, like the look an indulgent parent might bestow on a rebellious child. "It's called conversation—you know, polite small talk? That's where I ask you unimportant questions and you answer them, then you ask me some and I answer, and maybe in the process we get to know each other a little better."

He was patronizing her. Annoyance crept over her, banishing the pricklings of suspicion. "Conversation?" she said with an incredulous huff of laughter. "You must be kidding. We shouldn't even be talking at all— about *anything.*"

He was silent for a moment, then said quietly, "I'm not trying to trick you into anything, if that's what you're thinking. My asking didn't have anything to do with you having secrets…me trying to find out who you are. Maybe I shouldn't be asking *any* kind of questions—most likely I shouldn't—hell, Lord *knows* I shouldn't. But look, you're a newcomer in a town where everybody knows everybody and half are related by blood or marriage. I'd like to learn more about you. That's it—that's all it is." He was frowning when he finished, maybe realizing how many contradictions there'd been in what he'd said.

Mary studied his rugged profile, cast in bronze by the setting sun. The dent in his cheek was a purple shadow, his hair burnished gold. The skin on his forehead had a rosy glow that looked as if it would be warm to touch…and she couldn't keep herself from thinking of the ways she might. *Brushing that thick silky hair back, my fingers burrowing through it…holding him close while I…*

Shimmering heat crept through her. *I shouldn't be doing this,* she thought, but she heard herself clear her throat. "I don't know many people in town—other than clients, that is. In the evenings I watch television…read… listen to music—"

"Yeah? Me too." The smile he threw her was spontaneous—the first of its kind she'd seen. It softened his face, warmed his cold-steel eyes. Her heart gave a hiccup of surprise. "What kind of music? Not country, I'm thinkin'."

Without knowing she was going to, she smiled back. "No. Classical, I guess...pop... Broadway...and anything you can dance to."

"You like to dance?"

"I used to," she said. Her smile faded and died.

"You ever go dancing on the weekends? We've got a few places around here. Naturally, it's gonna be country, though."

She stared blindly at her hands and shook her head. "On weekends I usually catch up on chores...go grocery shopping. When the weather lets me, I go to the firing range... maybe for a walk." The remembered loneliness of those solitary walks came creeping over her like nighttime fog, banishing the lovely shimmering warmth, and only now that it was leaving her did she recognize the warmth as happiness.

"You ever ride?"

"What? Ride—oh, you mean horses?" She shuddered, and when she looked up, found she'd almost missed another of his oddly endearing, crooked grins.

"Well, yeah, this bein' Montana."

"Oh—God, no." She looked at him with such horror that he laughed out loud. This time when he glanced at her, his eyes were bright with curiosity.

"Mean to tell me you've never ridden a horse before?"

She shook her head. Her skin was crawling with new prickles of warning.

"Why is that? Never had the chance, or scared to try?"

She gave a short, high laugh, considered for moment, then decided to ignore the warnings. "Both, I guess. Maybe a cause and effect in there somewhere."

"Ah," he said, nodding wisely, "must be a city girl."

She turned her head sharply and looked out the window as a memory came from nowhere, unexpected and shocking as a slap.

"You think you want to be a city girl!" My father's voice, thundering down like the wrath of God from somewhere above me—his pulpit, maybe. I remember the church smells of old wood and linseed oil and dead flowers as he shouted, "Cities are dens of wickedness and degradation, girl—remember what the Lord did to Sodom and Gomorrah. No! My

answer is no, and no, and a thousand times no! No daughter of mine will ever follow a path that can only lead to sin and death! Not while I have breath!"

She thought, *Goes to show how much you know, Sheriff.* But the warning prickles were too insistent now to be ignored, and they kept her from saying it out loud.

The SUV turned sharply, jounced off the pavement and into a packed-earth parking lot, and came to a halt.

Mary glanced around in surprise; she'd been too fogged in by memories to notice they'd gone beyond the turn-off to her street. "Why are we stopping here?"

The sheriff pulled the keys from the ignition and turned to look at her, his hair and features weirdly highlighted by the flashing multicolored glow of the animated neon sign on the roof of Buster's Last Stand Saloon. "It's dinnertime. I'm hungry, and I'm guessing you are, too. I'm also guessing—well, hell, to be honest, I happen to *know* you haven't done any grocery shopping since you got out of jail. Since I'm told you like the cooking here, thought you might like to stop in…pick up something to take home for dinner."

She stared at him, trying to read him, wondering whether he'd meant to be cruel… whether he could really be so devious. But his expression, thanks to the flickering light of the neon sign, had nothing to tell her.

She turned to stare instead at the sign—a cowboy on a rearing horse, which was said to be something of an antique, though not as much of one as the original, which Mary had been told had depicted an Indian wielding a tomahawk. It had been replaced sometime in the latter part of the twentieth century when changing sensibilities had rendered it politically incorrect.

She gazed now at the rearing horse, half-hypnotized by its flashing animated sequence that seemed to keep time with the thumping of her heartbeat and the throbbing ache in her throat, and wondered why her vision should suddenly blur with unshed tears. Because his kindness had seemed real to her… because she'd trusted him…because she felt betrayed? Or something else entirely?

"Why are you doing this?" She was so used to keeping silent…so used to keeping her secrets, she almost didn't believe it was her own voice. "What did you hope to accomplish by bringing me here?"

"What?" He jerked back from her as if she'd struck him. Feigned innocence, she wondered, or genuine surprise? "Ah, Mary, come on, now—"

"Were you hoping I'd... I don't know, be overcome with guilt at seeing the place where Jason and I had our...confrontation, break down and confess I shot him? Save your county the expense of a trial?" She glared at him, relieved it was anger that had brought these forbidden tears. Anger, she could deal with.

"Ah...hell. Mary..." He drew a hand over his face, then turned so that he was facing her, one arm across the back of the seats. "Look, I've an idea you've got good reasons to be so suspicious and cynical about a man's motives. Maybe I can't expect you to trust me, or believe me when I tell you I'm just not that devious." His voice was a low, hypnotic rumble. She didn't want to listen to it...didn't want to sit unmoving when she felt his hand on the back of her neck. And yet...she did. "But I'm not," the mesmerizing voice went on, while his hand slipped under her straggling hair to lay its comforting and intimate warmth on her bare nape. "Swear to God. Kind of wish I'd thought of it, but the fact is, all I was trying to do was get you something to eat before I took you home. I am truly sorry I upset you."

She nodded, eyes closed, and struggled to push words past the ache in her throat. "It's okay… I'm sorry…it's just that…"

But how could she explain to him that in the darkness and the flashing neon lights it had all come back to her, that she could feel hot, moist hands on her body, the rough scrape of beard stubble, cruel wet lips and searching tongue…the choking stench of beer breath…the coppery taste of blood in her mouth. She felt nauseated and cold; all the feelings she'd suppressed that night rose up in her now, and it took every ounce of will she had to keep from tearing open the car door and vomiting onto the hard-packed earth… then running away as fast and as far as she could get from that soothing voice and gentle hand. So compelling was the desire to crawl trembling and sobbing into this man's arms… to allow herself the unimaginable luxury of his comfort and protection.

"It's okay," he murmured. His fingers stroked the side of her neck…his warm palm massaged its base. "It's okay. How 'bout if I go in and get you a sandwich? If you promise you won't run off while I'm gone." She could hear the ironic smile in his voice and gave a small answering spurt of hopeless laughter.

"Where would I go?" She shook her head and huffed in a shallow breath. "Thanks, but... I'm not really hungry. If you could just take me home...."

"I can do that—if you're sure." She could feel his eyes searching her face. She nodded, and felt the warmth and weight of his hand leave her neck as he turned and reached for the key.

She told herself she was relieved, and she was. Oh, she was. But then why, somewhere deep inside, did she feel a sharp bright tug of pain, as if something she'd become attached to had been roughly ripped away?

He drove her home in frowning silence, one hand clamped across the lower part of his face, the other tapping a restless cadence on the steering wheel, while Mary tried to watch him without letting him know, wondering what he might be thinking that had darkened his thoughts so. Wondering how it was that she should feel his silence as a kind of abandonment, and why she should feel *this* loneliness so acutely when she'd been accustomed to loneliness for years. Was it the contrast, perhaps, between this withdrawal and the unexpected intimacy they'd shared a few minutes ago? And who was this foolish stranger inside her recklessly crying, *Yes— yes, I want more of that! Please, oh please... touch me again!*

Seductive and dangerous thoughts...and she would put them out of her mind for good. She *would*.

But when the SUV drew to a gentle stop in front of Queenie's small clapboard house, she didn't get out right away, but sat with her hands clenched in her lap, staring up at the lighted front porch...at the lilac bush where Jason had crouched in ambush that night...

"Would you like me to come in with you for a minute?"

She almost laughed. Thankfully, she found the self-control to keep from it, and simply shook her head. If she laughed, how would she explain to him why? How could she tell him that, in her present vulnerable state, her greatest fear was that if she were alone with him she'd throw herself into his arms?

Instead, still gazing out of the window, she said softly, "What's going to happen now? Do I just...go on about my life—as much as the news media will let me—as if nothing's happened?"

She heard an exhalation…a small throat-clearing sound. "Well, the wheels of justice don't grind quite as slowly here in Hartsville as they do in the big city, but it's still apt to be a while before this comes to trial. Luckily for us, the media people have short attention spans. Most of 'em have already cleared out—except for the diehard papparazzi, maybe." There was a pause, and a smile came back into his voice. "Guess it's a good thing you have me to drive you back and forth to work."

She turned to look at him. "How long are you going to keep doing this? Until the trial?"

In the darkness she couldn't see his eyes, but the quiet voice had a silvery edge. "As long as I need to, Miss Mary."

She gave him a small bitter smile. "Thanks for the ride, Sheriff." She opened the door and climbed out of the car.

His voice stopped her before she could slam the door shut. "We're gonna be seeing quite a bit of each other in the next few weeks. Do you think maybe you could call me Roan?"

She hesitated, holding the door and gazing into the deepening dusk where a few of last year's leaves, caught by the breeze, were swirling in the SUV's headlights. Her throat tightened. "Isn't that unusual, considering who we are to each other?"

From inside the SUV came a short huff of laughter, and then the rumbling drawl: "Miss Mary, not one thing about you and me is *usual*."

The motor fired. Mary closed the door and stepped back from the car. Folding her arms around herself, she watched as it rolled slowly away.

It was Saturday morning, and Roan was having an altercation with Susie Grace. This had been happening with some regularity of late, and it was beginning to be a concern to him. His relationship with his daughter had been a source of comfort and joy to him up to now, and he didn't like to see that change. At least, he acknowledged, not any sooner than it had to.

The bone of contention on this particular occasion had to do with Boyd planning on taking some steers to the sale, and Roan feeling a compelling need to keep an eye on his murder suspect, and Susie Grace not wanting to accompany either one.

At the moment she had both elbows planted

on the breakfast table and an expression on her face of the type that would have prompted Roan's mother to tell him he'd better hope his face didn't freeze that way. She'd eaten the middle out of a piece of toast and stuck her finger through the hole and was twirling it like a lasso in the vicinity of her left ear.

"I'll stay here by myself," she announced, in the manner of a queen issuing a royal proclamation.

Roan blew on his coffee, sipped it, said, "No, you won't," and watched his beloved child morph instantly from monarch into whiny seven-year-old.

"Da-ad, *why?* I'm old enough, I can take care of myself."

"No, you're not," said Roan.

Susie Grace hurled the piece of toast across the table, tumbled from her chair and ran out of the room, bellowing like a just-branded calf.

Roan sighed and set his coffee cup down on the table. "What am I doing wrong?" he asked Boyd, who was standing at the stove tending to the last of a batch of hotcakes.

With his back to him, Boyd said, "It ain't what you're doin', it's what you're *not* doin'."

"Which is?"

His father-in-law flipped another hotcake. "Spendin' time with her. You ain't been home much since the Holbrook kid got killed. She's missin' you, is all."

Roan's snort of protest was prompted more by guilt than disagreement. "Well, there's not much I can do about that," he muttered into his coffee cup. "I'm doing the best I can."

Boyd scooped up the hotcakes and stacked them on a plate, turned off the gas burner, then looked over at Roan. "How long you gonna shadow that little ol' gal from the beauty shop?"

"I guess until a jury finds her innocent or guilty." Roan looked at his coffee with distaste and set the cup back on the table, though he knew good and well it wasn't Boyd's coffee that tasted so bitter in his mouth.

"You tellin' me you really think she did it?" Boyd's sharp eyes speared him, and he shifted irritably under their gaze.

"Didn't you already ask me that?"

The older man shrugged and turned back to the stove. "Just wonderin', since you been spendin' so much time with her..." He gathered up frying pans and dropped them into the sink full of soapy water. "Thought by now you mighta got to know her a little better, mighta changed your mind."

"Ah, hell, I don't know." Roan gave a gusty sigh as he pushed back from the table, got up and carried his breakfast plate and coffee cup to the sink. "Truth is—and this goes no further than this room, you understand—I am having a hard time believing the woman could be guilty of killing anybody. But if not her, dammit, then *who?* Everything I've got points to her, and there isn't anybody else around here that had a good enough reason to kill Jason—not like that, like it was a personal grudge. An execution, even."

Boyd nodded and went on scrubbing at a frying pan. Roan clapped him on the shoulder and said with a breeziness he didn't feel, "Good thing it's not up to me to decide. I'm gonna let a jury do that. Listen, good luck at the sale. Right now I think I'm gonna go have a little talk with my daughter. You might want to wish me luck on that, too."

Boyd grunted. "Yeah, you think she's hard to get along with now, just wait till she hits puberty." He looked at Roan and pointed a soapy spatula at him. "What that kid needs is a mother. You know that, don't you?"

Roan said, "Huh," and walked away. But

as he headed down the hall to his daughter's bedroom, he felt like he'd been kicked by a mule. *What that kid needs is a mother.* Dammit, he knew that, and he didn't know why those words had hit him so hard just now. It wasn't like he hadn't said it himself a time or two before.

Maybe because it had come from Boyd, father of the woman any new mother of Susie's would have to replace? Or because the face that had sprung unbidden and unwanted into his mind when Boyd said it was that of a woman he'd recently arrested for first-degree murder.

Saturday promised to be a busy day for Mary. It was prom weekend, and she was booked solid from opening in the morning until the last possible moment before the big night. She'd scheduled herself more tightly than she normally would, too, right through lunch and without even a coffee break. Maybe it was because she hadn't had a prom of her own, but she felt a responsibility to make sure every single girl went off to the dance feeling beautiful.

Who knew better than than she did what

it was like to feel beautiful…and what it was like not to?

And so, when Cat woke her earlier than usual—in his customary fashion, landing on her bed with a thump that shook the mattress, and then, vibrating the very air with his grinding purr, plodding the full length of her body to bump his head against her chin hard enough to make her see stars—she was more than happy for the opportunity to get a head start on the day. The sun was shining, the cold spell had passed, and she saw no reason why she should wait for Sheriff Harley to drive her to work when she could just as easily walk the half-dozen blocks and spend an extra hour getting things organized and prepped for the onslaught to come.

Which was why she was in her shop, immersed in the task of laying out gloves, smocks, wraps, curlers, scissors and all the other tools and supplies and magic potions she would need to transform two dozen or so highly emotional and self-conscious teenaged ducklings into self-confident swans, when she heard the back door of the salon open, then bang shut. She barely had time to glance up before the sheriff came bursting through the curtain, looking like a fighting bull in search of the matador.

He checked when he saw Mary and said, "Ah, there you are," in a calm voice that might have been convincing if his eyes hadn't glittered so brightly, and if she hadn't heard the sharp exhale of a breath through his nostrils.

She gave him a brief smile and went back to her sorting. "Did you think I'd left town?"

The sheriff folded his arms on his chest and strolled slowly toward her. "The thought crossed my mind."

"Mine, too," Mary said lightly, not looking up. Dismayed at the way her heart had quickened. "I couldn't very well go today, though—it's prom night."

He nodded and said, "Ah."

As if he truly understands, Mary thought, with a little tickle of surprise.

And why shouldn't he? No doubt he remembers his prom. She felt a twinge of envy for the girl who had been his childhood sweetheart...and eventually his wife.

"You might have called me," he said, from unexpectedly close behind her, in an undertone that was unnecessary in the empty shop. And perhaps for that reason seemed strangely intimate.

"I...didn't think of it." She felt too warm. Nervous, and hemmed in. He was too close...

she could feel the heat from his body...smell his clean, just-shaved, just-showered smell.

She started to turn, needing to find more room to breathe, and when she did, a movement caught her eye—the curtain across the back entrance to the salon, twitching back into place, as if someone was watching furtively from behind it.

She halted and said, "Oh—" and the sheriff turned, too, following her startled gaze.

He made a gesture toward the curtain. "Come on out here, Susie Grace, she's not gonna bite you."

There was a pause...the curtain quivered, billowed, and then was snatched aside by a small hand to reveal a girl, possibly seven or eight but small for her age, dressed in jeans and a blue pullover with yellow butterflies appliqued on the front. She was wearing blue cowboy boots and a look that was half wary and half defiant. Her hair was pulled into two tight braids that hung stiffly to just below her shoulders. Hair the color of fire...copper pennies...autumn leaves.

Mary's breath caught, and as the child moved reluctantly into the room, she felt the earth shudder under her feet. Thirty years fell away in an instant, and she found herself looking through a window into her own past—or was it a mirror? Except for the scars that puckered and crinkled the skin on the little girl's neck and chin and one side of her face, Mary was gazing at herself...the child she had once been.

Chapter Nine

"My daughter, Susan."

It was the sound of Roan's voice, clipped and cool rather than his usual throaty rumble, that finally pulled Mary's gaze away from the child. Throwing him a guilty glance, she saw that his mouth had tightened, and she realized he must have completely misinterpreted the look on her face, realized he must think it was the child's scars that had made her go shocked and still. Dismayed, she caught a quick breath to steady herself and returned the little girl's sulky glare with a smile.

"Come on in here," her father said impatiently. "This is Miss Mary. She's not gonna bite you."

"Hi, Susan," Mary said, putting out her hand, "I'm very glad to meet you. Your dad has told—"

She was interrupted by the trilling of a cellular phone. Muttering under his breath, Roan snatched it from his belt and flipped it open. "Yeah." He turned a shoulder to his audience of two, and then, after a brief pause, looked back at Mary, his eyes bright and intense. He gestured with the cell phone toward the salon's back door. "I'm gonna have to...uh, I'll just step outside for a minute, if that's..."

"Yes, sure," Mary murmured, tearing her gaze from his daughter's face...and those coppery braids, so much like her own, once. "Go ahead."

The sheriff vanished behind the swaying curtain, abandoning her to the company of his sullen and distrustful child. She listened to his footsteps thump through the storage room, and the outer door creak open, then click shut.

There was a brief, vibrant silence, and then Susie Grace's small scarred chin lifted a notch. "Go ahead and stare if you want to," she said valiantly. "Everybody does. I don't care."

Mary's stomach gave a queer little lurch. "I wouldn't do that, Susie Grace—it would be rude."

"Well," Susie Grace returned with a shrug, "you were."

"I was *looking* at you. Because I just met you. That's natural. But I think it's natural that I would want to know what happened to give you those scars. Don't you?"

Susie Grace wrinkled her nose and eyed her skeptically. "Don't you know?"

"Maybe I heard something," Mary said with an offhand shrug. "But I'd rather *you* told me."

The child cocked her head and did a sort of half pirouette, the way Mary had seen children do when they felt self-conscious. "I got burned in a fire. So did my Grampa Boyd. So did my mom, but she died." She threw Mary a resentful look over her shoulder. "I suppose you're going to feel sorry for me now. Or else try to be really nice to me, so my dad will like you."

Wow, Mary thought, and decided she might be forgiven a lie. "Actually, I don't care whether your dad likes me or not," she said with an airy toss of her head as she turned back to the work station she'd been setting up. "And why would

I feel sorry for you? I was thinking what a lucky little girl you are." She was startled to realize that last part, at least, wasn't a lie.

And she was pleased when, watching from under her lashes, she saw the little girl's expressive features register first surprise and then uncertainty. "What do you mean?"

Mary cleared her throat, which had grown unexpectedly tight. "Well, you've got a nice home, with a father and grampa who love and take care of you—I think that makes you *very* lucky." She turned to study the little girl's upturned face—drawn by curiosity, perhaps, she had cautiously crept close to her side. "Plus, you have gorgeous blue eyes, and I'll bet you have a nice smile, too, when you want to use it." Casually, she reached out to touch one coppery braid, then lifted and drew it over the child's shoulder. "And, you have beautiful hair."

Susie Grace jerked her head, flipping the braid back over her shoulder. "I hate my hair."

Unperturbed, Mary laughed softly. "I used to have to wear my hair in pigtails when I was a little girl."

"You did?" Susie Grace was doing the suspicious, wrinkled-up-nose thing again.

"Yeah—I hated them, too."

Susie Grace giggled, clapping a hand over her mouth and ducking her head the way little girls do when they share delicious secrets with each other, and Mary shivered inside with something she hadn't felt in a very long time. *Sheer delight.*

Roan wasn't in the best of moods when he finished his call and returned the cell phone to his belt. The U.S. Marshal's Office, apparently overwhelmed and in a state of reorganization due to some personnel shortages and recent scandals, still hadn't been able to locate either a case file for Mary Owen, or the marshal assigned to her case. Never thrilled to be dealing with federal bureaucracy at the best of times, right now his inability to make any headway in solving the mystery of his murder suspect's identity had him ready to spit bullets.

He also wasn't happy about the way that particular murder suspect had been occupying his mind of late…her face, those shimmering green-gold eyes coming into his thoughts in the dark of night when he lay alone in the bed he'd shared with Erin. It had been a long time since he'd shared his bed with a woman— any woman. He hoped that was all this was about. Guilt…the notion that he was betraying his wife. Lust…the natural awareness a man has for an attractive woman. Those he could handle.

He for *sure* wasn't happy, though, about the pain that had knifed through his belly this morning and turned his blood to ice and his heart to stone when he'd arrived at her house to pick her up and found her gone.

All those things were on his mind as he made his way back through the storeroom, flicked aside the curtain and stepped into the powder-pink salon. All that, plus a niggling measure of guilt at having left his murder suspect to babysit Susie Grace, who Lord knew didn't care for strangers at the best of times, and in the mood she was in this morning…

He halted. His jaw went slack and that and every other intelligent thought flew right out of his head.

Momentum had carried him several long strides into the salon before his brain registered what he was seeing: Susie Grace, his ornery tomboy daughter, sitting high in one of Mary's chairs with a pink drape around her neck. She had her eyes all squinched up, closed tight, and most of what had been her long braids was lying in a copper-colored pile at Mary's feet.

He must have made some sound, because although she didn't open her eyes, Susie Grace's face lit up with a grin. "Hi, Dad."

He cleared his throat, stalling while he collected his wits—though his first attempt at speech didn't show much evidence of success in that respect. "Uh…what's goin' on? What've you guys been up to?" The answer to which was pretty damned obvious, even to a man not much accustomed to the mysteries of beauty salons.

"I'm getting my hair cut," said Susie Grace.

"I can see that," said Roan, nodding. "How come your eyes are shut?"

"Mary told me to keep them closed 'til she's done. But it's okay, 'cause I'm scared to look anyway." She gave a theatrical shiver.

Mary glanced at him, pushed her glasses up on the bridge of her nose and went on with what she was doing. Roan winced as he watched another wet hank of red hair tumble to the floor.

"I'm giving her a layered cut," Mary explained. "When it's dry it's going to feather around her face and neck, see?" She managed, with subtle motions of her hands and the scissors, to show him what she wouldn't say aloud: *And it will hide and soften the effect of the scars.* "And," she added, tilting Susie Grace's head in order to reach a new spot, "it should be short enough so it won't get in her way."

"Yeah, 'cause I don't like hair in my face," said Susie Grace, scrunching up her face again in disgust.

Mary laid the scissors aside and picked up a blow dryer. She turned it on and blew away the stray locks of hair that had fallen on Susie Grace's face and on the shoulders of the pink drape. Then Roan watched, with emotions he couldn't name quivering in his stomach, while hands that seemed almost magical tousled and fluffed and coaxed the damp strands that remained into soft shining waves that swung and floated...then settled like the petals of a flower against the puckered, silvery skin that marred his little girl's cheek and neck.

Mary turned off the dryer, laid it aside, then turned the chair to face the mirror. "Open your eyes, Susie Grace."

Roan held his breath. Susie Grace slowly opened her eyes. She looked at herself for what seemed like forever...with absolutely no expression on her face, in a silence so complete he wondered why they all couldn't hear his heart pounding.

Then she stuck out her lower lip. "I look like a *girl*."

"A very *pretty* girl," Mary said softly.

Susie Grace, being...well, Susie Grace, stubbornly shook her head. But her eyes were glowing, and her face...

It was suddenly too much. Roan pivoted sharply away to hide the emotions that must have been visible on his face...coughed to ease the ache in his throat...rubbed at the back of his neck where it burned with the embarrassment of so much emotion.

"Don't you like it, Dad?"

The doubt and disappointment in her voice tore at him. He didn't know how he managed to come up with a smile before he turned back to her, but he did. "Yeah, peanut, of course I like it. You look real pretty. You look—" he had to cough again to get the words through his throat "—just like your mother."

He hurled one desperate look at Mary, then yanked his sunglasses out of his pocket and shoved them onto his face. *Damned* if he was going to let his murder suspect catch him with tears in his eyes.

But where did he go from here? His shocked mind was casting wildly about for an answer to that when he was saved, literally, by the bell—the one on the salon's front door. It jangled merrily as several high-school girls burst in, bringing with them the cool spring air and all the noise and laughter and brightness only a bunch of teenage girls can.

They turned the volume down considerably when they saw the sheriff standing there.

To put them at ease Roan nodded and smiled and said affably, "Mornin', ladies."

Having got his feet back square on the ground again, he turned to his daughter and the woman who'd knocked them out from under him in the first place. He held out his hand to Susie Grace, who ignored it and hopped down from the chair without help, brushing at her face and shaking her head to feel the way her hair moved on her neck. Her eyes were shining like it was Christmas morning.

"We'd best be getting on," he said gruffly, before he could get choked up again. "Looks like Miss Mary needs to get to work." He looked at her, glad he had the sunglasses to hide behind. "How much do I owe you?"

She made a startled, distracted gesture. "Oh—just call it even for the gas." A smile flickered, then quickly died. She didn't have the benefit of dark glasses like he did; behind the transparent lenses her eyes seemed uncommonly bright.

"We're going horseback riding," Susie Grace announced, oblivious to rampaging adult emotions. Roan saw her glance warily at the high-school girls, but at least she didn't try to hide behind his legs, as she usually did. Instead, she reached for Mary's hand and said shyly, "You could come with us."

He wasn't surprised she didn't answer. He thought she must be more than a little bit distracted, though, because she sort of strolled along beside them as they walked outside, letting Susie Grace lead her by the hand.

So there they were—his daughter holding Mary's hand on one side and his on the other—like one little happy family. He didn't know what to feel about that picture—whether it made him happy, or angry, or sad, or just confused as hell.

When they were outside in the alley, Susie Grace tried again, wheedling the way she did when she was trying to get her way and knew it wasn't going to happen. "Come with us? *Please?*"

Mary gave a little gurgle of a laugh. "Oh,

honey, I can't—I have a lot of other girls' hair to fix today." She shot Roan a look with more than laughter in her eyes, the kind of look that passes between a man and a woman when they share secret thoughts without saying a word—and he knew then she was remembering what she'd told him about her feelings about horses.

And he didn't know how to feel about that, either.

"We'll be back in time to take you home," he said, bringing himself back to earth and a warning note into his tone.

She nodded and wrapped her arms across her waist. Her smile was merely wry now. "No rush—I'm sure I'll be here until late."

"Tomorrow's Sunday," Susie Grace said hopefully, looking from one grownup to the other and back again, fidgeting in the natural way of little kids, now that they were away from curious eyes. "Nobody works Sunday, right? You could come with us tomorrow! Right, Dad? Can she come?"

"Well, I don't—" Mary sucked in a breath and shot Roan a look of pure panic, and once again he knew right away what she was thinking.

"Not horseback riding," he assured her dryly. *"Shopping."*

"We're going to the mall in Bozeman to buy me clothes 'cause I outgrew all my old ones," Susie Grace explained, hopping excitedly. "Can she come with us, Dad? *Please?*"

Roan looked at Mary, and she looked back at him, and her eyes seemed to shimmer in the soft spring sunlight. The same sun touched her cheeks with a warm ivory glow, and her lips slowly parted and grew lush…and ripe, and he swore he could see a pulse beating in her long, slender throat. Standing right there in that alley he could feel his own pulse thumping low down in his belly, where a ball of heat had formed and was growing hotter and heavier by the second, making him feel scorched from his scalp to his toes.

He for damn sure knew how he felt about *that,* and he was not so sure he was going to be able to handle it after all.

Because what he felt was scared to death.

"Don't know when I've seen her so happy," Roan said, narrowed eyes following his daughter's progress through the food court tables on her way to the video arcade. He coughed and frowned at the coffee-flavored ice cream cone in his hand. "It was a nice thing you did, fixing her hair like that. Don't know if I said thank you or not, but…thank you."

Mary smiled, the cool sweet miracle of pistachio almond ice cream lingering on her tongue. "No thanks necessary. Every girl needs to feel pretty."

He threw her a look, bright with a father's anguish. "Yeah, I know. That's why I… I mean, how can she—"

Without thinking, she reached across the table to put her hand on his arm, and the sensation of warm wiry muscle beneath a soft cotton shirtsleeve sent a flash of tingling heat through her fingers and hand. It had already spread into every part of her before she could snatch the hand away, and she laid her palm against her chest in a vain effort to still the turmoil it had kindled there.

"Roan, *feeling* pretty isn't about what's on the outside—it's in *here.*" The quiver of emotion in her voice wasn't only from the words, or the memories they recalled. "It doesn't matter how pretty she *is,* if she doesn't *feel* pretty…and vice versa, of course," she finished in a more casual tone, when she saw he was studying her with bright and unreadable eyes.

To avoid that scrutiny, she turned her attention to her ice cream cone, turning it to find the spot most in need of licking. But she found licking it only intensified her awareness of that keen blue gaze....

Then, having taken care of all incipient drips, she didn't know what to do with the cone. If she lowered it, which would be the natural thing to do, it would expose her lips, which all of a sudden felt ridiculously swollen, to his discerning gaze. She would feel... naked. And her lips were glazed, now, and sticky with the ice cream's sweetness; yet licking them while he watched seemed almost unbearably seductive. What if he thought...

"Another way of sayin' kids need to feel good about themselves." He licked his cone unselfconsciously. Above it his eyes grew lazy and soft, as if behind the cone his mouth was smiling.

Out of the blue it occurred to Mary what his deep rumbling drawl reminded her of. There'd always been something about it... the tone, the pitch...that set pleasure vibrations humming inside her. It was like Cat's purring. His voice made her feel happy and warm and safe.

"Yes," she said, and smiled.

Roan frowned at his ice cream cone to hide

the fact that he felt like he'd just been bucked off a horse. *Oh Lord, that smile...*

He thought it probably hadn't occured to her what she must look like when she did that. Or that she wasn't supposed to bc beautiful.

"Well, shoot," he said belligerently, "I think Susie's pretty, even with her scars. I've told her, but I don't think she believes me. She just tells me, 'Oh, *Dad....*'"

Mary nodded, and he watched her smile grow crooked. "That's because everybody knows all dads are supposed to think their little girls are beautiful. It's a question little girls ask their mothers: 'Mommy, am I pretty?'" She studied her almost empty cone as if she'd lost her appetite for it. The sadness was in her eyes, now, too.

"Did you ask yours?" He smiled at her, wanting to bring the lovely green light back into her eyes.

She bit into her cone with a soft crunch and nodded. "Sooner or later we all do."

"And what did she say?"

Her throat moved as if it was rocks she'd swallowed instead of a bite of sugar cookie ice cream cone. After a pause, looking past him she said in a voice without expression, "She told me the devil loves a pretty face.

Then she told my father. He made me kneel on the church floor—I don't know for how long…hours, I guess. Maybe all day. I remember the floor was hard… I remember my knees hurt, and my back. I remember being cold and hungry. I remember crying."

Roan was used to hearing shocking things, but he couldn't remember anything he'd ever heard on the job that hit him as hard. Luckily, he'd had a lot of practice keeping his feelings to himself, so he was able to respond in the quiet, even tone he'd use with a distraught witness. "Your father was a preacher?"

She nodded.

And there it was, finally—a small thing, but after a week of subtle probing his mystery woman had just handed him a piece of her past. A piece that might even help solve the puzzle of who and what she was, if he could take the time to look at it closely.

But right then he felt no flare of triumph at the revelation, no sense of achievement or success. Right then his mind was occupied by only one thing: the image of a little girl with shimmering tear-filled green eyes and the face of an angel, on her knees in a cold empty church, shivering…crying…praying. Wondering what she'd done that was so wrong.

As the shock slowly faded, rage took its place. The same rage, he told himself, that filled him every time he had to deal with a case involving abuse of a child. He never had been able to understand that kind of cruelty—never had and never would.

Stiffening his facial muscles and avoiding the eyes that gazed past him, veiled in a misty sheen that reminded him of dewfall on a gray spring morning, he tried to think of something to say, something that might restore the gray to sunlit green. His inability to do so had begun to eat dangerously at his self-control when he saw Susie Grace wending her way toward them, wearing the remnants of her Rocky Road ice cream cone as a chocolate goatee.

A final little skip-hop brought her to a halt beside the table, already launched into her appeal. "Dad, I used up all my quarters. Can I have some more? *Please?* I only need—"

"What's this?" Roan touched her sticky chin with his knuckle. "Looks to me like you need to wash your face, kiddo."

Susie Grace stuck out her tongue in a mostly fruitless effort to comply with that suggestion.

It felt good to watch his kid being a kid and be thankful for it. Laughter shivered inside his chest as he said sternly, "Nope, 'fraid it's gonna take more than that. Come on—I'll take you to the restroom."

Susie Grace gasped as if he'd suggested she strip right there on the spot. "Da-ad, it's the *girls'* bathroom. You can't go in there!"

"How about if I take you?" Mary said.

His daughter's reply was a radiant smile, made downright impish by that chocolate goatee.

"Is that okay with you?" Mary asked Roan in a low voice as she scooted back her chair, nudging aside the pile of shopping bags that were stacked around and underneath it.

He shrugged and said, "Sure."

Susie Grace threw him a look of pure glee. She reached confidently for Mary's hand, Mary looped the strap of her purse over one shoulder and the two of them began to make their way through the maze of tables toward the restrooms on the opposite side of the food court.

Roan followed them with his eyes, followed them until the image was seared on his brain: little girl with tousled red-gold hair, dressed in a spanking new spring-green outfit, hopping and skipping with barely contained exuberance as she held on to the hand of a tall, slender woman…a woman who dressed in shapeless clothes, with her hair hanging down her back in a lank brown ponytail, yet who walked with beauty and grace and confidence in her step.

Then…that image seemed to shimmer and sizzle and melt like butter on a griddle, and another came to take its place: *Same little girl, four years younger…same joyful exuberance as she clings to the hand of a tall, slender woman with fiery red curls tumbling untamed down her back…as she smiles down at the child…and walks with beauty, grace and confidence in her step.*

And for some reason he thought again about the old Blackfoot horse trainer and the Spirit Messenger. He didn't believe in such things—he didn't. But *something* shivered across his skin and filled the inside of his head and every part of him, and he wondered whether it was a warning…or a promise.

He waited until he was certain Mary and his daughter weren't going to look back, then buried his face in his hands.

God help me… God, or Spirit Messenger… Bear, Wolf, Buffalo or Raven…whoever you are: Help me. I think I'm in danger…of falling in love with a murder suspect.

* * *

It was late afternoon when the SUV pulled to a stop in front of Mary's house, but at that time of year the sun was still high in the sky. Susie Grace had fallen asleep in the back seat on the drive back from Bozeman, stuffed full of ice cream and lulled by the sunshine and the quiet and the lazy beat of the music from the car radio Roan had tuned—with apologies to Mary— to a classic country station.

Mary didn't mind that Roan seemed disinclined toward conversation, or worry about what might be weighing so heavily on his mind as he drove with his elbow resting on the windowsill and his hand covering the lower part of his face, eyes narrowed behind his sunglasses in that way they had of seeming to be focused on something far beyond the road ahead. She didn't worry about anything, actually, not even her own bleak future, and the silence didn't seem awkward or burdensome to her.

Perhaps, like Susie Grace, she'd fallen under the spell of a lazy spring Sunday afternoon, and it was only lethargy that made her content to listen to the music—which she'd grown accustomed to if not fond of during the past ten years—and gaze through the car window at the cattle and horses grazing in spring-green pastures, and new foals frisking awkwardly alongside their mothers. And to allow herself, for the first time in many, many years—and only for a little while—to dream…

This. Yes, this life…this man, who makes me feel excited and happy…young and alive… and yet somehow…safe. This child, who makes me feel needed, and makes me laugh. Yes…this.

Like a child glimpsing a forbidden garden beyond a locked gate, she could allow her mind to drink in the fragrance of the flowers, bask in the loveliness…just for a little while.

She couldn't hold back a sigh when Roan pulled the SUV to a stop and turned off the motor. The smile that hovered on her lips as she turned to him felt fragile and precariously balanced, like a butterfly in a breeze.

"Thank you," she said softly, mindful of the sleeping child. "It was nice of you to let me do this."

She couldn't read his eyes behind the dark lenses, but his smile seemed wry. "I should be thanking you. Susie Grace had a great time. I know that was about the easiest time clothes shopping with her I've had in a while."

"She's a great little girl. And it was nice to forget…for a time."

"Yeah." He looked away for a moment, and she could see a muscle rippling in his jaw.

She stared at it, knowing she mustn't, while her own jaws grew tight and her throat began to ache, and all her forbidden thoughts and dreams thrummed inside her head like imprisoned bees. That thrumming grew ever more insistant, until it seemed to hang in the air between them…until she couldn't stand it anymore.

"Yeah, well—" Roan said, at almost the same moment Mary was saying, with a bright little laugh, "Well, I guess I'd better—"

He cleared his throat and slapped the gear lever into Park. "I know some of those bags back there are yours." He reached for the door handle.

"Don't get out," Mary said quickly, nodding toward the back seat. "I'll get it—there's just the one."

Her chest twinged with the guilty knowledge that somewhere in the jumble of shopping bags full of little girls' clothes in the back of the SUV was a department-store bag with a lovely pale-green silk sweater in it. A woman's sweater, slinky and sexy and feminine. It was the first becoming thing she'd allowed herself to buy in years—almost certainly a mistake, especially now. But it had been impossible to resist both the sweater *and* Susie Grace. Mary had just been telling her that redheads look good in green when Susie Grace had spotted this particular sweater. She'd insisted Mary should buy it. "You'd look good in green, too," she'd declared, "'cause you've got green eyes."

A mistake.

Heart pounding, vision shimmering, she reached for the door handle and yanked it open. And froze, half in and half out of the car as a sleepy voice came from the back seat.

"Mary? What's goin' on? Are we home already?"

"We're just dropping Miss Mary off at her house," Roan said. "You can go back to sleep, peanut."

"I don't *want* to go back to sleep." There was the click of a seatbelt and Susie Grace was scrambling out of her seat, struggling to open her door—which Roan, of course, had locked with the master switch for her safety. She pushed on it, frantic and wobbly from interrupted sleep, crying, "Mary, wait—I don't want you to go. I didn't get to say goodbye.

And who's gonna help me with—*Da-ad!*"
She gave up on the door and turned to glare at
Roan, face flushed, eyes dangerously bright.

Mary gave Roan a look and a gesture of
mute appeal; the last thing she wanted was for
such a lovely day to end with Susie Grace in
tears. Evidently Roan was of the same mind.
He capitulated with a shrug and released the
door lock. Susie Grace tumbled out of the
car and threw her arms around Mary's waist.

She wasn't prepared. Not for this. Too
many emotions, emotions she didn't want and
didn't know what to do with. Emotions...feel-
ings...thoughts she hadn't allowed herself in
so many years. *Why is this happening? Why
now?*

She didn't dare look at Roan. She gazed
down at Susie Grace through a shimmering
mist, patted her back awkwardly and said
with a light laugh, "Well, I'm not going to
the moon."

"I don't want you to go *anywhere*," Susie
Grace said fiercely. "Can't you come home
with us? You could have dinner with us.
Dad—"

Mary took a deep breath. Reaching deep
inside herself for the strength, she put her
hand under the little girl's chin and tilted it

so she could look into her face. "Susie Grace, you know I can't. Not tonight. Maybe we can get together some other time, okay? If it's all right with your dad."

"Promise?"

"Promise." Mary closed her eyes and begged forgiveness for the lie. "And now…if you want, you can help me find—"

But Susie Grace was appeased for the moment, and with moods as mercurial as only a seven-year-old's can be, was already on to other things.

"Is that your kitty?" She was hopping and skipping her way across the grass to the front porch, where Cat sat on the topmost step, looking down upon them like a statue of an Egyptian god. "What's her name? Does she bite? Can I pet her?"

"*His* name is Cat," Mary said as she went to open the back of the SUV. "He very well may bite—he's pretty cranky. I doubt he'll let you pet him…" Having retrieved her shopping bag, she closed the door, turned around, and gave an astonished laugh.

Susie Grace was sprawled on the porch steps, nose-to-nose—literally—with Cat. As Mary watched, the little girl reached out, wrapped her arms around the huge tomcat and hauled

him into her lap like a baby doll. To which in-
dignity Cat responded with his usual display of
affection—a head-butt to Susie Grace's chin.
Mary could hear the animal's buzz-saw purring from where she stood. "Oh, for heaven's
sake," she muttered, laughing.

The sound of a car door slamming penetrated the edges of her consciousness…then
awareness came prowling over her skin, raising goose bumps, quickening breath and heartbeat.

"She's good with animals," Roan said, his
quiet rumbling voice so close behind her she
felt its vibrations in her bones. "Always has
been. She's always the one to find where the
barn cats hide their kittens."

Laughing, she turned her head to look at
him, and his eyes were soft as he smiled back
at her. The lowering sun was warm and gentle
on her face, the breeze flirted with her hair
like a lover's fingers…and Mary knew she
had never in her life been happier than she
was at this moment.

So lost was she in the sweetness of those
moments that when, a short time later and a
little way down the street, a car started up
and sped away, it never even registered on
her consciousness.

Chapter Ten

Susie Grace was the only one in Roan's household watching television Monday morning when the news story broke. Boyd had installed the small set, one of the under-the-counter, fold-down flat-panel kind, so he could keep up with the news and his favorite programs while he was doing the cooking or cleaning up the dishes. Since this was Monday morning, though, he was still digesting Sunday's newspaper, and Roan was around the corner in the bathroom mopping up after shaving and trying to decide if it was time to drop in at the barber shop or not.

Susie Grace had been keyed up and fidgety all morning, which Roan figured meant she was feeling either excited or apprehensive about the prospect of her first school day sporting her new hairdo. Consequently, she'd been doing more playing with her bowl of cereal than eating. She was picking raisins out with her fingers and sucking the milk off them when Boyd looked up from his paper long enough to tell her to quit fooling around and eat her breakfast or she was going to miss the bus.

"I don't like the cereal. It's *soggy*," Susie Grace said crossly.

"Not surprised," Boyd said, and went back to his paper.

Lacking a better target, Susie Grace glared at the TV set, lower lip sticking out, arms folded across her new green top with the yellow and white daisies on the front. A moment later, she sat up straight, sulks forgotten. "Look, Grampa, it's Mary."

"What? Where?" Boyd flicked the newspaper over, looking around as if he thought someone might be hiding underneath it.

"Not there." Susie Grace giggled, then pointed. "Right *there*. On TV." Boyd put down the paper and picked up the TV remote. Susie Grace tumbled out of her chair and ran out of the kitchen yelling, "Dad! Come quick—Miss Mary's on TV!"

Roan poked his head out of the bathroom and frowned at her over the towel he was using to pat his freshly shaved jaws dry. "What are you talking about?"

With patient emphasis she repeated it. "Mary's on tee vee. I saw her. Come on, *hurry*—you're gonna miss it."

Roan felt the blood draining out of his head and his body going cold, but there wasn't time for his mind to form coherent patterns. It was a little like being caught up in an earthquake or volcanic eruption—while it was happening there was only one thought possible: catastrophe.

Boyd was staring intently at the small TV set, the remote control he'd used to turn the volume up still pointed at it. "Didn't realize that little ol' gal was such a looker," he muttered without looking up.

"What's going on?" Roan asked in a low voice, ignoring Susie Grace, who was dancing and chattering excitedly somewhere on the edges of his awareness.

Boyd clicked the remote and turned the sound up another notch. "See for yourself."

Roan glared at the set through narrowed

eyes. It was one of the network morning shows...two well-known faces, one belonging to the morning show's female host, the other the classically chiseled features of the evening news anchor...sitting in chairs opposite each other in standard interview fashion.

"...did you first realize the woman in the photograph was your—I guess I should say *our* former colleague?"

"Well, as you know, the photo came in on the wire yesterday evening, after I'd signed off the evening news broadcast. I recognized her right away. There was no doubt in my mind that it was Yancy."

The photograph that had caught Susie Grace's eye filled the screen, and Roan felt a sharp squeezing around his heart. Because he knew, almost to the second, when the picture had to have been taken. Mary's clothes were the ones she'd been wearing the day before, during the shopping trip to Bozeman. And the smile...ah, the smile. It was the one he'd only seen a time or two...the one that took his breath away. The last time he'd seen it was the evening before, when she'd turned to him with her face full of joy and laughter and light, and he'd been so blinded by the radiance of it he'd forgotten to pay attention to what was going on around him.

"How well did you know Yancy Lavigne?"

"I'd just started with the network as a reporter. My beat was the west coast—L.A., San Franciso—and of course hers was fashion, which meant she covered all those 'red-carpet' events. So our paths crossed quite a bit. I guess I knew her as well as anybody did. She seemed like a genuinely nice girl, which is why we were all so shocked when we heard she'd gotten mixed up with the South American mob."

"Yes, but if I remember correctly, didn't she testify against some members of the Del-Rey family? Wasn't she the key witness, and instrumental in getting the main kingpins of that cartel convicted and sent to jail?"

"Yes, she was. And after doing so, apparently vanished off the face of the earth—or, as we now know, into the Witness Protection Program. I guess we know now where she's been all these years."

There was more, but Roan didn't hear it. He was too busy cussing under his breath, half-choking on the anger that was billowing up from the cold, burning place inside him, like smoke from dry ice.

And then his phone rang.

* * *

On Florida's Gulf Coast, Joy Cavanaugh, also known as Lynn Starr, creator of the Asia Brand series of bestselling murder mystery novels, was enjoying one of her favorite moments of the day. Her husband Scott, chief homicide detective for the county sheriff's department, was already at work, and their nine-and-a-half-year-old daughter, Carrie Jane, had just left for school. This was the time before she tackled the household chores, and then had to face the computer and the overdue rewrites on her current novel, that precious hour—which admittedly sometimes stretched into two or more—when she allowed herself the luxury of curling up with someone else's book.

She poured herself a second cup of coffee, then settled on the sunroom couch and tucked her bare feet up under the edge of her bathrobe. She heaved a happy sigh as she picked up the hardcover romance she was currently reading, her place marked with the flap of the dust jacket. The television was on, tuned, as always, to her favorite network morning show. It didn't interfere with her reading pleasure; she enjoyed an ability to tune it out when it didn't interest her. And she liked to catch the local news and weather every half hour or so.

She read, contentedly sipping her coffee, the television making companionable noises in the background...until a word, a name, penetrated her shields like a steel-tipped arrow and stabbed straight through to her heart.

Coffee slopped onto her robe. The book slipped unnoticed from her hand. Trembling, clutching the coffee cup to her chest, she stared at the image on the screen...the face of a woman well-remembered, beloved as a sister, lost to her for ten long years.

When her brain resumed functioning she picked up the phone and, with hands still shaking, dialed her husband's number.

Mary woke on Monday morning to a yawning emptiness...empty house, empty schedule, empty future. After Sunday's glimpse into the secret garden, the barren landscape of her own life seemed to stretch around her in every direction, as far as she could see... emptiness and only more emptiness.

Since she stayed open on Saturdays, the shop, like most beauty salons, was closed on Mondays. Normally, she filled the day doing the countless routine chores necessary to keep herself, her household and her business functioning—collecting the trash, watering the plants on the kitchen windowsill, cleaning the litter box, dusting and vacuuming and laundry, washing the car, raking up leaves and pine needles, bookkeeping, making out lists of supplies to order for the shop.

Today she didn't feel like doing any of those things.

Normally, she would have grocery shopping and banking to do, maybe a scheduled appointment with the dentist, or to have her car serviced. But her car was in the sheriff's department's impound yard, and she couldn't carry groceries home without it.

Normally, she might look forward to a drive or a hike in the mountains, or a trip to the firing range, both of which were now out of the question.

Yesterday, strolling through a shopping mall with Roan and his daughter, picking out clothes for Susie Grace, eating ice cream cones in the food court, for the first time in so many years she'd felt…almost happy. Carefree. *Normal.* But of course, she realized now—had known even then—it had all been no more normal for her than a day at Disneyland. Her life, her real world, had been waiting for her beyond the magic gates.

That's what you get, Mary, for letting yourself dream.

Depression settled over her like a blanket.

When Cat came to wake her in his usual manner, she pushed at him irritably, muttered, "Go 'way, dammit," and pulled the covers over her head. Cat's response to this was to park himself on her chest and make kneading motions with his forepaws in the mound of blankets where he calculated her face should be.

"I think I liked you better when you hated me," Mary grumbled, pushing both blankets and the cat aside and reaching for the TV remote. She aimed it at the small portable set on the dressing table across the room and clicked On.

A moment later she was sitting bolt upright in her bed, awash in adrenaline: jangled, head ringing, body gone clammy and cold. She stared at the screen, unable to tear her eyes from it, and this time when Cat came to rub against her she gathered him unthinkingly into her arms and hugged him close, trying to warm herself with his small furry body.

* * *

Joy's legs had stopped shaking, pretty much. Now she was pacing back and forth through the rooms of her house, talking on the phone and making wild, out-of-sync gestures with her free hand like a mishandled marionette.

"I have to go to her," she said, sniffling into the phone. "She needs me. Oh, Scott… poor Yancy."

"You don't need to be running off up to Montana and getting into the middle of this," her husband said calmly but firmly. "There's nothing you can do anyway, except make things worse."

"I can *be* there. She shouldn't be alone through something like this."

"What makes you think she's alone? It's been ten years, honey, she's probably married, with a family of her own."

Joy was silent for a moment, brushing away tears. Then she said in a low, choked voice, "She didn't do it—shoot that senator's son. You know that—she couldn't have. Yancy couldn't kill anyone."

There was a soft exhalation, a pause, and then, "I know."

"I have to do *something*. Please—I can be on a plane by—"

"Joy, absolutely not. I mean it. What am I gonna have to do, handcuff you to the bathroom plumbing again?"

Joy gave a watery squeak of laughter and a grudging sniff. "Yeah, look how well that worked the last time you tried it." But she'd heard the genuine concern in her husband's voice. They were both remembering what had happened last time she'd been hell-bent on rescuing Yancy.

"Look, dammit—" Joy winced. It wasn't like her patient teddy-bear husband to shout. "What do you think *you're* gonna do if Junior DelRey comes for her? Jump in front of a bullet?"

Her heart gave a sickening lurch. "Junior? But—I thought he was in prison."

"Oh, no. His father and uncle got life—I think they both died in prison. Diego DelRey was sent up as accessory. He's been out for... I guess it'd be two years, now." Scott's voice was grim.

"Oh God...if he sees that news broadcast— Scott, you have to do something!"

"Yeah." There was another, gustier exhalation. "Okay, look, I'll see what I can do. I'll try and get hold of the sheriff up there—what was the name of the place again?"

"Hartsville," Joy said with a relieved sniffle. "Hart County, Montana."

Roan argued with himself as he drove into town. Not out loud—he wasn't that crazy—although at the rate he was going, he figured that was coming, it was only a matter of time. Right now, thankfully, there was still a rational, grown-up part of him that demanded to know what the hell the rest of him thought he was doing.

It was way too late to try to pretend he hadn't compromised his objectivity where Miss Mary Owen—or Yancy, or whatever the hell her name was—was concerned.

Much harder to admit he might be in over his head.

Easy enough to admit learning the truth about his mystery woman had hit him hard. What man *wouldn't* be ticked off to find out the woman he was teetering on the brink of falling in love with, to the point where he'd convinced himself she wasn't a murderer, had been in bed—literally—with the South American mob? He could admit to being mad as hell, feeling like he'd been conned, made a damn fool of.

It was harder to admit how much it hurt.

He'd *trusted* her, dammit—ironic, too, when he considered how he'd started out trying to get *her* to trust *him.* Instead, he'd come to trust and believe in her innocence enough to introduce his daughter to her, and even, God help him, include her on a family outing. Clearly, he *had* lost his mind.

Temporarily, he told himself grimly as he jerked the SUV to a stop in front of Queenie Schultz's little clapboard house. Which was something he'd almost begun to look forward to, these past few mornings…pulling up, tapping the horn, then watching Mary emerge from the house like a little brown mouse from its hole. And he'd be smiling to himself, enjoying the secret knowledge that the mouse was really an enchantress in disguise. *Enchantress? What the hell was that? Now I'm weaving fairy-tale fantasies about my murder suspect?*

He sat staring at the house, girding himself. He told himself he was through being blinded by a pair of green-gold eyes and that he was seeing everything clearly now. He told himself this morning's development was the wake-up call he needed to get himself back on track, remember who and what he was and get back to doing the job the people of Heartbreak County paid him to do. He told himself he was damn lucky he'd come to his senses when he had.

He stared at the house and the front porch and the lilac bush and told himself he wasn't seeing her there, that breath-stopping smile and those shimmering eyes lifted to his, and hearing his little girl's laughter. He told himself his heart wasn't thumping like a jackhammer inside his chest.

"Time to quite actin' like a lunatic and start actin' like a sheriff," he growled to himself as he opened the door and reached for his Stetson.

She answered the door wearing a flannel bathrobe, an ugly blue and purple plaid the color of bruises. She wasn't wearing her glasses—had they been part of the lie, too, he wondered? Without them her eyes had a dazed, unfocused look, and there was a purplish-blue smudge, like a thumbprint, below each one. Her skin had the almost translucent quality he'd noticed that first night, with only the faintest lingering hint of the bruises Jason had given her, and no trace at all of a blush. Her hair was loose and tousled, as if she'd just gotten out of bed. It was the first time he'd seen it that way, tumbled down around her shoulders, and he couldn't help but notice it was longer and thicker than he'd thought it would be, and had a little bit of a tendency to curl after all.

"It's Monday—the shop is closed," she said, gathering a handful of her hair and raking it back. She lifted her chin and her eyes darkened and her face closed up like a fortress preparing for battle. "I won't be needing a ride."

"I didn't come to give you one," Roan said between clenched teeth. He opened the screen door and moved past her into the house. He pitched his hat onto the back of the sofa, then turned and arrowed a look at her. "Is it true?"

It wasn't what he'd meant to say—at least, not like that, with his voice sounding like a rusty gate hinge. But it was out, now; there was nothing he could do but wait for her answer.

He *needed* the answer, dammit. Which was maybe why he did what he did when she seemed about to brush past him without giving him one. He grabbed her arm. Not acting like a sheriff, for sure, and maybe not a lunatic, either. Maybe just a man caught up in an emotional confrontation with a woman, and there was no use kidding himself this had anything to do with the job. Not any longer.

She flicked a glance down at his hand, then lashed it back at him, and he swore he could feel the burn of that look on his skin. He didn't fold, just stared back at her, his own eyes on fire in their sockets.

"I just got up," she said very softly. "I was going to get some coffee. Do you mind?"

"Hell with the damn coffee! The story on the news this morning—is it true?"

There was a long pause. His heart knocked against his ribs, and he could feel his pulse in his fingers where they circled the sleeve of her robe.

"Some of it." She spoke as if her lips were made of glass.

The smile he gave her felt no less rigid. It cramped the muscles in his jaws. He said with exaggerated patience, "Well, let's start with your name. I seem to recall you swore to me it was Mary. So who is Yancy? Huh? *Now* what's the truth?"

"Roan..."

The sound of his name coming so softly

from her mouth hit him like a blow. He felt sick. It shamed him to realize he'd tightened his grip on her arm, but he couldn't seem to let go. "Oh, well, hell—I forgot. What good does it do me to ask *you* for the truth? How am I even supposed to know what the truth is, coming from you? 'My name is Mary,' you told me, and you didn't kill Jason. Since you lied about the one—"

She gave a sharp, angry gasp, and he felt the muscles in her arm go rigid. "I *didn't* lie. My name *is* Mary. Mary Yancy." Her chin came up, *en garde,* once again ready for battle. "Yancy Lavigne was my professional name."

But he was too angry to absorb such a simple explanation, and instead plowed on. "Yeah, and I was right about you being a city girl, wasn't I? That story you told me—your father, the church—how does that fit with your New York City glamour-girl—"

"That was true—every bit of it." Her eyes had darkened, but he couldn't let himself acknowledge the pain in them. If he did, the anger would go out of him like air from a leaky life raft, and right now it was the only thing keeping him afloat.

"My father's name was Joshua Yancy,"

she went on, speaking rapidly, breathlessly, wounded but defiant. "He was the pastor of a church—strict fundamentalist—in a small town in upstate New York. My mother's name was Rebecca. She played the organ. I was their only child. My father was fifty and my mother was in her mid-forties, I think, when I was born. My arrival must have been a tremendous embarrassment for them, indisputable evidence, you see, that they'd been engaging in Pleasures of the Flesh." She said it as if it had been written in capital letters, her lips twisting into a bitter smile. "It didn't help matters that I turned out to be pretty, but I think the capper, the final disgrace, was my red hair. Neither of them had it, so they—"

"You had…red hair." He felt as though he'd gone deaf—and numb. He didn't feel the flannel robe beneath his fingers anymore—wasn't aware he was holding her by both arms now.

She shook her dirt-brown hair back on her shoulders. He felt the warm tickle of it on his hands. "Oh, yes—fiery. I'm sure they thought I must be the Devil's spawn. They certainly never let me forget it."

Roan was barely listening to her. His head was full of the sounds of his good intentions and common sense colliding with concepts of some sort of Fate or Destiny he'd never even believed in before. Logic and common sense told him this woman's hair being the same color as his wife's and daughter's had nothing to do with anything. And yet, why did he feel like he'd just been bucked off a bronc...shaken, bruised, and not sure which way was up?

He shook his head, and when the dust began to clear, realized his fingers were woven through locks of silky brown hair they'd found all on their own, and were testing the texture of it against their tips as if it were some rich and rare fabric he was thinking of buying.

He thought of her skin...that particular translucence, clear and pale as porcelain. The way her eyes could go in an instant from rain on the ocean to sunshine on meadow grass. The fact that she hated pink.

"My God," he murmured. "My God. How—"

"I dye it, Roan," she said, gently sardonic. "It's not that hard to do, considering I'm a hair stylist."

She jerked away from him, and his hand, thoughtlessly clutching, caught the sleeve of the flannel robe. Her momentum pulled it off her shoulder. What lay revealed, then, like the unveiling of a lovely work of art, was a gentle round of creamy white faintly shadowed, as was her face, with freckles. And the narrow strap of a silky nightgown, the exact color of the lilacs beside her front porch.

Something slammed him in the gut—he told himself it was anger. It ricocheted through him, blowing all thought from his mind the way a gunshot sends a flock of birds exploding from a tree. Thoughts of Erin and Susie Grace vanished, along with any notion he might have had about behaving like the professional lawman he liked to think he was. The only thing in his head right then was the image of that pale, lovely body...and the Mob.

He followed her into the kitchen, his skin sizzling and blood pumping hot in the bottom of his belly. "Tell me—how did you get from singing in church choirs to sleeping in a drug lord's bed?" he said with a cruelty that shocked him.

She didn't seem to notice it. She fussed with the coffeemaker, putting in a filter, counting out spoonfuls of coffee. She waited until she'd finished, then muttered without looking up, "It's a long story."

"For God's sake, Mary—why didn't you tell me about this?"

She shook her hair back and tilted her face toward him— another unconscious gesture of a beautiful woman. "Apparently you're not acquainted with the protected witness's first rule." Her smile was faint and sardonic. "*Tell no one.* It's the first thing they tell you: if you break security they can't protect you. They hammer that into you until you're afraid to admit even to yourself in the privacy of your own bedroom who you really are—" her voice caught "—or who you *used* to be."

He wouldn't let himself hear the pain. "My God," he said, almost shouting—something he did so rarely he didn't recognize his own voice. "Do you know what this does to the case against you? You were the mistress of a mobster. Not only does that make you look like the kind of person who might kill somebody, at least in most people's minds, but the prosecution can make a helluva good case for blackmail. How's this? Jason found out about you somehow—is that what happened, Mary? He threatened to expose you unless you gave him what he wanted, so you *shot* him?"

Her eyes had gone the dark slate-green of thunder clouds, and the way they were glaring at him now, he wouldn't have been surprised to see lightning bolts shoot out of them. "I…

have…never…shot…anyone…in…my…life," she said in a voice pressed between clenched teeth, enunciating each word separately as she advanced across the kitchen toward him. "In fact—I think the only wrongdoing I've ever been guilty of in my life is being *stupid*. Stupidly chasing after the wrong dreams, maybe. And you know what?" Almost nose-to-nose with him now, she punched his chest with one finger. "I know for a fact I don't have to take this from you. In fact, I want you to *leave*. Right…*now*." The finger punched him again.

In full retreat, backing up with his hands held out to his sides in surrender, Roan found himself wondering how in the hell this firebrand had managed to pass herself off as a mouse for so long.

"I want you out of my house," she finished, folding her arms on her heaving chest. "And I'm calling my lawyer."

The funny thing was, watching her work up such a spectacular head of steam, Roan could feel his own temper cooling down. Something began to hum deep inside him—excitement, maybe, or anticipation…appreciation…respect…who knew? What he did know was he suddenly had to fight an urge to grin.

"Look… Mary," he began, and was on the

verge of putting his hands on her shoulders again, with the memory of what was under that flannel robe all too fresh and vivid in his mind.

So it was maybe a good thing his cell phone picked that particular moment to ring, although he didn't see it that way at the time. Some adrenaline squirted into his system, just enough to make his heart do a little hop-skip and his skin tingle with the disappointment of missed possibilities, and he was swearing as he snatched the trilling phone from his belt. He glanced at it to make sure it wasn't Boyd or Susie Grace's school calling, then thumbed it on and barked, "Roan."

"Uh, yeah, Sheriff," came the cigarette-raspy voice of Carol Butterfield, the morning dispatcher, "sorry to bother you, but I've got somebody on the line here I think you're gonna want to talk to. Fella says he's a deputy sheriff down in Florida, has some information on the Holbrook murder—or rather, on the woman you arrested for it. You see the news this morning?"

"Yeah, I did." He glanced at Mary, who gave him a hostile look, then whirled and marched back to the counter and the coffeepot. "Okay," he said, "put him through."

* * *

Mary leaned against the countertop, sipping her coffee and watching the tall, lean, golden-haired sheriff restlessly pace the two stingy steps the confines of her back stoop allowed him. *Two steps...turn. Two steps...turn.* Now and then he'd throw a glance her way, and when he did, some sort of electric current would shoot along her nerves and her muscles would tense and shiver, her heart would skip, her breathing quicken, and threatening tears sting her eyes and nose like pepper.

Just tears of anger, she told herself. Tears of confusion.

Confusion. Oh yes. She couldn't think. Inside her head there was nothing but noise, a babble of voices all shrieking at the top of their lungs, like a town hall meeting gone berserk.

I want him to leave!

I want him to hold me....

I want to be alone!

I'm so tired of being alone....

I want to run away, far, far away!

But I'm so tired of running.

All this emotion—I hate it! I was calm before—I want to feel calm again!

Maybe you weren't calm, just dead.

At least I didn't hurt!

That's what dead is, dummy. It's pain that tells you you're alive.

Outside on the stoop, Roan was folding his cell phone, ready to come back in. Mary watched him through the divided panes with narrowed eyes and pounding heart, quivering inside. Turning the volume down on the voices, she prepared herself, ready to stoke up the fire of her anger again, because at least anger was a *choice*—something that let her be in control.

He came through the door, tucking the phone into its holster on his belt. He closed the door behind him, then looked at her and said, "That was somebody you know."

Her stomach flip-flopped and her body went cold. She didn't know she'd set her coffee cup down until it hit the countertop with a clunk that jarred to her elbow. "Not..."

He shook his head, confusing her all the more. *I thought he was angry with me. Why are his eyes so gentle?*

"A sheriff's detective from down in Florida—Scott Cavanaugh. Says he only met you once, but you know his wife real well. Her name's Joy? I guess the two of you used to be roommates?"

"Joy?" It came from her mouth but she didn't recognize it, that dazed and bewildered voice, like the cry of a lost child beholding a familiar face.

Then, everything inside her simply…crumbled.

In some disconnected but still-functioning part of herself she understood she was falling apart, but like a spectator watching a train wreck unfold before her eyes, she was powerless to stop it. She began to shake, then to laugh, and finally, to cry—all three happening to her at once, and while she could wrap an arm across her waist to contain the shivering and clamp a hand over her mouth to hold back the laughter, there was nothing she could do about the tears pouring from her eyes like a summer sunshine-and-rain squall after a long, long drought.

Roan started toward her and she backed away from him, putting out her hand in what he knew must be an instinctive effort to ward off the inevitable, the way someone facing a gunman throws up his hands to stop the bullets. And with about as much effect.

He folded her into his arms, though she fought him—fought desperately, folding up and barricading herself behind a wall of hands and arms and elbows. He knew to ignore all that; long years of experience dealing with a redheaded woman had led him to understand she was apt to fight hardest against what she needed—and wanted—most. And it had taught him to be patient with those kinds of contradictions.

So he corraled her with strong arms, gentle hands and soothing words, stroked her back and her hair, cradled her face against his thumping heart, smiling over her head and a little misty-eyed himself because there was a poignant familiarity about the feel of her quivering body in his arms, the little snuffling, hiccuping sounds, and even about the damp spot she was making on the front of his shirt. Erin had been prone to rain squalls like this. Some of his best memories of his life with her involved their sweet, sweet aftermath...which was possibly why, when he felt Mary's shivering and tears subside and her body begin to relax, it seemed so natural to him to gently tilt her face up and kiss her.

Chapter Eleven

He kissed her eyelids first, the taste of her tears cool and briny on his lips...and so sweet it made his heart ache. He heard her breath catch and his muscles quivered with response, even as his mind was being slammed with the full realization of what it was he was doing.

It hit him like a power surge—the awareness that this wasn't his wife's face he held, cradled like a precious treasure between his two hands. It froze him for a moment, shorted out his circuits, so he couldn't think about *who* this woman was...only that her face was damp and warm from the tears she'd shed, the ivory perfection of her skin delicately blotched with pink like the petals of some exotic hybrid flower. He couldn't let himself think about who *he* was, either...only that the woman he held in his arms smelled good... felt good...tasted good...and he'd been hungry a long, long time.

He wiped away the dampness on her cheeks with his thumbs, let his lips caress that gentle curve...find the corner of her mouth and sip the drop of salt-sweet moisture pooled there. He felt her lips part...her breathing cease. And he paused...hovered there, his lips not quite touching hers, the suspense and the yearning an ache in his bones and a quivering in his muscles...a prickling behind his eyelids and a tingling in his skin. Breathing her in...lost in the forbidden wonder of it all.

He heard the faint sound she made—a whimper of impatience. And then her head moved in his hands...turned slightly...seeking. Not moving closer, not demanding, simply *feeling*. Waiting...breathless...the way the world at dawn seems to hold its breath in anticipation of the sunrise.

I can still turn back... I can stop this...now.

But, it seemed, he could no more stop it than he could have stopped the sun from rising.

He moved...or she did...just a little, enough

so that their lips touched...breath mingled... and again he froze there, each of his heart-beats a hammer blow. He hadn't known how painful it would be, this coming back to life after being numb...asleep...dead for so long. The blood running through his veins was like wildfire; there wasn't any part of him that didn't feel the burn. The roar of it in his ears drowned thought. All he knew was pain... and a need that was a thousand times greater than pain.

He felt her trembling but couldn't let himself wonder or care why she did. He knew she could have moved away from him if she'd wanted to. But she seemed as spellbound by what was happening as he.

To test himself—and her—he let his hands fall away from her face, not holding her, still not claiming her mouth, neither moving away from her nor closer, releasing her if that was what she wanted. But she didn't move, and pausing there with only breath between them, he let his hands come to rest on her shoulders...then move inward to caress her neck before making the return journey, taking the edges of her robe with them.

He didn't ask, but of her own accord, and moving no other part of her body, she slowly lowered her arms to her sides. Delicately, like someone trying to mold moonlight in his hands, he eased the robe over her shoulders, over rounded flesh the velvety texture of rose petals, and heard the fabric rustle as it fell to the floor. It whispered to him like a blessing.

He didn't know how long they stood like that, facing each other, eyes closed, lips and bodies scarcely touching, hands down at their sides. Mary's face was tilted up to his and her hair streamed down her back, and he thought they could almost feel each other's hearts pounding. And then, like lovers finding one another in the dark, their hands came together...fingers touched...twined... then joyfully clasped. A gasp came from her lips—and at the same instant from his—and at last, at long last, he brought them together, his mouth sinking into the sweet welcome of hers like a lost soul coming home.

The sense of profound relief and pleasure he felt lasted only a second. It hit him like a bomb blast—first the white-hot flash of awareness, the heavy *thump* of need in the bottom of his belly. Then desire blew through him like a shock-wind.

He felt powerless against it...didn't know

when he let go of her hands. He was aware that they touched him, though only on the edges of consciousness. He had already lost himself in her...the taste of her mouth, the texture of her skin, the sweet moist warmth of her body. It had been so long since he'd held a woman's body in his arms.

He gathered her in, his hands roaming hungrily, sweeping across the valleys, swells and plains of her body that was at once strange to him, yet seemed achingly familiar. His hands were marauders, roving where they pleased... pillaging her lush curves...taking...wanting more. Wanting his clothes and her nightgown *gone,* wanting her skin touching his skin and her long sleek body under his and the rich, dark mystery of her female body folding close around him...embracing him...inviting him in. It had been so long since he'd lost himself in a woman's body.

Thoughtlessly, heedlessly, he gathered the nightgown's silky fabric in greedy handfuls, gathered it until he'd uncovered what he wanted. He heard her gasp when he cupped her nakedness with his hands, and she clutched at the back of his neck as if the earth had dropped out from under her feet. He took advantage of the moment to plunge his tongue deep into her mouth and felt her fingers tangle in his hair and her soft breasts pillow against his thumping heart.

It shocked him to realize how close he was to taking her then and there, how much he wanted to make love to her in her frilly pink kitchen with sunshine streaming through the windows and the smell of fresh-brewed coffee in the air. Shocked him...but not enough to make him stop.

Stop him? Mary could have, but she was as lost as he.

And then, suddenly, they did stop. Both of them. Stopped, looked down and stared like dazed crash survivors at the moth-eaten yellow-orange tomcat doing drunken figure eights around their ankles.

For a few moments, except for those sinuous movements and the sound of raspy purring, everything seemed to stop. And as shocked as she'd been when Roan kissed her—and she'd kissed him back—for Mary the shock of stopping was a thousand times worse. It had been so long since she'd been kissed. So long since she'd been touched. So long since her body had felt the sting and ache of desire.

She felt her nightgown slither down to

cover her naked bottom, a cool, silky caress where a delicious rough warmth had been before. Her fingers cramped and ached when she withdrew them from the crispy softness of his hair…and oh, how hard it was to tear herself away from that warmth…that strength…from his hands, his arms…his chest…his mouth.

It might have been easier if he hadn't still been holding her, hands firm but gentle on her arms, as if he feared she'd topple over if he let her go. She heard a rumble that must have been an apology. She made similar noises and was careful not to raise her eyes too far. Not far enough to meet his. She couldn't bear to see what was in those keen blue eyes now. Would it be desire still? Or perhaps only contempt now…or worse, pity?

A moment ago she'd prayed he would go on holding her, touching her, kissing her, forever. Now she prayed for him to let her go— quickly, before he could feel how devastated she was. Before he could know the power he had over her…the power to make her tremble and ache…the power to make her cry. It had been a long time since anyone had held such power over her. She'd forgotten how terrifying it was.

But she couldn't hide it—the shaking, at

least. He must have felt it, because he muttered, "You're cold," and bent down and picked up her robe and draped it around her shoulders.

She murmured an acknowledgment…a thank you, and managed to salvage enough pride to pull herself away from him. She felt stiff and awkward as she made herself busy, getting out a can of cat food, opening it, filling Cat's food dish.

Her face felt hot, and every muscle in it hurt. She wanted, desperately, to crawl into a hole somewhere and cry.

It had been a long time since she'd cried. She hated to cry. Crying was defeat. Crying was giving in, letting the loneliness win.

But you did cry.

Yes, she'd almost forgotten! She'd cried because he'd told her about *Joy.* The once-loved name blew into her mind like a breeze bearing promises of spring. She dropped the cat-food can in the sink, turned on the water…took a breath, cleared her throat. Miraculously, words came. "You…said you…talked to Joy?"

She heard him take a breath…clear his throat. When it came his voice sounded normal, as if nothing untoward had happened between them. As if he hadn't just turned her world upside down. "I talked to her husband, Scott. He said to tell you Joy sends her love. I'm supposed to tell you she knows you didn't do it."

The tears were rising again. Mary pressed her fingertips to her lips...fought them down. Laughed instead.

His voice came gently from too close behind her. "The two of you were close?"

She nodded, and after a moment said without turning, "I guess Scott told you everything?"

"He told me enough." She didn't have to look at him to know his eyes would have that diamond-bright glitter again. His voice told her. "I need to hear the rest from you."

Mary nodded, sick, aching inside.

"First, though, you better go put on some clothes." And now a certain gravelly thickness in his voice made her look at him with quickened heartbeat and questions in her eyes, and when she saw the softening, and the off-center tilt to his smile, felt a new tremor begin somewhere deep inside her. "That's the ugliest damn robe I ever saw," he growled. "I can't be held responsible for wanting to tear it off of you again."

The squeak that flew out of her mouth

could have been laughter. Taking no chances, she touched the back of her hand to her nose and fled.

In the quiet and calm of the bathroom she stared at herself in the mirror…and felt herself go cold. Not because she didn't recognize the face looking back at her. But because she *did*.

Flushed cheeks…kiss-swollen mouth…eyes bright with laughter and hope… *Yancy's face.*

Gripping the edges of the sink so hard her fingers went numb, she watched the color drain from her cheeks and her eyes go gray as rain. "Stupid…" she whispered. "Stupid… stupid."

Stupid Yancy, who'd spent too many years chasing rainbows and fairy tales…certain happiness lay just beyond the *next* hill.

Stupid Yancy. Now stupid Mary…doing the very same thing.

A man makes you feel good…makes you feel safe and cared for…and you're ready to forgive him anything, go anywhere with him, do whatever he tells you. He kisses you… touches your naked body with his strong cowboy's hands, and you're already dreaming of happily-ever-after, thinking he holds the sunshine of your life in his smile.

Stupid—this isn't a fairy tale and he isn't Prince Charming. He's the sheriff who arrested you for murder, the one who showed the man who wants to kill you exactly where to look.

Stupid—maybe for you he's the forbidden garden, but he's not your happiness...or your future. Maybe you can trust him with your life—yes, okay, that, because he's a good man and a good sheriff—but for God's sake don't be stupid enough to fall in love with him.

While she was in the bathroom, Roan poured himself a cup of coffee and drank it standing at the kitchen sink, while he stared out the window and watched a jay pull nesting materials out of a brush pile in the yard next door. His body felt bruised...hypersensitized. The coffee felt like whiskey going down. It burned his throat and warmed his belly and he shuddered as if he'd just come in from a blizzard half-frozen to death.

It took a few minutes for the warmth and the caffeine to do their thing and his body to settle down and his brain to start hitting on all cylinders again, which was maybe why it took longer than it should have to occur to him how vulnerable the house was. No fences...

wide open to the neighbors' yards on each side and the cover of trees and scrub behind.

A killer wouldn't even have to break into the house to get at her. All he'd have to do is park himself out there somewhere and shoot her through the window. Any half-competent hitman could do it and be gone before the echoes died....

His body went cold again and the coffee turned bitter in his mouth.

He turned when he heard Mary's step and watched her come into the kitchen. She'd put on jeans and a long-sleeved pullover with no particular shape to it, with the sleeves pushed up to her elbows. Her hair was twisted up in back of her head in its usual any-old-which-way knot, but there wasn't a single thing mousy-looking about her now. Even dressed as she was and with her face scrubbed shiny as a child's and not a smidgen of makeup, she managed to look both elegant and sexy.

He wondered whether it was just *him,* that he saw her differently now, or if there really was something different in the way she carried herself...the way her head sat on her neck, and the tilt of her chin...

And it hit him then, what the difference was: She wasn't trying to hide anymore.

She went straight to the coffeepot and poured herself some, careful to avoid looking at Roan, though the image of him was clear as a color photograph in her mind: Long lean body in a casual slouch propped against the sink, ankles crossed, one hand holding a coffee mug and the other thumb hooked in a pocket of his Levi's…morning sunshine pouring through the window curtain behind him touching his hair and shoulders with a soft pinkish-gold, like a lover's blush.

Her heart tripped, her insides twittered, and her legs felt as though they might disconnect at the knees. And in spite of all her resolutions and warnings, her mutinous mind sighed, *Yes…this…forever this.*

She stirred sugar substitute into her coffee, tasted it, and thus fortified, turned to face him. Leaned against the counter as she sipped, and raised defiant eyes to his.

"You okay?" he asked softly. Kindly.

She lifted her eyebrows and replied in a tone of mild surprise, "Of course." Pretending she wasn't quivering inside.

"Feel like talking?"

A smile tugged at the corner of her mouth. "Would it matter if I said no?"

He drank coffee and regarded her steadily

across the rim of the cup, eyes slightly narrowed, but in a thoughtful way, not hard. He lowered his cup, paused a moment, then said in the same quiet rumbling voice, "I'll put it another way. Are you ready to tell me what I'm gonna need to know so I can protect you?"

She made an automatic gesture of protest and managed to choke out, "I don't need—" before he stopped her with a firm but patient, "Now, that's just stupid." As if she were Susie Grace talking nonsense.

Anger stung her, threatening the delicate web of self-control she'd woven around her emotions. She didn't want to talk, didn't know if she *could* talk without feeling it all over again. And she didn't want to feel any more, not today. Not right now. Not while he was anywhere near her. Because it would be too hard to keep from crawling right back into his arms, where every shred of sense told her she had no business being.

Far too easy to accept the comfort and kindness he offered and pretend it was something more.

But Roan was at the table, pulling a chair out for her, waiting for her. She went reluctantly, set her coffee on the table and let him seat her—and she thought again, as she had when he'd first given her a ride in his car, what irony it was—as if they were on a date, having dinner together.

"Besides which," he continued as he took the chair opposite her, "it's just not true. You sure as hell do need protecting. Look at this place. Look at where you work. If somebody wants to get to you, you'd be a sitting duck, and I'm responsible for your safety whether you like it or not. So let's quit wasting time. I want you to tell me everything you can about how you got into this mess, and maybe we can figure how to get you out."

Mary studied her hands wrapped around the coffee mug. She nodded, cleared her throat, using all her willpower to put her anger—and all the less definable emotions—on slow simmer. "Where do you want me to start?"

"You told me about your parents…you were a preacher's kid."

She had to use both hands to hold her coffee steady as she lifted it to her lips. "And you asked me how I got from there to being a… what was it you called it?" There was a rasp of resentment in her voice she couldn't hide, and she allowed her mouth to tilt in a sardonic little smile. "A mobster's…*girlfriend?*

But you leapfrogged right over the part where I ran away to the wicked city at seventeen to be a model."

"All right, let's start there." His eyes were resting on her again, narrowed in appraisal, keen as ever, but once again without that all-seeing cop look she'd come to dread.

Relaxing a little, she stared into her coffee for a moment, then took a deep breath and began. Though not where she'd expected to.

"You'll probably find this hard to believe, the way I am now," she said lightly, even laughing, "but when I was a little girl I was in love with pretty clothes. My own were hand-me-downs, ill-fitting, years out of style, and I hated having to wear them when I knew what beautiful clothes could look like. And I did know, because I used to steal catalogs from people's mailboxes—" she threw him a glance "—probably a felony, I know—and I'd sneak fashion magazines wherever I could find them and look at them at night under my blankets with a flashlight. I had to be careful—my father would have punished me if he'd known."

"He'd what—make you kneel in the church and pray for your sins?" Roan's voice was tight.

"Or worse." She smiled; it was getting easier, she could suppress the memories even while she spoke of them, now. She felt only a faint chill, like a frosty breath on the back of her neck. "But he could have done just about anything to me, it wouldn't have made any difference. I wanted the world I saw in those magazines, and I was determined to have it.

"Anyway, I was in my last year of high school when I answered this ad—some sort of model search—in a magazine. I nearly died when I was accepted. Then it was *completely* crazy, trying to keep the secret. I had to ditch school to go have pictures made. Borrow money from classmates to pay for them. But in the end it was worth it, because I was offered a scholarship to a modeling school in New York City—room and board and everything."

Roan pursed his lips in a silent whistle. "Wow."

"Yeah," she said flatly, "I was thrilled. Then I had to break the news to my parents."

"How'd that go?" he prompted when she didn't continue.

Her hands had gone clammy. She drew them slowly from the tabletop and into her lap, and began to rub them methodically on her thighs. Shielding herself, she said evenly, "I don't think it matters, does it? It doesn't have anything to do with what happened after." She tightened her lips, clamping down on the pain. "Suffice to say, I left home that night and haven't been back."

"What'd you use for money?"

She gave a brittle laugh and shifted in her chair. "Oh, well, now *that* I'm not proud of."

He put a hand over his eyes. "Lord—don't tell me—you robbed the church poor box."

"Something like that, yeah." She picked up her coffee cup, discovered it was empty and set it down again. "Anyway," she added, a surge of righteousness bubbling up inside her, "I paid it back—and then some—out of my first modeling check. It's not one of the things I still lose sleep over, that's for sure."

Without comment, Roan got up from the table and went for the coffeepot. He refilled her mug and his and brought her two packets of a sugar substitute and a spoon—a man who was comfortable in the kitchen, she noticed—then sat back down, picked up his coffee and blew on it. "So—you were a success at it? The modeling?"

"Oh, yeah." She managed a smile, but it slipped awry. "It happened pretty quickly. In fact, after the sheltered life I'd led, everything in the city came at me hard and fast." She lifted her coffee, frowned at him through the steam and said darkly, "And in case you were thinking about asking, I'm not going to elaborate on that, either. It was a tough time, and it's got nothing to do with anything now." She paused, looked down at her coffee cup and blinked. "I'm not sure I'd have survived it, though, if it hadn't been for... Joy." She clamped a hand over her mouth as the tears welled.

He didn't crowd her, she gave him credit for that. Just waited a moment to give her time to regain control, then said quietly, "The two of you were roommates?"

Mary gulped a swallow and nodded. "She advertised, I answered, we hit it off right away. She was..." She paused once more, cleared her throat. "She was the big sister I'd never had. There were times she seemed more like the *mother* I'd never had."

"What do you mean by that?" Again, giving her time, she thought. But she'd given up trying to stop the tears.

"Because," she whispered, blotting them with her fingers, "she loved me. Unconditionally. Nobody had ever given me that—unconditional love. *Nobody.*" She touched her nose with the back of her hand, then scrubbed angrily at her cheeks. "God knows, my parents never did. I'd had friends, growing up, but I always felt like I had to put up a front for them—be somebody I wasn't. Same with the people I met, working in the city. But not with Joy. She knew I wasn't perfect and loved me anyway. She'd have given her life for me—she almost did."

"Ah," said Roan. "Tell me about that."

She gave her head a fierce little shake. "Not yet. That comes later. That was after I met Diego DelRey."

"So, tell me about *that.*"

"Uh-uh—that comes later, too. First I have to tell you how I *got* to there. You have to understand…*why.*"

"Okay—make me understand." He said it gently. She was smiling at him now, winsomely through her tears, like a child hoping for a stranger's approval. And at the same time she seemed calmer…stronger, he thought, as if even the memory, the thought of her friend's love nurtured her.

"It's hard to explain," she said, intently studying her hands and the coffee mug they cradled. "The modeling career was going well, I had the job I'd always wanted, but I wasn't happy. I found out I really hated modeling, if you want the truth. I always felt like a...a product, rather than a person.

"Anyway, Joy was trying to become a writer, and she got me started writing, too. First it was just a journal—personal stuff. Then, one day during a break on a photo shoot for this huge fashion magazine, I was off in a corner writing in my journal, and one of the photographers saw me and wanted to know what I was writing. I told him it was just stuff about the shoot, and he asked if he could read it. I felt really shy about giving him my personal writings, but he was pretty persuasive. Then, after he'd read some of it, he asked if I'd mind if he showed it to his editor at the magazine. At this point, I figured, how much difference could it make?

"Well...as it turned out, a lot." She answered her own question with a dazed laugh. "The editor liked my stuff so much she decided to make an article out of it to go with the photo layout—kind of a model's diary of what a photo shoot was like." She shrugged... drew a hitching breath.

"That was it—the beginning of Yancy Lavigne, fashion reporter. Again, it came at me faster than I knew how to deal with it. Before I knew it, I'd entered this…this whole new world, filled with beautiful, glamorous, rich, exciting, famous people. I was talking to people whose faces everyone in the world knows—and getting paid for it. Me—poor, homely, awkward Mary Yancy from Nowheresville. It was like some kind of drug, I guess. Intoxicating. And, like drugs do, it really messed up my head. Because the more I was around that world, the more I wanted it for myself—not just to report on, but to *belong* to."

She jumped up from the table and paced restlessly to the window, rubbing at her upper arms. Roan shoved back his chair so he could watch her, his belly clenching with the urge to jump up, drag her away from those windows. Using all his self-control to keep his butt in his chair, he told himself to relax. *The news just broke a couple of hours ago—if they come for her, it won't be this morning. Not yet.*

Her soft voice drifted back to him; he had to strain to hear it. "I'm not proud of this. But… I knew I'd never be able to enter that world on my own, so I thought—I decided I could marry into it." She gave her head a little toss that almost…almost made him smile. "I'd never had any trouble attracting men—I just figured I needed to go where I could attract the right kind of man. Someone rich. Maybe even famous."

"Didn't you meet enough of that kind on the job?"

She threw him another one of her lopsided little smiles. "Oh, sure, but I was the *press,* the *media.* In that world, that's kind of the equivalent of the hired help—you're necessary, they treat you with courtesy, maybe even kindness…sometimes even what passes for friendship. But they don't make you part of the family. Like…they might have an affair, but they don't marry you." She didn't sound bitter about it, just matter-of-fact.

"Anyway, I decided on this resort down in Florida—new, very hip, very posh, a very hot destination for the rich and famous. I saved every penny I could scrape up, then I took a couple of weeks vacation time, and off I went—chasing the rainbow. Or a fairy tale, I guess. You know—Prince Charming."

She turned and came back to the table. Sat down and faced him again, back straight, no longer smiling, the way she'd faced him in his interrogation room…face pale, eyes cold and bleak. It was hard, seeing her that way. Remembering that evening left him with a sour, heavy feeling in his belly.

"And, I found him," she said. "At least, I thought I had. Diego DelRey was...everything I'd hoped for...dreamed of. He was handsome and charming, of course—very sweet, really, like a little boy, sometimes. A spoiled little boy. He was incredibly rich—or his family was. They actually owned the resort, and Diego managed it for the family. At the time, that's all I knew about Diego—that he was from some South American country, well-known and liked in the world of the rich, famous and beautiful people. And very, very rich. That, and the fact that he was crazy in love with me." She paused to glare at him. "And I don't care who you are, *Sheriff,* you don't need details about that, either."

"Fine with me," Roan growled, in complete agreement with her on that point, for reasons that had nothing to do with him being sheriff. He cleared his throat—not that it helped much. "Just one question, though. Were you in love with him?"

She smiled, a little sadly. "I wanted to be. You have no idea how much I wanted to be. At the end of my two weeks, when he begged me to stay, asked me to marry him, I said yes. He gave me a hugely expensive ring, and took me to his family's estate, on this private island." Her smile vanished—as suddenly as if she'd put her foot down and discovered the ground wasn't there. So suddenly, Roan had to fight an urge to reach for her. She gulped coffee. "Then…things changed."

"Changed? How so?" He leaned forward, focused on her, his hands clasped on the table in front of him. Heart quickening.

She waved a hand…frowned. "Oh…it's hard to remember now. Hard to put my finger on what it was, at first. The atmosphere just felt…wrong. Diego's father—they called him Señor—and his uncle…they were nice enough to me, I guess, but for some reason they scared me. Maybe it was their eyes… they seemed so hard. The fact that they never smiled. And there were all these dangerous-looking men around—I know they carried guns, I'd seen them—and everywhere I went, one of them seemed to be right there, watching me. I wasn't allowed to leave the island unless Diego was with me—I didn't mind that so much; after all, he was my fiancé, I didn't have any reason to go places without him. But then…they wouldn't let me use the phone, not even to call Joy. I didn't understand that. I knew she'd be worried about me when I didn't come home after my vacation. She'd even given me a prepaid phone card to use to call her." A smile flickered. "That was the way she was.

"Anyway, I began to realize I was pretty much a prisoner on that island. Diego tried to tell me it was just temporary, that the family was getting ready to close down the estate and leave for their home country—just for the summer, he said, and so I'd have a chance to meet the rest of his family. He told me we'd be married down there. I told him I wanted Joy to be there—to be my maid of honor. He promised me that once we got to his family home, I could call Joy and have her come for a visit. I really missed her—and that was another thing; there weren't any other women on the island—except Anita, the housekeeper." Her throat rippled, and she continued in a whisper, "She was nice to me. I liked her. She—"

"She was the one they killed—the Del-Reys?"

Mary nodded. She spoke rapidly, trying to get through it. Her voice shook. "And her husband, Eduardo. He took care of the grounds.

They—I think they killed them just to cover their tracks. As if they were *nothing*—loose ends to be tied up, trash to be thrown away. Because the feds were closing in on them and they didn't want to leave any witnesses behind. Or maybe they thought they knew things. They—" she swallowed again "—the DelReys—they'd rigged the whole island with explosives, probably to take out as many of the federal agents as possible when they came for them.

"I didn't know any of that at the time, of course, except… I knew Anita and Eduardo were unconscious, because I'd seen them—or maybe they were already dead. Anyway, that was when I understood, finally, who—and what—the DelReys were. All I could think about was how I was going to get away from them. How to keep them from getting suspicious of me. I knew they wouldn't hesitate to kill me too, no matter how Diego felt about me."

Her eyes focused on something far away, she picked up her coffee cup and took another thoughtless gulp. He could hear her swallow. "That evening a helicopter came for us—all of us. We were flying away in it when the house blew up—the whole island was exploding. It looked like a movie. Señor DelRey said the feds were responsible for it. Meanwhile, I was trying to act like I was so crazy in love with Diego I didn't care about anything else. Flying away in that helicopter…watching the fire, and the explosions…knowing Anita and Eduardo were down there—" Her voice rose to a squeak. "I didn't know Joy was there, too—on the island. She'd come looking for me. She was there—she almost got killed— because of *me*."

"Easy…" Roan gave up fighting it and reached for her hand.

Chapter Twelve

His hand might have been the head of a rattlesnake, from the way she shied back from it.

"Mary," he said in a gravelly voice, "You weren't responsible for your friend—"

"Yes—yes, I was." She was on her feet again, pacing the small sunlit room and throwing back quick, furious glances. "Joy came looking for me. She came because I hadn't called, and then I wasn't on the plane, and she was worried about me. She came because she loved me. And when she knew I was in trouble, she risked her life for me. Not just then, on the island, but later." She paused, one hand gripping the back of a chair, the other brushing at her cheeks and nose. "See, the helicopter took us first to one of the Del-Reys' manufacturing plants—there was an air strip there, and they were waiting for their plane to come and fly us out of the country. They didn't know the feds had them under surveillance all the time, that they were just waiting for the plane to land before moving in and arresting everybody. But what the feds didn't know was that I was there, too. They thought—"

"I got some of this from Cavanaugh," Roan said in a soothing tone. "The feds had found your purse with the housekeeper's charred body and assumed you'd been killed in the explosions and fire."

"But Joy *knew* I wasn't dead. She knew it, but nobody would believe her. The feds were ready to take down the DelReys with guns blazing, and Joy was sure I'd be hurt or taken hostage, or worse, so she—God, she's just this little tiny short person—you should see her—but she came for me. All by herself. And she got me out of there, Roan. She saved my life. And the worst of it is, I never even got to say thank you. I never even got to say goodbye." She rounded on him one last time, fists clenched, face blotchy, nose red, eyes streaming and at the same time shooting fire.

He thought it the most beautiful and amazing thing he'd ever seen, like witnessing a rare natural phenomenon—the northern lights, or a moonlight rainbow.

She went on in a choked voice. "Do you understand what that was like? They took me away that very night. I had to leave everything—didn't even have a toothbrush, a change of clothes. Nothing whatsoever that was mine—or that had been Yancy's. It was like… I'd *died*. My life—who I'd been, the people I'd loved—was over. I couldn't contact anyone—I didn't dare. They'd told me about cases where people had broken security, and then their bodies were found a few days later—God, Roan, they even showed me *pictures*." She had her arms wrapped around herself, her eyes focusing on horrors only she could see. But Roan had seen enough crime-scene photos to know the images wouldn't be pretty.

He sat very still, cradling his empty coffee mug with both hands to keep himself from doing something stupid—stupid and dangerous—like getting up and going to her and pulling her back into his arms. Some inner sense told him she wouldn't want that, not right then, anyway. And considering what had happened the last time he'd done that, maybe he didn't either. Shouldn't, for sure.

He cleared his throat. "Well, now your security's broken all to hell. If DelRey still wants to kill you, he knows right where to find you, thanks to me and that news broadcast."

"No." She turned to face him, the sunlight from behind haloing her hair so that for the first time he saw hints of fire in it that even the dye couldn't hide. "No—it wasn't your fault or the news media's or anybody's." She came toward him slowly, her body quiet… something different about the way she looked, the way she held herself.

Then she began to speak again, and once again it came to him what the difference was. The fear was gone.

"I've been thinking about it…after I heard the news this morning…before you got here. Just now. And what I think is, this is Fate." Roan made a sound, an involuntary gesture, and she held up a hand to forestall the protest. "No—these last ten years—they've been such hell. You have no idea. Running…hiding, afraid to trust anyone, afraid to get close to anyone, all with one purpose: Running away from my...well, Destiny, I guess you could call it. Only now I think all that time I thought I was avoiding Fate, I've actually been on a collision course with it. It's like... every step I've taken in the last ten years has been leading me to this. It's brought me *here*." She caught a hitching breath. "For better or worse, this is where it ends. I'm done with running. One way or another, it's going to end here."

Watching her, listening to her, he'd managed to keep his face blank, his body still and his mouth shut, while a whole kaleidoscope of emotions and sensations rolled through him—rage...both icy and hot; rejection and annoyance, tenderness and sorrow. And finally, a fierce and powerful resolve that should have surprised him, but didn't.

Nobody's going to take this *woman from me.* Nobody.

Once upon a time, someone had taken the life of the woman he loved and gotten away with it. It wouldn't happen again. Not while he had breath in his body.

"Don't know about Fate," he drawled as he pushed back his chair and stood up, emotions barricaded, now, inside a fortress of calm resolve, "but I'm gonna be arranging some protection for you, whether you like it or not. And that's not open for discussion," he added, when he saw she was about to speak.

Her smile was faint and wry. "I was going to ask if that would include giving me my gun back."

He gave a snort of laughter. "Can't do *that*—sorry." He strolled toward her, but kept his arms folded on his chest to stop himself from reaching for her, touching her. He halted an arm's length from her, frowning, knowing on the outside he looked the very picture of the strong arm of the law—steadfast, courageous, protector of the innocent—while his insides churned with fear and the knowledge that his starched sheriff's uniform and shiny silver badge and white hero's hat hadn't done a thing to save Erin's life. In spite of all that, someone had come into his home, killed his wife, maimed his child and he'd been powerless even to catch the one responsible. *Protector of the innocent...* The thought was a bitter pain in his heart.

"What I can do, though, is put someone watching this house, and your shop whenever you're there—goes without saying either I or one of my deputies will be taking you to work and anywhere else you need to go—and bringing you home. And you don't go inside either place until it's been thoroughly checked out—that clear? When you're here alone, I want you to keep all the doors and windows locked, shades down, curtains drawn. And stay the hell away from the windows. Don't—"

"Roan." She was smiling at him still, a patient little smile that made him want to shake her. "This is a small town. Don't you think someone's going to notice if a stranger—say, um...a hitman—"

"Don't. Dammit."

She closed her eyes and contritely whispered, "Sorry. I'm trying not to be scared."

"Hell, you *should* be scared." His throat felt raw. "Look, it's fine to try and be brave, but don't make light of this. From what Scott Cavanaugh told me, those were some seriously bad people you pissed off. Señor may not be around anymore, but his son sure as hell is. He's the one you hit where it hurts most."

The fine skin around her eyes flinched, and it struck him that without her glasses her face seemed open and defenseless as a child's. His willpower caved like a house of cards. He put his hands on her arms, felt the tremors she was trying to hide, and his insides melted like chocolate in the sun.

"Mary, Diego DelRey was released from prison two years ago. He's off the radar. He could be anywhere. He probably wouldn't come after you himself, but let's say he sends a—" his lips twitched wryly "—hitman. I wish I could tell you you're right about it being hard for a stranger to sneak into town without being noticed. Normally that'd be true. Thing is, for the next couple weeks, things aren't going to be exactly 'normal' around here. We've got Boomtown Days coming up. That's Hartsville's spring blow-out—maybe you noticed the stores downtown getting all spruced up for the big event? Happens every year around this time, same time as the college rodeo over in Silver Springs. We're gonna have all sorts of out-of-towners coming in." And there was no way in hell his department was going to be able to keep track and run checks on all of them.

He closed his eyes...let out a breath. And Lord, it was hard not to gather her in, wrap her up in his arms the way he wanted to... wrap her up in a nice little package and put her somewhere to keep her safe until all this was over....

Over? Just when and how was this mess she was in going to be over? When Diego DelRey was dead? And there was still a first-degree murder charge hanging over her head—the one he'd put there.

"Look," he said with gravel in his voice, "just…be careful, okay? Do those things I told you. Pull those shades. Lock your doors. Don't take chances." Hard as it was, he made himself let go of her, looked around for his hat, remembered where he'd left it and ran a distracted hand through his hair. "I'm gonna figure out something…if I have to, I'll put you back in jail."

"I won't go," she said unsteadily, lifting her chin and hugging herself, her own hands rubbing the places where his had been. "You have no right—not until a jury finds me guilty."

"Yeah, and that's not gonna happen either," he growled. "Not if I can help it."

His joints felt loose and his muscles jerky as he strode through the house, grabbed up his hat and let himself out the front door. On the porch he stood for a moment, hauling in great big lungfuls of the warm spring air… looking up and down the street of the town he'd lived in all his life, looking up at the trees leafing out and dropping flower fluff and pollen everywhere, looking past them at the sky…blue Montana sky. Thinking it all ought to look different to him, somehow.

Because he was definitely a different man coming out of that house than when he'd gone in.

Mary had no way of knowing how long she stood there propping up the kitchen counter. She knew there were things she should be doing—lock the doors, pull the shades, take a shower, make the bed—but she felt too battered, too emotionally drained to think or move. Cat, having completed his after-breakfast toilette, came to twine around her legs by way of saying thank you, and she couldn't even summon the energy to bend down and pet him. So, when the telephone on the kitchen wall rang, for a moment or two she simply stared at it, unable to think why on earth it should be making such a sound.

Then, when her brain did start to function, her body turned ice-cold. The phone here at home never rang. Who could possibly be calling her now? She thought about running after Roan—maybe he was still sitting out in front in his SUV, calling in to his office, as he often did. Then she scolded herself for cowardice. So much for putting up a brave front.

She walked to the phone and lifted the receiver from its hook with hands so wet and clammy she nearly dropped it before she got it tucked into its proper place next to her ear. "Hello?" she said in a hushed and husky voice.

Shaking, heart pounding, she listened to silence...some rapid breathing. And then... "Oh God—*Yancy?*" the caller squeaked. And burst into sobs.

Mary spent more than an hour on the phone with Joy. Afterward, she felt calmer, stronger, a thousand pounds lighter and ten years younger. And how strange it was, she thought, that she should feel this way when there was a murder charge hanging over her and someone—Diego or his gunman—possibly at that very moment on his way to kill her.

The truth was, the murder charge, the fact that her life was in danger—none of that seemed real. What was real to her was the profound sense of relief she felt to have finally stopped running. The tremendous feeling of freedom that came from laying down the burden of her secrets was like breathing fresh air and feeling the sun on her face after being locked in a dungeon.

With her spirits so high, it was hard, in the week that followed, for Mary to stick to the orders Roan had given her. Or, it would have been, if he'd allowed her any wiggle-room at all. She got used to seeing the sheriff's department patrol vehicles cruising the street in front of her shop, or parked in front of her house at all hours of the day or night.

The days fell into a routine. Every morning, a deputy would show up on her doorstep, escort her to his patrol car and drive her to work. She would remain in the vehicle while the deputy unlocked her shop and searched it thoroughly, then wait to be escorted inside. Deputies kept an eye on the front of the shop; the back door was always locked. At closing time, the process would be reversed, until she was once more safely barricaded inside her house with the doors and windows locked and the shades drawn.

It was always a deputy who drove her to work and brought her home again, never Roan. When Mary asked, she was told the sheriff was busy with preparations for the onslaught of visitors expected for Boomtown Days.

It was just as well, she told herself. But there

was a Roan-shaped emptiness in her heart, bigger than she'd imagined it could be. And the longing that came along with his image in her mind—and it came much too often, with blue eyes glinting, a wry smile deepening the thumbprints in his cheeks and his hair bearing the imprint of his Stetson—was the only cloud darkening her skies during those days.

Cat, she discovered, made a very good watchdog, since he growled whenever the deputies came to her door. He was a comfort in other ways, too, and she took to sleeping with him curled up on the foot of her bed.

Her shop was surprisingly busy. More people than usual seemed to be stopping in to make appointments in person rather than phoning. Regular clients popped in to say hello, or to drop off bouquets of flowers they'd picked from their yards, and people who'd never been in the shop before came to browse through the boutique.

Curiosity, Mary cynically told herself, because of the news story. After the first day or two, the constant jangling of the bell attached to the door got on her nerves.

Then she mentioned the steady stream of visitors to Miss Ada when she came for her regular appointment on Friday at five o'clock, and the elderly clerk of court patted her hand and said, "The town's behind you, dear."

Mary felt as if the wind had been knocked out of her. She put down her comb and scissors and fled to the back room, where to her own astonishment, she had a good cry. *The town's behind you...* Whether it was true or merely Miss Ada being kind, the notion that a community might open its heart to her, its people make a place for her among them after she'd wandered alone in the world for so long, seemed...almost unbearable. *To belong...*

But that was a hope too lovely even to whisper in the most secret part of her mind.

Saturday, which was to be the big kick-off for Boomtown Days, dawned warm and clear, with not a cloud in the sky and for once neither rain nor wind in the forecast. Chamber of Commerce weather, Tom Daggett, the deputy who drove Mary to her shop that morning, called it. Tom was one of Mary's favorite deputies, a very sweet boy, though it was hard to think of him as an officer of the law. To her, he looked barely old enough to drive.

Since pretty much everybody in town would be attending the parade and accompanying concerts, carnivals and food and artisan fairs, Mary had decided not to open the hair salon that day. Like many of the other shop owners up and down Main and the streets that crossed it, she planned to put some of her boutique items out on racks on the sidewalk, hoping to catch the eyes of browsing out-of-towners with extra money to spend.

She spent the morning deciding which items to put out, setting prices and hand-lettering signs, and by eleven or so had what she considered to be a rather nice display set up in front of the salon. There was a rack of clearance items from last winter marked down to fifty percent off, and another with some of her newer, flashier stuff, particularly some things with a Western motif she thought might go well with the theme of the day's celebration. She enjoyed a brisk business—mostly lookers, but a few nice sales as well—before the strolling crowds drifted off toward Main Street to watch the parade.

Mary was taking advantage of the respite to restore some order to the racks when Betty, from the art gallery next door, came wandering over to compare notes on the morning's business—like Mary, she'd enjoyed a whole lot of looky-lous and a handful of sales, but was satisfied by the day's take, overall. Betty was a grandmotherly but elegant woman who favored tunics and broom-stick skirts in bright peacock colors, and wore her thick salt-and-pepper hair in a Navajo twist which she had a habit of sticking writing utensils into.

She stayed to chat, making cozy small talk about her garden and her grandkids, and when they heard the thump of a marching band start up in the distance, happened to mention, with a sigh, that she hated having to miss the parade, since her grandson Cody would be riding on the Future Farmers of America float, and her granddaughters, Jennifer and Ashley, were both in the high school band. One played saxophone, the other, clarinet.

"Why don't you go?" Mary said. "I can keep an eye on your stuff for you."

Betty's face brightened. "Oh—that's nice of you. Are you sure you don't mind?"

"Of course not," Mary assured her. "Everyone's watching the parade anyway. Go on—hurry. You don't want to miss it."

"Thank you so much—I won't be long..." Betty was already hurrying down the sidewalk. She turned once to smile and wave.

Mary smiled and waved back, a lovely warmth spreading through her. *This is what it's like...belonging.*

She turned back to the racks, and as she did, bumped it just slightly. When she did that, a rather gaudy beaded suede jacket—one of the clearance items—slithered off its hanger and fell to the sidewalk. She muttered, "Oops," and bent over to pick it up.

At precisely the same moment, the window behind her, bearing in gilt letters the words, Queenie's Salon & Boutique—We Pamper You Like Royalty, disintegrated.

As the crystalline cubes of safety glass rained down around her, Mary's natural impulse was to rise and stare in utter bewilderment at the hole where her shop window had been. She never knew what it was that made her, after that first instant, drop like a stone and flatten herself on the concrete sidewalk underneath the rack of clothes.

Out on Main Street the parade was going by. She could hear the thump of a marching band, people clapping...cheering. Directly above her head, she could hear something hitting the clothes on the rack with sharp little thumps. Each thump made the rack jerk and twitch and rattle on its castors. She heard other sounds, like angry mosquitos, and felt the sting of something hitting her cheek. Her body was shaking violently; her chest and throat felt raw, as if she'd been screaming and screaming, the way people do in nightmares.

It seemed like a nightmare. Half a block away there were crowds of people, laughing, happy people...people waving flags, throwing confetti, calling out to their friends, children and neighbors riding on the floats, or on horses or marching in the band. There was no one to notice a woman huddled under a rack of clothes, no one to hear her terrified cries for help. All alone and caught in a killer's gunsights, Mary covered her head with her arms and waited to die.

It might have been seconds later, or minutes or an eternity... She heard the roar of an engine, the screech of brakes, the slam of a door. Pounding footsteps. But her shocked mind heard only more danger. Her body curled itself into a tight, trembling ball, and Deputy Daggett had to almost lift her bodily up off the sidewalk, repeatedly shouting her name, before she was able to comprehend that salvation truly was at hand.

"Go, go, *go!*" The deputy gave her a powerful shove in the general direction of the salon.

She lurched toward the door—there was no glass left in it, either—and managed to push it open…stumble through it on rubbery legs. From the relative safety inside the shop she looked back to see the impossibly young, downy-cheeked deputy in a half crouch behind the dubious shelter of the clothes rack, weapon in one hand, keying on his shoulder radio with the other and calmly shouting, "Shots fired, officer requesting backup at Queenie's Hair Salon. Repeat—shots fired…."

Slowly, as if in a dream, Mary lifted a hand to touch her cheek. She pulled her fingers away…saw blood and wetness. And only then realized she was crying.

Roan was in the emergency services command post that had been set up in the back parking lot of the courthouse when he got the call. He and Paul Gunther, owner of Gunther's Groceries, who also happened to be the deputy mayor and a member of the Boomtown Days planning committee for as long as Roan could remember, had just been congratulating one another on how smoothly everything was going this year. So far, the only arrests had been a handful of D and Ds last night, then the usual rowdiness this morning—including a couple of high-school kids who'd thought it might be fun to set off some firecrackers along the parade route just to see what the mounted units would do. Out-of-towners, Paul Gunther declared—city kids without a clue about the kind of havoc a spooked horse was capable of wreaking on a crowd of people, and what was the world coming to, anyway?

Roan's radio beeped at him, and both men fell expectantly silent, listening.

And he heard the words he'd half expected and hoped never to hear. *"Shots fired... Queenie's Hair Salon...shots fired!"* He was in his patrol car, tires spitting gravel, before the static died.

As the SUV bucked and jounced out of the parking lot and down the dirt alley he thumbed on the siren—something he rarely had cause to do—and spoke into his radio with a calm he couldn't account for—some kind of protective numbness, maybe.

"SD Mobile One responding to shots fired...requesting all available units..."

When he was done with that and had shut off the radio mike, he began to swear fervently and out loud, repeating every bad word he knew, over and over, almost like a prayer.

As the SUV fishtailed around the corner and onto Second Street, Roan could see Tom

Daggett's patrol car parked crossways down in front of Queenie's, lights on and flashing. At the far end of the street where the crowd had gathered to watch the parade go by, he could see a few people beginning to turn and look to see what all the excitement was about. He didn't see Tom, and he didn't see Mary.

He brought the SUV to a screeching halt alongside the curb next to some sidewalk displays of paintings and photographs in front of Betty's frame shop. Now he saw Tom crouched down behind a rack of clothes in front of Mary's place, his sidearm braced on the top crossbar, aimed in the general direction of the rooftops across the street. He saw the gaping hole where the store's front window had been, and the glass all over the sidewalk. He still didn't see Mary.

Tom looked over at him and straightened up a little, slowly and cautiously, darting glances back and forth between Roan and those buildings across the street. A couple of other units came screaming onto the street right then and skidded to a halt a half block back, effectively barricading it. Roan barked orders for the new arrivals into his radio, telling them to check out the buildings across the street, then grabbed his hat and exited his vehicle. He was pretty sure the shooter was long gone, but he kept his head down just in case.

He started over to where his deputy was, running bent over, dodging in and out among the art display easels, boots crunching on the broken glass with a sound that made his teeth grate and his skin shiver, like fingernails on slate.

Tom saw him coming and diverted him with a gesture, a sweep of his thumb toward the broken window. "She's okay, Sheriff—she's inside."

His voice was hoarse and out-of-breath, but Roan took note of the fact that it looked like excitement, and not fear, that had the kid's cheeks and eyes lit up like Christmas morning. His greenest deputy had come through his baptism of fire with flying colors, and Roan made a mental note to make sure he got commended for his bravery when all this was over.

Right now, he had other things on his mind. *One* thing.

Calling her name softly, he stepped through the broken-out window. The salon seemed dim to him after the bright midday sunshine, so he took off his sunglasses and tucked them in his pocket. He could smell some kind of perfume—hair products, he thought, from the different sizes and colors of plastic bottles that were scattered all over the place, oozing their contents onto the black-and-white vinyl tile floor. He walked over glass from a shattered display case, and shredded flowers from the blue-and-white vase that had sat on top of it. He saw a broken mirror, and a rack of magazines lying on its side. But he still didn't see Mary.

Well, hell. Vibrating with an urgent need to see for himself that she was all right, he crossed to the doorway and moved the pink ruffled curtain aside with the back of his hand. Called her name again. She didn't answer, but he could hear water running, and he could see a light on in the combination restroom and janitor's closet off the storeroom. The door was standing partway open. He went to it and tapped on it with his knuckle. "Mary? You in there?"

The door opened wider. He didn't know what he'd expected—to find her cowering somewhere in a corner, quivering like a trapped rabbit, maybe? He should have known that wouldn't be Mary's style—though to be honest, he didn't exactly know what her style might be. Most of the time he had known her, she'd been pretending to be somebody else.

She was standing in front of the sink, not cowering at all, calmly drying her hands with a paper towel.

"Are you okay?" Roan asked gently.

She turned her head to look at him. "Yes, I'm fine." Her voice was calm, but her eyes were too bright and the skin on her face looked stretched and shiny. Her color was uneven in a way that was too pretty to be called blotchy—shades ranging from alabaster to the delicate pink of seashells and rose petals, with some deeper pink edging her nose and around her eyes. She had a tiny cut on one cheek, still oozing blood. Roan's belly burned when he saw that.

Lord, how he wanted to go to her, put his arms around her. The desire to hold her was so powerful his muscles quivered with it. But there was something…a kind of shell around her—pride, maybe, or shock or self-control— he'd seen it before in victims of violence. He knew how fragile she was, and how much she didn't want to break.

So he kept to a safe distance and said in the gruff but gentle voice he used for comforting victims, "Everything's under control now, Mary. You're gonna be okay." He paused, dipped his head toward her, made a gesture with his hand toward the cut on her cheek. "You need to have that looked at."

She shook her head. "Just a scratch." She folded a fresh paper towel and pressed it against her cheek. Then she darted a look at him with eyes hard and green as glacier ice and softly asked, "Did you get him?"

He shook his head—once, quick and hard. "But we will," he promised grimly, then added in a gentler tone, "Right now, though, I'm gonna need you to come with me."

She didn't question, simply nodded. He moved aside to let her pass, reached to shut off the bathroom light, then closed in beside her again.

He couldn't have imagined how hard it would be, walking beside her like that, close enough to protect her, trying not to crowd her too much…wanting—*needing* to touch her, knowing he didn't dare…and the frustration of that gnawing at him, a sharp fierce ache in his belly.

"Is there anything here you need?" he asked her as they made their way through the ruined salon.

"My purse."

"Okay, where is it?"

"I'll get it."

He waited while she stepped carefully through the spilled bottles and broken glass to retrieve her purse from a bottom drawer in one of her stations, then motioned her toward the door and opened it for her. She looked up at him as she slipped past him. "Where are you taking me?"

"Someplace safe."

"Are you going to put me in jail?" Her voice sounded stifled, as if her teeth wanted to chatter and she was determined not to let them.

"No," Roan said, keeping his narrow-eyed gaze focused over her head as he took his sunglasses out of his pocket and put them on. "Not that."

He was pretty sure what he'd told her was right, and that whoever had shot at her was long gone, but just to be sure he kept his body between hers and the street as he walked her quickly to his car, hustled her inside and slammed the door. He went around to the driver's side, then waited for Tom Daggett to make his way over to him from across the street, jogging through the maze of parked police vehicles and crime-scene tape.

"No sign of the shooter, Sheriff," Tom said, and Roan could have sworn the deputy's voice had deepened some since the last time he'd heard it. "Found some shell casings upstairs in one of the buildings. And we got a witness a couple streets over says he saw a man run down the alley and jump in a cream-colored SUV, take off like a bat outa hell. Says the guy was carrying a huntin' rifle, but he didn't think anything of it, just thought he musta been in the parade."

Roan nodded. He could understand that reasoning well enough; there was more than one gun club participating in the parade most years. Boyd, his own father-in-law, would most likely have been marching with the Old West Gun Club he belonged to, if he hadn't had to stay home with Susie Grace because she hated crowds, particularly crowds of out-of-towners, crowds of strangers who weren't used to her and therefore likely to stare and ask insensitive questions.

"Keep on with the canvas," he said to Tom. "And get the description of that SUV to the State Police right away. Then get this place secured. You're gonna have your hands full with crowd control once the parade's over. Folks are gonna be coming to see what all the fuss was about. I'll leave that in your hands." He jerked his head toward the woman sitting like a statue in the front seat of his SUV. "I'm taking off for a while—taking Mary to a safe house. Nobody's gonna know where but me, so don't ask. If you need me, you know how to reach me, but unless it's a break in this case or a dire emergency, it can wait."

"Okay, Sheriff." Deputy Daggett all but saluted, trying hard not to look tickled to death Roan had put him in charge.

Roan got in the car and slammed the door on more of his deputy's earnest assurances all would be taken care of in his absence. Without looking at his silent passenger, he started up the SUV, put it in gear and backed out of the street along the curb, the way he'd come in. Once he had the vehicle pointed forward again, he glanced over at Mary and growled, "Fasten your seatbelt."

She obeyed, then fired back breathlessly, "What are you mad at *me* for?"

"I'm not—" He made a breath-sound like a tire going flat, then hit the steering wheel with the palm of his hand. "Dammit, Mary, I'm not mad at you. I'm just *mad*."

Scared, he silently corrected himself. Scared spitless. Because it had almost happened again.

Someone had almost taken the life of a woman he cared about and was responsible for protecting. Still could. Because it looked like he wasn't any better at keeping this woman safe than he had been Erin.

Chapter Thirteen

"Dammit, Mary," Roan said, "you were supposed to stay inside. What the hell were you doing out there? A sidewalk sale, for God's sake. What were you thinking?"

Belonging. I wanted to be a part of it...the town, the celebration. I just wanted to...belong.

But she thought that sounded pathetic, so she didn't say it. Instead, she cleared her throat and contritely muttered, "I'm sorry."

Roan glanced at her, then shook his head and gave a snort of laughter. "That has to be the worst hitman I've ever heard of—or you're about the luckiest victim. The guy had a hunting rifle with a scope on it. I don't know how the hell he missed."

"Luck," Mary mumbled; her tongue felt clumsy. She frowned and touched the sore place on her cheek. "Something—a jacket, I think—fell off the hanger. I bent over to pick it up. That's when the window..." She paused, a replay of that moment coming sharp and vivid to her mind. She fought to shut it out... had to shut it out, because right behind those images she could feel it creeping closer, the emotional meltdown she'd managed so far to hold off with a combination of willpower and denial. It was about to pounce...she could feel its cold grip on her throat when she swallowed and tried to laugh. "I guess I should be dead right now."

It seemed an eternity before Roan responded, in a voice between a growl and a murmur. "Yeah. You should." He paused, then added grimly, "He won't miss again."

She stared at him, swallowing repeatedly and fighting back tears. Wishing she could see his eyes, wishing she knew how to read him. But between his hat brim, the sunglasses and the hand covering most of the lower part of his face, his emotions were well-guarded.

He flicked her another brief glance and

his mouth twitched upward at one corner—a hard little smile. "That's why we're not going to give him a second chance. I'm getting you out of this town, right now. I'm going to put you someplace where you'll be safe until we get this guy."

Something shivered through her...a chilling blast of déjà vu. *The small, barren room... a strange man saying, "We're going to take you to a safe house...."*

"I'm not doing this, Roan," she said in a low, uneven voice. "I won't do it again. Not ever."

"Mary—"

"I don't care!" Her voice rose, both in pitch and volume; the monster was coming and there wasn't anything she could do to stop it. "I told you. I'm tired of running...tired of hiding. I'm not going to do it. I won't...be... alone...any...more."

"You're not going to be alone." His jaw looked the way his voice sounded—rock hard. "I'm taking you to my ranch. You'll be with me. And Boyd and Susie Grace. Think you can handle that?"

She stared at him, her mind gone blank. It was so far from what she'd expected him to say.

He let out a breath, uneven and impatient. "Look—I know it's a little…unorthodox. But it's the safest place I can think of right now. My place is out in the middle of nowhere, so unless this jackass comes for you by helicopter or horseback, we're gonna see him coming a long way off. Then he'll have to get by me or Boyd first."

"What—" She cleared her throat carefully. She felt as if everything inside her had shaken loose. Her emotions were vulnerable…uncertain and unformed, like something newly born. "What about Susie Grace?"

There was a pause. She counted heartbeats and watched a muscle work in the side of his jaw. "Like I said," he growled, "it's the best I could come up with on short notice."

Mary went on gazing at him, while those unformed thoughts and fragile feelings filled her head like a cloud of gnats…or soap bubbles. Any attempt to grasp them she knew would be futile, so she didn't even try. Finally she said in a soft, shaking voice, "I want to go home first." How strange to hear the word *home* coming out of her mouth.

"Too dangerous," Roan said. His jaw and mouth looked implacable again. "The shooter could be waiting for you there."

"What about my things? I have to pack."

He shook his head. "I can pick up whatever you need later."

Anger—with the Fates, with him, with herself for her own impotence—blew through her like pollen in the wind. She sucked in air like someone about to sneeze and gasped out, "What about Cat? I can't just leave him—"

"*Dammit,* Mary!"

"Dammit, *Roan!*" She shot it back at him between clenched teeth, her breathing quick and shallow. "I said I'm not doing this again. I mean it. I'm not running, I'm not hiding, I'm not leaving pieces of myself behind. I'll stay at your place, *temporarily,* if that's what I need to do, but I'm not going without my stuff, and I am *not* going without my *cat.*"

He gave her one brief, furious look, then stomped on the brakes, swearing under his breath. The SUV swerved to the side of the road and jerked to a halt. He turned his head to glare at her along his shoulder, and not even the sunglasses could hide the frustration burning in his eyes. After a long pause, he threw a glance over his shoulder, made a tire-squealing U-turn and headed the SUV back into town.

Roan was about as close to losing his temper as he ever got, though if he'd been honest with himself he'd have to admit the burr under his saddle probably wasn't anger at all. At the moment, though, he didn't give much of a damn about honesty. What he cared about was keeping it together, and anger seemed a whole lot easier to deal with than some of the other stuff rattling around inside him.

Stubborn woman, he thought, and wouldn't let himself think about the anguish, courage and vulnerability that were there in her voice too.

Wouldn't let himself think what a high-caliber slug would have done to her head but for a split-second quirk of Fate.

Wouldn't let himself picture it, anyway. He was definitely thinking about it when he pulled up in front of the little clapboard house. All his senses were on hair-trigger alert and the short hairs rising on the back of his neck. He wondered how in the hell he was going to be able to check out the house without leaving Mary alone and unguarded in the car.

As it happened, while he was silently grinding his teeth and pondering the matter, she took it out of his hands. Almost before the SUV stopped rolling, before he had any idea what she had in mind, she opened up her door and jumped out. By the time he got the motor turned off and the keys out of the ignition and his own door open, she was already halfway across the raggedy dandelion-studded grass, right out in the open, unshielded, unguarded.

With fear and fury propelling him, he caught up with her in about two strides. He grabbed her arm—ignoring her gasp of outraged protest—and steered her away from the front steps and around the side of the house to the back, where he shoved her down beside the stoop and told her to stay there while he did a sweep for intruders. He was almost as surprised as she was when she obeyed him. He could feel her seething about it, though, when he came back and hauled her up the steps and shielded her with his body while she unlocked the door.

Inside the kitchen, he locked the door and pulled down the shades, this time making sure to keep a good firm grip on her arm in case she had any more ideas about dashing off without waiting for him to check things out first. Again, it didn't make her happy; this time the look she gave him when he told her to stay put while he had a look around probably should have turned him to stone.

"You're not going to make this easy, are you?" he said mildly when he met her in the living room, feeling a little more relaxed now he'd made sure there weren't any hitmen lurking in her closets or under the bed. Somehow it didn't surprise him that she hadn't obeyed his order to stay in the kitchen.

"No," she snapped, "I'm not." She had her arms folded and one hip stuck out, and everything about her but the color of her hair screamed, *Red-Headed Woman—Handle with Care!*

It was an attitude Roan was well acquainted with, having spent a good part of his life in the company of red-haired females, but what he *wasn't* prepared for was the little hot spot that opened up in the bottom of his belly, like a slumbering coal flaring to life.

"I'm through being meek and mild," she bit out between heaving breaths, her eyes spitting green-gold fire, and the thought, *Meek and mild? You've got to be kidding!* flashed through his mind. But the urge to break into a grin vanished when she continued, and he saw the fire in her eyes was just one shaky step away from tears. "I'm tired of…of letting some— some *man* run my life. Like I'm a little child who needs to be told what to do.

Okay, I've let it happen, but no more. I'm not a child, I'm a grownup, dammit. *I* decide whether to go or stay, whether to hide or not. *My choice.*"

"Fine," he said, keeping his voice stern, grateful for the sunglasses that wouldn't let her see what was in his eyes. He folded his arms and faced her across a barrier of space so charged with electricity it seemed almost to hum. "You're right. You choose. Tell me what you want to do. Do you want to stay here, wait for Diego DelRey or his hitman to come for you? Or do you want to come stay out at my ranch where I can protect you?"

She stared at him through a long, vibrating silence, while the fire in her eyes slowly died. Finally... "I want to stay with you," she whispered.

The naked longing in her face hit him like a fist in the gut. Reaching for her was a reflex. But she'd already turned away from him, jerky as a mechanical doll.

Stupid, Mary thought. *Stupid! Oh God, Oh God, I hope I didn't let him see....*

But she had. She knew she had. She hadn't missed the way his face...at least the part of it she could see...had changed. She was only glad he was wearing sunglasses, so she hadn't had to see the pity in his eyes.

"I'll just be a minute," she muttered breathlessly as she fled like a coward to her bedroom.

She meant it, too—about taking a minute to pack; she had it down to a science. She began to pull clothes out of drawers and dump them into the suitcase she'd hauled out from the bottom of her closet, pausing long enough to call back to him, "I think I saw a cat carrier in the garage…maybe you could—"

She heard a growled, "I'll get it," then the thump of boots on hardwood.

She heard the kitchen door slam. And all the fight and defiance went out of her like air from a balloon. She let the pile of clothes slip from her arms and gripped the edges of the suitcase that was lying open on the bed, leaned on her hands, bowed her head and closed her eyes, weighed down by an overwhelming sense of grief and loss.

I don't want to do this.

The packing thing she may have had down pat, but the leaving…that was another matter. She thought of all the places she'd left… all the people, most of the time just when she was beginning to get to know them…never long enough to feel that sense of home…of belonging. She had a sudden fierce urge to pick up the suitcase and heave it through the nearest window.

No more. I don't want to leave again. Not this town. This is where I want to belong.

How insane was that, when this was the town where she'd been assaulted, nearly raped, arrested and charged with murder? Where, but for the sake of a sympathetic judge, she would right now be in jail?

All right, maybe not the town, but the people. Kind people, like Miss Ada and Betty. People who need me, like Susie Grace.

And Roan. You know very well this isn't about the town, or the people. It's about one person. Roan.

How insane was *that,* to fall for the sheriff who'd arrested her and put her in jail for a murder she hadn't committed?

It was all too much…everything coming down on her at once, happening way too fast. She could feel emotions looming, piling up in her like snow on a precipice. It wouldn't take much to bring it all tumbling down on her. And so what? she thought recklessly. Let it come. She would welcome it. After everything that had happened to her, after the long, long struggle to outrun Destiny, it would be almost a relief to finally let it sweep her away....

Without a car cluttering up the garage, Roan was able to find the cat carrier without too much difficulty. After sweeping off the worst of the dust, he carried it into the kitchen and left it there while he went to see how Mary was coming along with her packing.

He found her standing in the middle of her bedroom, frowning at a half-filled suitcase on the bed in front of her. She looked no less emotionally fragile than when he'd left her, so he knocked softly on the door frame and eased into the room much the way he'd have entered the cage of a sleeping lioness.

"Found the carrier," he said, keeping his voice to a neutral mutter. "Now all I need's the cat. Any idea where I might find him?"

She jerked around, her hair in tumbled disarray, her mouth forming an O of distress. "Oh—oh God. He could be anywhere—curled up asleep somewhere...hunting...visiting the neighbors... He always comes home when he knows I'm here, though. He'll be here—I know he will. If we wait—"

"Mary..." He said it with a sigh, knowing

the battle that was coming. "The longer we wait, the less chance we have of getting you out of town undetected. We can't—"

She held up a hand. "No—*don't*. Don't even say it."

Well, he'd known she was going to fight him on it, and she didn't disappoint him. Her eyes were getting the shimmer again—the fire-and-rain thing that grabbed him in some deep-down part of himself that didn't know how to say no.

"I'm not leaving without him, Roan. I mean it."

"Mary—" He put his hands on her arms, gently stroking. Meaning only to comfort her...make her see reason. Honest to God.

She shook her head rapidly, further dislodging her hair from its haphazard moorings and sending strands of it snaking across her face, giving her the wild look of someone fighting her way through a tempest. "He's not even mine," she said furiously. "He's Queenie's stupid cat. I know he's hateful and ugly, but she left him with me. I'm responsible for him. I can't just *leave* him here. What if someone comes for me and...and hurts him? I can't..." The words trailed off.

For a moment she simply stared at him, a

strange fierce light in her eyes. He'd seen it before, that look, during his skydiving training. It was the look of someone about to jump out of an airplane...terrified, but committed. Then, to his utter astonishment, she reached up and took off his sunglasses. For another few seconds she burned that look into his eyes...then hooked a hand around his neck, leaned up and kissed him.

He barely felt the soft pillowing of her mouth against his before it burst like ripe fruit in the sun, flooding him with her warm, sweet essence. The taste and smell and feel of her woman's body blew through him like summer winds, and remembered heat and sweat and desperate lust of the golden summers of his youth collided with the cold and barrenness of the recent past to form a storm cell within him of epic intensity. It slammed into him with a concussion like thunder. Heat raced through his blood, electricity crackled along his skin.

For a moment, stunned, he merely took what she offered. Then suddenly he was plundering deeper, greedily...driving his hands into her hair while his mouth bore down on hers, demanding more...and more still wasn't enough. There was desperation in the way his mouth devoured her, recklessness in his exploring hands, fostered by a need greater than anything he'd ever known before.

But then…he'd never been hungry for so long, and this was a need only a starving man could know.

She tore her mouth from his at last and clung to him, sobbing…gasping for breath. Holding her, he returned to his senses slowly… first to discover they were both shaking, then that his hand was molded to the shape of her breast and his work-roughened skin separated from the delicate silkiness of hers only by the thinnest layer of lace. Not surprisingly, the sweater she was wearing had been no barrier to him at all.

"I'm sorry." She gulped the words in a tear-thickened voice, not pulling away from him but lowering her face so his lips, already burning with thirst for her, could only find solace in the smooth moist skin of her forehead.

Breath gusted from his chest and stirred her hair. "Mary…"

She gave her head a quick, hard shake… pressed her hand against him, trembling— pushing him away or imploring him to stay? He could feel the battle raging inside her as she said with a heart-rending travesty of a laugh, "That wasn't—I know there must be rules against you...against us doing this."

"Probably," he said, laughing with her, in too much turmoil himself to realize how much she wanted him to deny it. "I don't think the situation's come up before."

He caught only a glimpse of her ravaged face before she turned away from him. One glimpse of pride and despair, hope and grief... And it hit him then, like a nightmare he hadn't had in so long he'd forgotten how terrible it could be—a sense of loss like a huge dark hole opening up in front of him where his future ought to be.

I can't lose this woman. Even if it means my job, my career. I'm not going to let her go.

Before the thought had completely formed in his mind his hand lashed out, caught her by the arm and spun her back to him. She came against his chest with a force that drove a gasp from her lungs, and his mouth was there to take it from her. She made a sound— a cry, a whimper, a sob—and he took that, too. Took it, and gave her back everything that was inside him he hadn't been able to find words to say.

At first, he cradled her head between his

two hands, afraid if he let go he might lose her again. Holding her like that, he kissed her mouth, her throat, the wound on her cheek, her eyelids…and when his lips tasted moisture there, felt a stinging in his own throat and the backs of his eyes. Only when he felt her hands tugging at his shirt did he scoop his hands underneath her sweater to reclaim the sweet, aching pleasure of skin on skin. His hands on her skin…her hands on his…oh yes, it was pleasure, and a fierce wild joy he'd sorely missed.

But it was also a strange kind of relief he felt—relief in knowing at last and beyond any doubt that he and this woman were both of like mind and had crossed an invisible line together…two people on a toboggan that had been balanced on the lip of a mountain but had now tipped irrevocably and begun its dangerous, exilarating journey. For better or worse, there was no getting off now. No turning back.

Treated to the sensory wonder of his hands on her nakedness, he couldn't get enough, couldn't get her clothes out of the way fast enough. The fact that she seemed caught on the same snag didn't help matters; the soft whimpering sounds she made, the cool slide of her hands over his fevered skin were like throwing gasoline on a conflagration. Or maybe it was just *her,* this woman who'd been called mousy, this redhead who wasn't…this proud woman with a panther's walk and fire-and-rain eyes and a mouth that had almost but not quite forgotten how to smile. Without doing a thing, she was more than enough to set a man on fire.

He pulled back from her a little, needing a respite from the sledgehammer pounding of his heart, and she took advantage of the space that opened between them to pull her sweater over her head and drop it to the floor. She stood there and looked at him then, eyes hot and vulnerable at the same time, and instead of quieting down, his heart leaped into his throat. Her breasts, rising and falling with her quick, shallow breaths, were just barely covered by the thinnest and most delicate lace.

Desire shuddered through him. He cupped her breasts in his palms as if they were gifts he'd been given…stroked the beaded tips through the transparent fabric and murmured, "Wow… Miss Mary, it appears you have unplumbed depths."

A breathy giggle somehow broke loose from her ragged respirations. "Feel free to plumb them—" her voice caught, and she finished in a choking whisper "—if you want."

"Oh, I want." He hooked his thumbs in the straps of her bra and drew them slowly over her shoulders. "I definitely want." Dazed... humbled by the beauty of what he'd uncovered...what she'd offered, he lifted his eyes to hers and said in a thickened voice, "That's... if you want, too."

It was another thing he'd forgotten—the vulnerability. Intimacy never had come easy for him. He and Erin had been kids together, played naked in the sprinkler together. Skinny-dipped together. Yet he remembered the first time they'd made love—virgins, both of them—how scared he'd been, not just the usual kind of performance anxiety most of the guys he knew wouldn't ever admit to having, not in a million years, and probably did a whole lot of bragging to cover up. No... the kind of fear he'd felt had been more in the nature of *awe,* an overwhelming sense of wonder at the magnitude of this step he was taking...that *they* were taking. He and Erin. That this woman would open up the most private and personal, intimate part of herself... to *him.* That he would allow her to see him without any of his defenses…utterly naked in every sense of the word.

After Erin, he'd thought he'd never go through that with another woman, ever again. And yet…here he was.

"I want," she whispered.

He released a breath he didn't know he'd been holding…closed his eyes and lowered his head…pressed his mouth to her throat… her breasts…moistening her skin and the lace alike with his essence. Inhaled deeply…he'd forgotten how good a woman's skin smelled. Tasted. Felt.

The desire to bury himself in her warm body and lose himself there was so intense he felt dizzy with it…hollow, as if he hadn't eaten in days. His stomach growled, and it made him think again of Erin, other times, before they'd made love, when they'd been necking and his stomach would growl, and she'd tease him about being hungry. *Oh, yeah…but not that kind of hungry.*

That memory led to another—the reason for those frustrating make-out sessions when he'd been so hard and hot and young enough to think he'd surely die from it: he'd been too afraid to buy condoms, because he figured if Boyd found out—and he was sure to find out, in a town where everybody knew everybody's business and the only drug store was owned by Boyd's late wife's cousin—he'd kill him.

Then one day when they were cleaning out the stables together, Boyd had handed him a packet of condoms. Roan could still hear the rancher's crusty voice, could still recall, word for word, what he'd said: *"You care about a gal, you take care of her. You hear me, son? You take care of my girl."*

Take care of her... Well, he'd done his best. To the best of his knowledge, his father-in-law hadn't ever held it against him that his best hadn't been good enough.

"Mary..." He pulled away from her with a groan of regret he felt deep in his belly... his groin...all the way to his toes. "We can't do this. Not now. I don't have anything. I'm sorry..."

"There's a package of condoms in the medicine cabinet," she said in a strangled voice. And quickly added when his startled stare jerked to hers, "Not mine—they came with the house. I guess Queenie forgot them." There was a different kind of light in her eyes, one he'd never seen there before. "Either that, or..."

"A housewarming gift?" He managed to

say it with a straight face, though he'd already realized the light in her eyes must be laughter. It seemed so improbable, so rare, that glint of wicked humor, his impulse was to shelter and nourish it with secret delight, like an orchid found blooming in a dark wood.

"Talk about unplumbed depths," Mary murmured solemnly.

And suddenly they were holding each other again, clinging hard, her face buried in the curve of his neck, his in her hair, both of them shaking with smothered laughter, giddy relief and maybe fear.

"Do you want to go get them," he whispered finally, "or shall I?"

"You go. Just don't…" She tipped her head back and her eyes, fathomless and green as oceans, searched his. "Don't be too long." Again her voice was unsteady, and he knew what she'd left unsaid.

Don't take too long…don't think too much… don't lose this.

"Count on it," he growled. He kissed her long and deeply, then left her.

It's because of moments like this, Mary thought as she waited for Roan to return, lovers consider darkness a friend.

Darkness would have spared her the agony of wondering how to wait for him...whether to undress or not...whether to wait for him in bed or not. How humiliating it would be if she did those things, and he changed his mind. Came to his senses.

Nothing like putting on a condom, she thought, fingers lingering uncertainly on the zipper of her slacks, to shine the cold light of reality on an insanity like this.

But, looking at it from the other side, how would it be if he came back dressed and ready, so to speak, to find her dressed and *not?* How embarrassing would that be for him?

Resolute now, and before she could change her mind again, she kicked off her shoes, pulled down the zipper and stepped out of her slacks. One issue decided.

She was still debating the second, standing beside her bed wearing nothing but a scrap of lace and trying to keep herself from shaking like a leaf, when Roan came into the room. She half turned, eyes filled with all the questions she couldn't ask. And one look at him told her all she needed to know—that he hadn't changed his mind, that what she was wearing, or he was wearing, or where she waited, in daylight or darkness…none of it mattered at all.

He'd taken off his boots and uniform belt and shirt, but not his pants. His hard, muscular body, pale as a marble sculpture except for the dark V of tan at his throat and a dusting of mink-brown hair, seemed to shimmer in the mist that came suddenly to cloud her eyes. Even so, she couldn't mistake the glitter of desire in his…or the naked vulnerability.

Her heart gave a leap she feared would send it through the wall of her chest. She had time for one glad cry and then his arms were strong around her, and his body hard against her softness, scorching wherever it touched her. His mouth opened with hers, both of them ravishing…hungry. His heartbeat thumped against her breasts. One big hand scraped down her naked back and skimmed roughly over her hip, taking the scrap of lace with it… then turned gentle as it slipped between her legs. Warm fingers cupped her, found their way between folds already moist and ready for him…stroked, tested…then pushed inside. The sensation tore through her…jolted her…stunned her. He captured her gasp in his mouth.

It had been too long, the sensation was too

raw. The penetration brought her almost instantly to shuddering, knee-buckling climax.

She was sobbing when he laid her down… trembling when he coaxed her legs apart, opened her to him and held her there with gentle hands and insistant thumbs…whimpering when he licked into her and stroked her once again to the brink of madness. And when he slid inside her at last, hard and hot and full, she sobbed again as she cried out his name.

Chapter Fourteen

He'd forgotten the feeling. Or had he ever known this desperate, driving need, this lust so savage it was like a wild animal clawing at his belly? The sensation of being wrenched inside-out, hollowed-out, pumped dry? And he'd forgotten, too, the relief that came afterward, relief so complete, exhaustion so overwhelming he wondered whether he would ever move again.

Wished he'd never have to move from where he was at that moment...a woman's long sleek body beneath him, pulsing warm around him, heart tapping lightly against his chest, hands gliding over his sweat-slicked back, shallow uneven breaths stirring his hair. *This woman. Mary.*

Mary. The name quivered through him like a seismic shockwave. What had he done?

He raised himself and looked down at her... mouse-brown hair spread across the flowered bedspread, porcelain skin still stained with the flush of passion and dusted across the bridge of her nose with tiny jewel-like drops of sweat. Her eyes were closed, the lashes clumped together in wet spikes, and her mouth was swollen and glazed with moisture from his kisses. He stared at her...framed her face with his hand and lightly brushed his thumb across her lips...and waited for the regrets to come. *What have I done?*

What had he done? Made love to a woman for the first time since his wife died, a woman in his protective custody, a woman he'd arrested, a woman accused of cold-blooded murder. Surely, there would be regrets... shouldn't there?

But all he felt was a tremendous sense of awe, and pride, and yes...of ownership. For Mary he felt warmth and tenderness, and maybe something deeper. Yes...time to admit it was definitely something deeper. And instead of feeling scared or ashamed or guilty about that, he felt...*happy.*

He leaned down to kiss her and felt her lips curve under his with her smile. "I'm trying to think of something to say," he said softly between light, brushing kisses. "Guess what I am is speechless."

"Yeah, me too." She nudged his lips with hers.

He felt her stir beneath him and instantly tensed. "Am I too heavy?"

Her arms tightened fiercely around him. "No—I love the way you feel...inside me. I wish—" She didn't finish it, but he knew what she meant. He felt that way, too. "It's been...a very long time," she whispered brokenly.

His throat tightened. Frowning into her eyes, stroking her wounded cheek with the backs of his fingers, he asked thickly, "Did I hurt you?"

Her eyebrows rose in surprise. "No—oh, no. I'm fine— really." Her smile was like a flash of sunlight, and he felt it warm his soul as he kissed her.

Then, with the tightness still gripping his throat, he murmured, "It's been a long time for me, too. First time since my wife died, actually."

"Really?" Her eyes widened with shock. "Wow—why? I mean, I know why I didn't, but…"

"Why didn't you?" He didn't want to talk about the terrible grief and rage that had left him a hollowed-out shell for so long. He'd tell her someday. Not now. "Surely not…ten years?"

This time her smile was a faint flicker, without any joy. "No, not ten years. At first I wanted a relationship. I was lonely, you know?" She turned her face away from him, so he eased his weight away from her and propped his head on his hand, leaving his other arm draped across her, keeping her close while she talked. "I'd accepted this would be my life from now on, that there was no going back. And I sure didn't want to spend the rest of my life alone. So I tried it, a few times. But always…at a certain point there'd be this… I'd have this need to share who I really was, even if it meant breaking security. And I knew I couldn't do that, so… it was really hard." Her voice broke, and she jerked back to look at him with shimmering eyes. "It was…like having to wear a mask all the time, even during the most intimate times. It felt awkward...suffocating." She looked away again and whispered, "In the end, it was just too hard. Intimacy—real intimacy—was impossible. And without it...well, it just wasn't enough. So... I'd break it off and move on. Eventually I stopped trying."

There was silence, then, while Roan stared down at her face, lashes quivering on her cheek, moisture pooled in the corner of her eye. He cleared his throat and said huskily, "Well, seeing as how I already know all your secrets—" he bent down and touched his mouth to the tear puddle, dispersing the salty sweetness over his lips and her eyelid like dew "—there's no mask necessary anymore. Not with me."

She turned her face to him; her eyes searched his and slowly came alive with wonder. "No..." she breathed, like someone beholding a miracle. "I guess...that's true."

He lowered his mouth to hers and kissed her deeply, taking a long sweet time about it. Desire for her was welling up hot in him again, like steam in a geyser, and when he rolled onto his back and brought her on top of him, her body already felt familiar to him. Her soft warm body slid over his hardness like an all-over caress, as she settled herself with a pleased little wiggle and a chuckle of surprise.

"Told you it's been a long time," Roan growled.

The SUV sped along the two-lane paved road that wound between pastures nestled among foothills studded with junipers and carpeted with wildflowers. Along the summits, pine trees stood like dark sentinels against a pale-blue sky streaked with feathery clouds. Roan drove with the windows down, and the air was warm and smelled of grass and pine needles and grazing cattle and all sorts of new growing things. It teased Mary's hair and stirred across her skin like a lover's caress, reminding nerve-endings of sensations reawakened such a short time ago.

Memories of that reawakening blew through her with a blast of heat that took her breath away. She glanced over at Roan, biting her lip to hold back a smile. But he was driving, as he had been since they'd left Hartsville, with one elbow planted on the window ledge, his hand resting across the bottom part of his face, eyes narrowed behind his sunglasses and focused on something far beyond the road ahead. He'd done that on the way back from Bozeman, she remembered—it seemed an age ago now, the day she'd first known she was falling in love with the Marlboro Man—the Sheriff of Hart County, Montana.

Heartbreak County, she thought, and felt the heat inside her dissipate before a wicked little chill of fear.

"Regrets?" she asked softly.

He threw her a quick surprised glance. His eyes were shielded behind the glasses, now, but a smile deepened the little depressions in his cheeks in a way that made her heart wallow drunkenly. "Regrets? Nah...worries, maybe." Eyes back on the road, his smile grew wry.

"Worries?"

He chuckled. "Yeah, like how I'm gonna keep my hands off you when you're sleeping under my roof, living with me in my house, right along with my father-in-law and my child."

Her stomach was quivering with something that felt oddly like butterflies, and she didn't reply.

After a moment Roan threw her another glance, this one without the smile. "Truth is,

Mary, I don't know quite what I'm gonna do about you." She couldn't think how to answer that, so she didn't. He faced front again and gave a gusty sigh. "I don't know if you have any idea how you've complicated my life."

"*Your* life!" It burst from her on a gust of incredulous laughter. "What about mine? I've got a hitman after me and a murder charge hanging over my head!"

"Yeah," he growled, "and I'm the one that's got to keep you safe and at the same time find some evidence that'll clear you."

Happiness burst inside her and spread through her whole being. She felt breathless with joy and hope. "You believe me? That I'm innocent?"

"Well, yeah, I thought I made that pretty clear a little while back." He glanced at her, forehead creased in a puzzled little frown, then shifted as he faced forward again, as if the seat was getting uncomfortable for him. "Never did think you were guilty, to tell the truth."

"Then why—" She shook her head, unable to finish it. Her lips felt numb. Her face and throat ached. She couldn't think of that dreadful humiliating time without feeling sick.

"Why did I arrest you?" This time the look

he gave her was dark with anger, though she felt fairly certain it wasn't directed at her. "Because," he said in a quiet and dangerous rumble, like the grinding of rock, "if I hadn't, someone else would have." And she watched his face—the part she could see—close up as dramatically as if a curtain had been whisked across it. After a moment he said in a voice as expressionless as his features, "I figured if I did it I'd at least have some control over how it was done. How you were treated." He flicked her another brief glance. "Hope it wasn't too bad for you. I tried to spare you where I could."

There was an ache in her throat she couldn't explain—unless it was a response to the emotions she could sense simmering beneath the surface of his icy calm...intense emotions she couldn't begin to understand. There was hurt, there, too.

She opened her mouth to answer him, but the words weren't there. What she really wanted—desperately longed to do—was reach across the console between them and take his hand... touch his arm...rub the back of his neck. But she didn't know if she had the right to such gestures of intimacy.

Intimacy. They'd shared a kind, certainly—

the physical kind, thoughts of which made her whole body blush even now. But this was different. Emotional intimacy...intimacy of the heart and soul. The difference between sex and love. For a long time she'd thought the two were one and the same. She knew better now.

She gave her head an ambiguous shake and looked away.

Roan cursed himself in silence. Helpless fury simmered in his belly. *Hope it wasn't too bad.... Yeah, right.* If he'd had any hopes of kidding himself about how bad it had been for her, being arrested, processed and jailed for murder, the memory of Mary's pinched, pale face would have set him straight.

He knew one thing: He couldn't let her go back to jail—and it would be state prison, next time, not Hart County's relatively friendly lockup. He couldn't even let himself think about that.

One more thing he knew: Whether or not he'd gotten her into the mess she was in, he for damn sure was the only one who could get her out.

Simple enough, really. All he had to do was get the guy who wanted her dead, put him away and find Jason Holbrook's killer.

As he thought that, the SUV topped the last rise before the long sweep down to the ranch. He heard Mary's breathing catch, then a long soft sigh, and his heart lifted under his ribs at the thought that she was seeing it the way he did every day of his life, only for the very first time...foothills layered with pine and aspen rolling away to hazy purple mountains capped with snow even in the dead of summer. He never got tired of that vista. Erin had loved it, too. Was it too much to hope for, that he might find another woman who would love it as much? Who'd be as happy here as Erin had been?

The road dropped away beneath the wheels of the SUV, but the hollow sensation in Roan's stomach was from something else entirely.

It *was* too much to hope for. So far out of the realm of possibility he was a fool even to think about it. Mary Owen was a woman living in exile. She'd had a life and a career she loved in the big city and would undoubtedly wish to return to it, if she could. If he made it possible. And what bitter irony, he thought, that by eliminating the threats hanging over Mary's head and giving her back her life, he was sure to lose her.

* * *

"Are you sure this is going to be all right with, um…the rest of your family?" Mary asked as the SUV rolled past corrals, feed silos and majestic cottonwoods wearing the soft new green of spring.

The thumbprint in Roan's cheek deepened with a smile. "You mean Boyd, I imagine— you know Susie Grace is going to be tickled, uh, pink. She's been pesterin' for a week to have you over for dinner."

"All right, Boyd, then." She drew an uneven breath; the quivering in her stomach was definitely butterflies. She'd never met Boyd Stuart, but she knew who he was. Original owner of this ranch, father of Roan's murdered wife. And how was he going to feel about his son-in-law bringing a strange woman into his daughter's house? His granddaughter's? A woman accused of murder, at that?

Roan's grin widened as he pulled the SUV to a stop in the shade of another of those giant cottonwood trees. "Ah, hell, don't let Boyd scare you. He might be crusty on the outside, but his insides are pure puddin'." He took the keys from the ignition and turned to look at her. "He knows all about you, by the way—

thinks you're innocent, too. Calls you 'that little ol' gal.'"

Mary touched the back of her hand to her lips to contain a helpless gurgle of laughter. Roan took off his sunglasses and tucked them in his shirt pocket, and the softness in his eyes, so different from their usual piercing glitter, brought an unexpected sting to hers.

He jerked his head toward his side window. "Well, here it is. It ain't the Ritz, but for the next little while you're gonna be calling it home."

She ducked her head to look out the window and saw a handsome house trimmed with white siding and natural stone, with a wide and welcoming porch skirted with holly and evergreens across the front. Lilacs bloomed along the split-rail fence that separated the yard from the driveway. "It looks lovely," she said. Then, because of something she'd heard in his voice…seen in his eyes, she looked at him and added quietly, "Actually, I've never been that fond of the Ritz."

There was a pause while they looked into each other's eyes, and Mary wondered whether he was any better at figuring out her feelings than she was his. Then Roan said brusquely, "Well—no sense in sitting here in the car." He opened the door, but paused a moment before getting out to nod toward the front of the car. "Here comes the welcoming committee."

Oh dear, Mary thought. Much as she'd have liked to accept Roan's assessment of his father-in-law's nature as gospel, she couldn't see any part of the man ambling toward them down the shade-dappled lane that might be described as "puddin'." Crusty, yes. That part she could definitely believe.

Boyd Stuart was angular and rawboned, small in stature—very likely smaller than he'd once been, thanks to decades of having his spine pounded on by a hard leather saddle. He walked with the bent-over, bandy-legged cowboy's gait she'd grown accustomed to seeing in the years she'd been living in the Great American West. He wore the rancher's uniform of boots, Levi's, long-sleeved blue work shirt and a sweat-stained baseball cap with a tractor manufacturer's logo on it. A pair of mottled gray cattle-herding dogs trotted along beside him.

"Oh, Cat's going to love this," Mary said as she gathered her courage, opened her door and climbed out of the car.

"What, you mean the dogs?" Roan threw

her look across the roof of the SUV. "They're used to the barn cats. They won't bother him."

"Tell that to Cat." She could hear a loud growling sound emanating from the back seat as the dogs came ranging up to lick Roan's hands. Having said their hellos, they then ambled over more slowly to check her out. She stood still, murmuring hopeful reassurances, while they sniffed her avidly—smelling the cat, no doubt. Having evidently decided she was Friend, they bumped and snuggled against her legs, begging to be petted. She bent down to oblige them with pats and coos and ear-fondles, and when she straightened up, Boyd was coming to a halt a few yards away.

The rancher took off his cap, wiped his pale forehead with his shirtsleeve and put it back on again. He flicked her a glance and a nod, then looked at Roan and gestured toward the sheriff's department SUV. "What's the law doin' out here this time a' day?" His growly voice reminded her of Roan's, only rustier.

Roan looked over at Mary, flashed her a reassuring smile. "Got somebody here I want you to meet. Boyd... Mary Owen— or, I guess it's Yancy, right? Anyway, Mary, this is my father-in-law, Boyd Stuart."

Mary nodded and smiled, uncertain whether to offer her hand or not. But the rancher nudged the bill of his cap back with his thumb, swiped his gnarled hand across the front of his shirt and then held it out to her with a gruff, "I know who you are. How-do, miss."

And that was when she saw that the hand he offered her bore the silvery discoloration of burn scars, and that above the grizzled jaws and weathered, leathery skin that covered the lower two-thirds of his face, his blue eyes were filled with a bottomless sadness. Kind eyes, she thought, that would never really smile again.

She took the scarred hand and murmured, "I'm so happy to meet you."

"So," Roan said, raking a hand through his hair in an uncharacteristically awkward gesture, "where's your sidekick?"

"Little bit?" Boyd scowled and made a cranky gesture with his hand that failed to override the affection in his voice. "Ah, she's off somewheres—barn, probably. One of the cats had a litter, and she's bound and determined to find her nest. She'll come a'runnin', once she knows you're here."

"I can't stay." Roan shot Mary another look,

one she couldn't read. "I need to get back to town. A lot going on I need to tend to."

The rancher took off his cap again...put it back on. "Yeah? How'd that go—the big parade?"

"Parade went fine," Roan said, and his eyes were hard and flinty. "Somebody took a shot at Mary, though."

Boyd's head rocked back as if someone had thrown a punch at him. "You don't say."

"'Fraid so. That's why I brought her out here. She's gonna need a safe place to stay until we can get whoever's responsible. You mind getting her settled in? Show her around? Like I said, I need to get on back."

"Sure," said Boyd. "No problem. Where you wanna put her?"

Mary opened her mouth, but her panic-stricken cries—*Don't go! Don't leave me!*—were all inside her head.

Roan had the back of the SUV open and was hauling out her suitcase and the cat carrier and the large shopping bag with the cat supplies in it. He set them beside the opening in the split rail fence, then looked up and said, "Put her in my room." This time Mary managed to produce sound, but no discernible words. He opened the car door and paused, half in and half out, to give her a long, burning look. "I'll sleep on the couch."

He slid behind the wheel and slammed the door, and the SUV roared to life. Mary and Boyd stood side by side without speaking and watched it execute a wrenching three-point turn, then accelerate down the lane, crunching gravel and spitting dust.

For a few more seconds the dust and the silence hovered in the air. Then Boyd made an abrupt beckoning gesture with one hand, picked up her suitcase with the other and said gruffly, "No sense standin' out here in the yard. Come on in the house—I'll show you to Roan's room." He started across the enclosed yard, moving surprisingly quickly in his odd crabbed gait—rather like the oldtime Western movie star, John Wayne, in a hurry.

Mary picked up the cat carrier and the shopping bag and followed. "Oh, please don't put him out of his room," she said, puffing a little as she hurried to catch up. "The couch—anything will be fine for me."

Boyd glanced over at the cat carrier, apparently ignoring that remark. "What you got there?" When the carrier's occupant responded with a furious growl, he chuckled and said, "Oh—big old fella." Then he looked up at Mary, and there was a gleam in his sad old eyes.

"Shoot, Roan don't hardly ever use it anyhow, the hours he keeps. Waste of a perfectly good mattress, you ask me." He opened the front door and held it with his backside while Mary slipped past him into the house, then pulled the door shut and clumped ahead of her across an entryway of polished pine. She barely had time to notice the large open rooms with vaulted ceilings, a sense of warmth and light and natural colors, a feeling of the outdoors brought inside, before following her host down a wide carpeted hallway that ended abruptly at a plywood barricade. Halfway down the hall, Boyd turned into an open doorway. Mary followed him into a room that was much smaller and plainer than she'd expected.

Boyd set the suitcase down with a thump on a Navajo patterned rug. "There you go," he said, then straightened, hooked a thumb in the pocket of his Levi's and surveyed the room with narrowed eyes, scratching his stubbled chin. "You'll most likely be wantin' clean sheets and such. You'll find some in that chest a' drawers over yonder. Bathroom's around the corner, next to the kitchen. You think of anything else you need, give me a holler."

"I wish you'd just let me have the couch," Mary murmured absently, trying not to look with too much curiosity...trying not to think about the fact that she was standing in Roan's bedroom. His private space. *Intimacy*....

"Couch is comfortable enough," Boyd admitted, hitching one shoulder. "Use it myself now and then, when Roan's in town late and I need to stay here with the little bit. Most a' the time I have my own place up the road—foreman's cottage. Suits me fine." He paused, then shook his head in a way that brooked no further argument. "Woman needs her privacy. You let Roan take the couch—he's young, won't hurt him none. And you've got the cat. Cats don't like strange places. You'll be needing to shut him up, I reckon." There was a definite twinkle in his eye as he nodded toward the case Mary was still holding. "Tell you a trick my wife used to use, to get a cat to settle in a new place. What you do is, you put butter on his paws."

"Really?" Mary said over Cat's outraged yowl. "That works?"

Boyd bobbed his head. "M'wife swore it did. Said the cat'd be so busy cleanin' the butter off his paws, he'd forget all about bein' in a strange place." He turned to the door with one of his abrupt hand gestures. "Well—I'll lct you get settled—" he turned back in his bent-over, arthritic way "—unless you'd like to see around the place first…"

"I'd like that," Mary said, with silent apologies to Cat. She'd wait to let him out of the carrier until she could stay to keep an eye on him. No telling what kind of damage he might do, the mood he was in.

Out in the hallway, she paused to look questioningly at the plywood barricadc. Boyd's hand gesture as he turned away from it was even more blunt and dismissive than usual.

"Used to be the master bedroom back there—Roan's den…baby's room…" His crusty voice had thickened. "Burned down a few years back. Roan never has got around to rebuilding it."

Mary sucked in air, but he left her no time for apologies, or to dwell on the dreadful images that came swarming into her mind. Chilled, she followed Boyd through a cursory tour of the house, and was glad when they came again into the warm spring sunshine, where the scent of lilacs and boistcrous greetings from the dogs helped to banish the ghost of past tragedy.

The dogs' names, she learned, were Rocky and Bear. They were Australian shepherds, and she could tell them apart easily enough because Rocky had one blue eye. Completely accepting of her now, they trotted at her heels as often as they did Boyd's, as they walked down the cottonwood-shaded lane between storage sheds of all shapes and sizes, corral fences and horse stables, most of them painted a dark red with white trim.

"You ride?" he asked, as they were walking through one of the stables, empty and remarkably cool and quiet for late afternoon. It smelled—not unpleasantly—of leather and straw, manure and something faintly salty Mary could only assume was *horse*.

"No," she said quickly, repressing a shudder—not wanting to be impolite, "not really."

Boyd chuckled. "Well…little bit'll have you mounted up in no time, I expect."

Not if I can help it, Mary thought.

Last stop on the tour was a huge old barn at the end of the lane. Again, the interior of the barn was cool and dim, shot through with fingers of sunlight from cracks in the siding and tiny dust-clouded windows high in the walls. Stacks of hay bales filled most of the space, along with a lot of tools and other mysterious objects that appeared to be very, very old. Antiques, Boyd explained proudly. Relics from the Old West he'd collected over the years.

He halted and called up toward the rafters, "Hey, little bit, come on down here, now. We got company."

There was a pause, and then a small face framed with tousled red hair appeared at the very top of the tallest haystack. The face split into a wide, off-center grin. "Hi," Susie Grace called down in a hoarse whisper. "I can't come down right now. I'm holding kittens. You want to see them? They're really cute. You can climb up here, if you want to."

Mary opened her mouth. Looked at Boyd, who grinned and shrugged his shoulders. She drew a quivering breath, the feelings inside her as hard to pin down as the dust motes dancing in those shafts of sunlight. Then she shrugged, stepped up onto the lowest layer of bales, and began to climb, Susie Grace calling encouragement and helpful instructions in her raspy whisper. She reached the top of the stack, weak-kneed but triumphant, and turned to wave at Boyd, who touched his cap with a finger, then turned and stumped off on some chore of his own.

Susie Grace scooted back to make room for Mary on the bales, crossing her legs under her Indian-style. She was cradling two tiny black-and-white kittens against her chest. She waited until Mary had settled herself, then peeled one of the kittens off of her T-shirt and commanded, "Hold out your hands."

Mary obeyed, holding her breath. She let it out in an awed and inarticulate whisper as the kitten's warm squirmy weight settled into her cupped palms.

"Hold it like this," Susie Grace said. "They like it under your neck—see?" She giggled. "It *tickles*." She eyed Mary, who was laughing, too. "Didn't you ever hold a kitten before?"

"Not this little," Mary said shakily. The kitten's tiny round head was bumping under her chin.

"I love kittens. They're my favorite animal. Well…second favorite, after horses. I like all animals, actually. I'm going to be a veterinarian when I grow up."

"Where is the mother?" Mary was busy now, trying to keep the kitten from climbing up her sweater, over her shoulder and down the other side.

"Probably hunting mice. Or gophers or

something. I waited until she left before I started searching for the nest. Mother cats don't like it when you bother their babies. Sometimes they move them, and then you have to start looking all over again."

"You certainly know a lot about animals," Mary said, smiling at her.

Susie Grace accepted the accolade with a nod. "I like animals because they don't care what people look like. They only care about smell and if you're nice to them or not."

Mary watched the kitten cuddle happily against the little girl's scarred and puckered skin and felt her heart swell with emotions she'd never felt before. Was this what it meant to love a child, she wondered? She hadn't thought it would hurt so much. "You could have surgery," she said huskily. "To make your scars better."

"I know." Susie Grace took a breath and quickly huffed it out again. "But I don't want to. I'm afraid it will hurt. It hurt really, really bad when I got burned."

"Well," Mary said with care, lest her emotions leak into her voice, "maybe you'll change your mind someday...when you grow up... have a boyfriend."

Susie Grace shook her head. "I'm not going to have a boyfriend."

"Why not?"

"Because...boys like pretty girls." Susie Grace shrugged.

A wave of anger took Mary's breath away. "You *are* pretty."

Susie Grace rolled her eyes. "That's what my dad says."

"Well, maybe you should believe him." Susie Grace's reply was another shrug. "Look," Mary said firmly, peeling the kitten off her sweater and placing it in Susie Grace's lap, "I'm not your dad. And I used to be a model. So I think I ought to know what pretty is. And I'm telling you—you *are* pretty. You can believe that."

Susie Grace didn't say a word. Keeping her face averted, she carefully put the kittens back in their straw nest. "Let's go see the horses," she said, and turning onto her belly, slipped over the edge of haystack.

Mary sat where she was for a few moments, fighting back the furious tears that were burning her eyes and throat. Then, a resolute smile pasted firmly on her face, she followed the little girl down the stack.

Horses again, she thought. *Wonderful.*

* * *

"This one's mine," said Susie Grace, reaching through the corral fence to stroke the face of an animal roughly the same color as her hair and tall as a small mountain. "Her name's Tootsie—isn't she beautiful?"

"Mmm," said Mary. *And big. Very big.*

Susie Grace giggled. "Here—give her some grain. She likes to eat out of your hand. Only you have to keep your fingers flat, or else she might bite them. Not on purpose, though. Horses can't see what's down there by their mouth, you know. It's kind of hard to tell fingers from something good to eat, just with the end of your nose. You should try it sometime." She shot Mary a look full of mischief as she held out the bucket of grain.

"Thanks—I'll take your word for it," Mary said dryly. She scooped a handful of grain from the bucket, closed her eyes, sent up a prayer, and thrust her hand between the boards of the fence. And gave a little gasp of surprise. It felt as if somebody was nuzzling her hand with a velvet boxing glove.

"You can pet her," said Susie Grace. "She likes it when you scratch her under her chin—like this."

Not wanting to disappoint the child, Mary

did…then, when nothing terrible seemed about to happen, ran her hand along the hard round jaw…then daringly over the neck…then the shoulder. Shivering inside with fear and wonder and excitement. She thought again of velvet, except this was warmer and damper than velvet, and underneath the velvet was a whole lot of muscle. Mountains of muscle.

Another velvety muzzle bumped against her arm, demanding a share of the attention, and Mary said, "Oh—" and laughed as she transferred her stroking to the newcomer. This one was a lovely mottled gray, like dappled shade on snow. It had a darker gray muzzle, and the softest darkest eyes she'd ever seen. "What's this one's name?"

"That's Angel." Susie Grace's eyes were on her scarred hands as they methodically stroked Tootsie's neck. "She's my mommy's horse. Her name used to be Dancer when she was a barrel racer, but now it's Angel, because my mom is an angel, too." There was a pause, and then she looked up at Mary and said, "She's real gentle. You can ride her if you want to."

Mary's heart dropped into her shoes.

After that, what could she do?

Which was how it happened that the next

morning, a bright sunny Sunday in May, Mary found herself where she'd have been content never in her whole entire life to be— in a saddle on the back of a horse. A horse named Angel.

Chapter Fifteen

Roan had about decided he believed in miracles. He'd never been so inclined before, but lately there'd been too many things happening in his life that couldn't be explained any other way.

Take last night. Coming home past midnight and not finding Boyd snoring away on the sofa had been a bit of a shock, before he'd remembered there was no reason for his father-in-law to stay over when there was another adult in the house to look after Susie Grace. Which was another kind of shock entirely. But that wasn't anything compared to the jolt he got when he went in to kiss his daughter good night and found a big ugly orange tomcat curled up next to her, purring like a buzz saw.

Then...pausing beside his bedroom door, hand on the doorknob, heart pounding like a teenage boy's, thinking of the lush and lovely body tucked between his sheets and aching with wanting to be in there with her. Wanting to kiss her awake and stroke her to shuddering arousal, make love to her until they were both laughing and crying like a couple of kids and too exhausted to move a muscle... then fall asleep with her softness still cuddled against him, her heartbeat tapping against his arm and her body's sweet perfume in every breath he took.

He wasn't sure if that qualified as a miracle or not, but he knew there'd been a time not so long ago when he'd have bet his life he'd never know those feelings again.

Then this morning...waking up to the familiar Sunday-morning smells—bacon and coffee and maple syrup—walking into the kitchen to find Boyd and Mary both there, Boyd trying to show Mary how to flip hotcakes and Susie Grace watching them and laughing so hard she had milk coming out of her nose.

But the capper, the biggest miracle of all, had to be this one before his eyes this very minute, shimmering like a mirage in the hot May sun—Miss Mary on the back of a horse.

And not looking too unhappy about it, either, now she was over her initial fear. Fear? No—he'd seen fear before, but this was sheer terror. Terror Roan had thought was going to send her running for the house like a scalded cat before he'd even got the horses saddled. He didn't suppose he ever would know what had given Mary the courage to get up on that horse. He'd have gladly given her an out rather than look at the fear in those eyes, but she'd refused to fold. And right now he had to say she looked awfully damn good, up there on Erin's dapple-gray mare, ambling through the wildflowers alongside Susie Grace on Tootsie. Looked as if she might have been born to ride all along, and just hadn't known it.

"Seems like she's doing okay," he said to Boyd, his voice gruff with the sheer joy it gave him just to have her here in his world… his place.

Boyd snorted. "Told her little bit'd have her up horseback in no time." He shifted in his saddle. "Don't you worry about that gal. She's gonna be just fine."

Something…an unformed thought, a question, an unfocused awareness…shivered through Roan's insides. Something in the old man's voice that made Roan look over at him with narrowed eyes. But Boyd's gaze was fixed on the two riders up ahead, and his jaw was set in a way that made Roan think of immoveable things, like rocks and mountains.

He shook off the vague uneasiness as he pulled up at the top of the saddleback ridge— from long habit; he was too distracted to appreciate the view this particular day. He had enough on his mind right now without worrying what might be troubling his father-in-law.

"Hard not to worry," he said as Boyd reined Foxy in alongside him. "Still haven't found whoever it was tried to shoot her yesterday. Then there's the little matter of how I'm gonna keep her from going to prison for the rest of her life."

"You'll get him," Boyd growled. "She ain't gonna go to prison."

Again Roan looked over at him with those questions he couldn't quite pin down floating in his mind. But the old man was leaning on his saddlehorn, squinting at the blue mountains off in the distance.

Something stirred across the back of Roan's neck. His Spirit Messenger again? It had been awhile since he'd felt that particular touch, and he was about half amused and half annoyed with himself for entertaining such superstitious nonsense.

He wondered what it was trying to tell him this time.

He didn't have much time to wonder, though, because right then he heard a shout, and at the same time Boyd rose up in his stirrups and said, "Oh hell."

Roan looked where he was looking and saw Susie Grace had gotten impatient, as usual, and taken off across the meadow at full gallop. Right behind her was Mary on the dapple-gray mare, bouncing up and down and holding on for dear life.

"Kid needs a good paddlin'," Boyd said as he nudged his horse forward.

Loping along beside him, Roan was too busy watching Mary to answer that, though at the moment he pretty much agreed with the sentiment. His heart felt as though it had lodged in his throat, and this time it wasn't his daughter he was scared breathless for. "Why the hell is she taking off after her like that? What's she trying to do, *race?*"

Boyd snorted. "Probably wasn't her idea. That horse always did like to run."

"Once a barrel racer, always a barrel racer," Roan muttered.

"Better go after her, boy. Need to be a better rider than that little gal to stay on a cuttin' horse if it takes a notion to change direction."

Roan had already kicked Springer into full gallop.

For Mary the world had become a bouncing, quivering blur that rushed past her at the speed of a runaway train. She couldn't breathe, couldn't scream, though her mouth was wide open. She could feel air rushing into her lungs but couldn't seem to push it back out again. Insects smacked against her face, tears welled up in her eyes and were torn away by the wind. Hard leather spanked her backside and bruised her in even more sensitive places, and all she could do was grip the saddlehorn and hang on, too paralyzed with fear even to pray.

The wild ride ended abruptly, in a slow-motion, nightmarish sort of way. There was an extra hard jolt, and Mary felt herself flying through quiet space...turning gracefully, silently, like a windmill, head over heels. Then she slithered along warm, slick horsehide to land in tall, tickly grass with a thump that jarred her teeth and turned the world blank for a second or two.

She was staring up at the pale-blue sky, brain still on lockdown, when she felt something bump gently against the top of her head. Hot moist breath smelling strongly of masticated hay gusted through her hair. She tilted her head, rolled her eyes back and found herself gazing up at the mottled gray underbelly of a whale. A whale with legs. She whimpered feebly, certain she was about to be trampled to death.

Especially when she felt the ground beneath her shake.

Instead, she heard a voice, deep and growly and hoarse, calling her name. She heard heavy, huffing breaths, the slap of reins and creak of saddle leather, thumping footsteps, and then a pale Stetson blotted out the sky.

"Roan?" she croaked, and heard a sharp exhalation and a whispered, *"Thank God...."*

"Wha' happened?" Was that her voice, so thin and frail? She couldn't seem to get enough air behind it.

"Shh," he said gently, "don't talk. Lie still." He took off his hat and laid it on the grass, then bent over her and looked into her eyes.

She gazed back at him, sure she'd never seen a face so beautiful, even with the mouth hard and tight and eyes narrowed and burning like fire. *No, ice. Fire and ice—that's what he is. Ice on the outside, fire on the inside.*

"I guess I fell off, huh?" she said, answering her own question since he didn't seem inclined to.

The thumbprints in his cheeks deepened, though it would have been a stretch to call the curve of his lips a smile. His hand gently smoothed her hair back from her forehead. "Yeah, you did—wasn't your fault, though."

"I'll say it wasn't!" She struggled to sit up, but Roan's hands kept her from it. "The…stupid horse just…took off. Why'd she do that? I didn't tell her to."

"Your horse took off because Susie Grace's horse did. Herd instinct." He was frowning as his hands roved quickly over her body… her arms, her legs. "All horses like to race— that one in particular. You hurt anywhere?"

"Everywhere," she groaned, but it was a lie; nothing hurt now that he was touching her. Nothing had ever felt so good as those hard, gentle hands.

"Good—pain's good. Means it's not likely your neck's broken." He paused to tilt his head toward the dapple-gray mare, now placidly chomping a mouthful of grass a few feet away. "She used to be a barrel racer."

"Susie Grace mentioned that." Mary had lived in rodeo country long enough to know what barrel racing was. She'd just never realized what that meant. "How does something that *big,* moving that *fast,* stop so *suddenly?*"

Roan's frown relaxed, and his chuckle sounded warm, relieved. "That's a quarter horse for you." He sat back on his heels, one hand draped across his knee, and his eyes caressed her with a light that was like sunshine to growing things.

And like those growing things, she felt herself—not physically, but inside, her whole being—yearning toward him, being pulled to him, nourished by him.

What happens to growing things when the sun goes away?

She glared at his hand, angry with herself for wanting it not to be so far away. For wanting it touching her again.

"Nothing seems to be broken," Roan said,

smiling at her finally. "Guess you can get up now."

"Thanks," Mary muttered, lifting an arm to pillow her head, "but I'd just as soon stay right here." The thought of getting back on that horse made her stomach turn over.

As if he'd read her mind, he brushed her cheek with the backs of his fingers and said softly, "You're gonna have to do it sometime, Miss Mary."

She closed her eyes and stubbornly shook her head. The feel of his fingers on her cheek made her whole face ache. And her heart. *How did I do this? How did I let this happen?*

The ground under her had begun to shake again. She lifted her head and saw Susie Grace galloping toward them up the gentle slope, her blue cowboy hat bouncing against her back. Boyd was there, too, she saw now, sitting on his spotted Apaloosa horse a little way off, leaning on his saddlehorn, watching.

"Mary! Mary—are you all right?" Susie Grace yelled as she reined Tootsie to a jolting, jarring halt. "What happened? I didn't see you. Did you fall off?"

"Stay right where you are, Missy." Roan had risen to his feet, ominous as a thunderhead. He caught the red-gold mare's bridle, patted her sweat-soaked neck and soothed her as she snorted and tossed her head. "What did you think you were doing? Haven't Grampa and I both talked to you about running off like that?" His voice was as stern as Mary had ever heard it.

"I'm sorry," Susie Grace hunched her shoulders, looking small and contrite.

Roan didn't soften an inch. "Sorry's too late. Mary's lucky she didn't break her neck. What would you do if she had, Susan? Tell me that. Sorry isn't gonna fix a broken neck."

Susie Grace, whose face had been crumpling by degrees, opened her mouth and began to wail at the top of her lungs.

"That isn't gonna help," Roan said darkly, raising his voice over the noise. "You're still gonna be grounded a good long while." He looked over at Boyd and jerked his head toward the howling child. "You mind taking her back? Mary and I'll be along in a while."

Boyd clicked to his mare and made a "Come here" gesture with his head. "Come on with me, little bit. Quit bellerin'. This's what happens when you don't do what you're told."

Roan let go of Tootsie's bridle and the mare

trotted off after Boyd, tail switching, Susie
Grace bouncing in the saddle, still wailing.

"She didn't mean to hurt me," Mary said
as she watched them go, more upset from the
child's distress than her own fall.

"I know she didn't." Roan had scooped up
the gray mare's reins and was brushing her
down, checking the cinch, adjusting the stirrups. "That's not the point. She's been told not
to go running off like that, and she did it anyway. Showing off in front of you, I guess, I
don't know. But that's no excuse for not mind-
ing." He glanced at her, then quickly away,
but not before she saw the pain—a parent's
anguish, she realized. She'd never thought
before how hard it must be to discipline a beloved child. "Boyd and I are both pretty easy
on her—maybe too easy. But when I do make
a point to tell her not to do something, there's
generally a damn good reason for it."

He gave the cinch a final tug, patted it flat,
then turned to her and held out his hand.
"Come on—up you get."

He wasn't smiling, but his eyes held something…a glowing warmth, a kindling promise…that made her inside yearn toward him
even as her outside cringed away and her

voice, dark and cracking with suspicion said, "Up where?"

He patted the saddle, the smile coming slowly, now, though still a little wry. "Everybody falls off a horse from time to time. Happens. When it does, what you do is get right back on."

"Uh-uh." She scrambled to her feet, ignoring his hand and trying not to moan as bruises and abused muscles screamed in outrage. "That's what *you'd* do. I, on the other hand, have no intention of getting back on that horse—or any other horse—ever again, thank you very much." She brushed at her rear and glared at him—which wasn't easy, when he looked at her like that.

"How're you gonna get back home?" His face now was serene, and he stood there smiling at her like some kind of cowboy angel, one hand on the back of the saddle, breezes riffling his hair and the sun glancing off it like tiny light-swords.

Her stomach went hollow, then hot. Juices pooled in her throat. "I'll walk," she said doggedly, standing her ground.

He chuckled. Mary sucked in a breath and drew herself up, bolstered, now, by both anger and pride. She peeled a wind-blown lock of hair away from her mouth, then shaded her eyes with her hand. "It's that way, right?"

His laughter was soft as his hand snaked out and caught her arm before she could take the first step...though to be truthful, had she really wanted to? He pulled her to him gently, and her heart began to knock so fiercely against her ribs she could hardly breathe. He captured her face in one big hand; his fingers stroked her hair away from her forehead, his thumb lightly grazed her lips, which parted helplessly under his touch. Her lips felt swollen...hot, as if they'd been stung.

"I'm not getting on that horse," she mumbled.

"Ah, Miss Mary..." His soft growl vibrated deep inside her, seemed to fill all the spaces inside her...like a cat's purr, and between the words he paused to touch warm smooth lips to her forehead, her eyelids, her cheeks, her nose and her chin. "Who'd have thought... you could be...so contrary?"

She whimpered helplessly, already lost. Then...he took her mouth. Not roughly, not greedily, just...completely. His arms came around her, and his body was hard against her breasts, and his mouth was inside and outside...everywhere. It felt warm and fierce...

but gentle, too…warm and sweet and good. It didn't feel like being lost, at all. It felt like coming home.

He kissed her until she was shaking all over, until she thought her legs wouldn't hold her, that she would crumple to the ground if he let her go. But he didn't let her go, only turned his mouth from hers and, gasping, pressed her face against the hollow of his shoulder. And it wasn't his strength and substance and virility that made her throat ache and tears spring unbidden to her eyes. It was the tiny vibrations she could feel coursing through his muscles and deep inside his powerful body…and the realization that it was *she* who'd caused this strong and self-reliant man to tremble.

She felt his chest deflate and a gust of breath stir her hair. "I've been wantin' to do that."

"I've been wanting you to," she whispered.

Holding her body close to his, he leaned his head and shoulders back to look down at her. "Really?" His grin was wider, the dents in his cheeks deeper than she'd ever seen them.

Her heart turned over. "Stop looking so smug," she said, melting inside. "You know I have. I haven't been able to think about anything else since…yesterday."

"No kidding? Not even getting shot at?"

"Not even that," she lied; it didn't seem like the moment to tell him about the nightmares that had plagued her sleep.

"Miss Mary… I'm gonna kiss you again." His voice rumbled from his chest into hers. He touched his lips lightly to the tip of her nose…then her eyelids…then her smile, and she turned her face blissfully upward like a thirsty flower to the rain. "Then… I'm gonna put you up on this horse and take you to a quiet place I know of and make love to you. That okay with you?"

She murmured something drunken in response, no longer caring whether she had to get back on a horse or not. She'd have ridden a buffalo if it meant she could stay with him just a little longer.

He brought her to a meadow glade he knew, where a friendly chuckling creek meandered and the grass was thick and warm and the air smelled of pine needles baking in the sun. He could be alone with her here, and for a few precious hours pretend it was all the world that mattered.

"So beautiful," Mary sighed, walking slowly through the grass, looking around her at the pine trees' sheltering walls.

"Yes," Roan agreed, looking only at her.

He tied the horses in the shade and took off their saddles, then untied the blanket roll on the back of his saddle and spread it on the tall soft grass beside the creek. He turned to Mary and held out his hand. She came to him slowly, like someone in a dream, and he drew a deep, wondering breath, half-afraid to believe this could be real, that he could be here in this place with this woman in this moment, and that he could feel, for the first time in four years, so utterly and completely happy.

He took her face between his two hands and lowered his parted lips to hers, and felt hers stir lazily, drunkenly into a smile. He felt her hands come to lie on his sides…felt the delicate trembling of her body. He made himself kiss her only lightly, at first, holding still and brushing his lips over hers as if it was the very first time, as if he was only now learning the shape and textures of her, testing his patience and self-control. And then, failing the test joyfully, he sank into her warm sweet depths and lost himself there.

"Been wantin' to do this," he mumbled as

he resurfaced dizzy and intoxicated, quaking with need of her already.

"I think we are," she whispered, laughing faintly.

"No...*this*." His fingers felt for the buttons on her shirt...began to work their way down. He drew back a little, asked the question with his eyes, and receiving his answer in her shimmering golden gaze, watched his hands pull the two halves of the shirt apart, then push them over her shoulders.

He undressed her slowly while her eyes clung to him and his to her, skimming his hands and mouth over each part as he uncovered it, touching her lightly the same way he'd kissed her at first, learning her body in its finest detail, committing each detail to memory, taking the taste and texture and smell of her into his pores, his mind, his *being*. And in introducing himself to her body's secrets in sensitive and clever ways, made her his in the only way he knew how.

When she was trembling too hard to stand and begging him in shaken, inarticulate whispers, he laid her down on the blanket, then undressed quickly and stretched himself alongside her, head propped on one hand so he could look down at her, lying golden, flushed and dewy in the sun. Her lips were swollen and moist from his kisses, and when she smiled at him, his heart quivered.

She reached up and touched back a fallen lock from his forehead, then seined through his hair with her fingers, like a weaver. Her lips parted suddenly, urgently, and her breath snagged on the words that didn't come.

"What?" he said tenderly, when he saw something flare, bright and desperate, in her eyes.

For a moment it hovered there, whatever it was she'd wanted to tell him, balanced like a raindrop on the tip of her tongue. Then her face spasmed, so lightly he might have missed it if he hadn't known its shapes and moods so well. Her eyes darkened with something that looked like pain, but she smiled at him brightly and whispered, "I want you to kiss me again…please."

So he did, tenderly as he knew how, his heart swelling inside him with longing and hope…the possibility that the words she couldn't bring herself to say might be the same ones locked inside *his* mind, the ones he still felt he had no right to say. Not yet. Not until he'd made things right for her again.

I love you…stay with me forever.

It was all there in his heart, though, as he kissed her, and she kissed him back eagerly, laughing with tears, as if she heard him.

He took his mouth from hers and moved it to her throat, paused to measure the tripping beat of her pulse…faster, even than his own… then left it to wander down her body. He let his hand lead, cupping each breast before his mouth could find its tip…fingers spreading across the silky skin of her stomach, making patterns for his tongue to follow, while she held his head lightly against her, neither guiding nor impeding, fingers weaving through his hair, warm as blessings on his scalp.

He stroked between her legs and they shifted to allow him access…but she winced when his hand brushed the inside of her thighs. He found the chafed red places where the saddle had rubbed and gently laved them with his tongue, and when she whimpered and squirmed and clutched him closer, he laughed softly and gave the same attention to other parts of her the saddle might have touched.…

Then, mindful of the abuses her tender body had suffered and of the hard ground and meager grass beneath them, he lay back on the blanket and pulled her over him. "Come to me, love," he whispered brokenly, words all but impossible now. "If you want me…inside you now. I really want…need…"

He groaned when her warm hand found and guided him home.

She couldn't stop the tears…it felt so good, the sweet hot sting of him coming inside her. He would wonder—let him wonder. She couldn't breathe, couldn't speak…the only outlet she had for the emotions swelling inside her was tears.

She shuddered, the pressure inside her building, so intense now, even tears weren't enough to relieve it. The delicious sliding pressure of his body…the pressure of her own body's arousal…sensations so exquisite she wondered how she could endure them without going insane. Pressure from emotions so enormous she couldn't contain them…wanted to scream them to the sky…feel their echoes rolling back on her like thunder.

Pressure from emotions so powerful they stunned her to silence, so that all she could do was gaze down at the face of the man beneath her and whisper them in her heart.

I love you…never dreamed I could love anyone so much. How did this happen?

Her body clenched, tighter…tighter. Desperate for release, she couldn't even sob; her breath was trapped high in her chest. Her mind spun her in dizzy circles, as if she had a fever. She was only dimly aware when Roan's strong arms encircled her…pulled her down onto his chest…when his mouth covered hers and captured her struggling breath…and then her high, keening cry as her body let go at last, and came apart in rippling waves.

She felt his body buck beneath her as he held her tightly and rode the waves with her… felt his chest heave and his muscles grow taut with strain before he surged up into her, gave himself to her in his own magnificent release.

In the aftermath they clung to each other, laughing and wiping away tears, rocking each other like giddy children.

Chapter Sixteen

The sun was hot on her back, but she felt too drained to move. Roan's hands, stroking and gentling her, felt the warmth.

"You're gonna get burned," his lion's purr voice rumbled as he nudged her forehead with his chin. Getting only a contented murmur in reply, he chuckled and rolled her over onto the blanket, then eased himself away from her and stood up.

Sunk deep in blissful lethargy, she watched from under a sheltering forearm as he walked naked to the edge of the creek, the hard muscle of his back and buttocks gleaming like marble in the sun. When he dropped to one knee and reached to scoop water from the creek with his cupped hand, she thought of statues of ancient Greek athletes, and didn't even consider it strange to be daydreaming such romantic nonsense when for so many years she hadn't allowed herself to dream at all. Today, her life was filled with wonder and magic, and even miracles seemed possible.

He splashed the crystal-clear water over his face and neck, shoulders and body, then turned to her, smiling, and held out his hand. Droplets of water clung to his hair and eyelashes and gleamed like oil on his cold-flushed skin. She rose to her feet and walked to him in a daze, too deeply under the spell of his warm and worshipful gaze to feel any self-consciousness at all. She was thinking only of him and how beautiful he was, and of how much she loved him and how much she wished they could be like this forever, just the two of them in a perfect little universe of happiness. Like Eden, before the Fall.

The icy water took her breath away, but didn't shatter her fragile joy…only made it shiver and shine more brightly. He gently bathed her face and body, smoothing the crystalline water over her skin like lotion, and she did the same for him, shivering with delight and learning his body with all the fascination of a child with a new toy, until both their bodies glowed rosy pink all over.

A black-and-yellow butterfly flitted past, and Mary uttered an enchanted little cry and reached for it.

"Uh-uh," Roan said, "come here… I'll show you how to catch a butterfly." Dipping water again from the creek, he stood behind her and brought her close to him, then dripped the water from his hand into hers. "Stand still," he murmured against her ear. "Hold out your hand."

She did as he told her, hardly daring to breathe. Moments crawled suspensefully past while she waited, and then…the butterfly fluttered drunkenly out of the sunlit sky… dipped and floated and swayed around her like a small plane trying to land in a high wind, and came to rest on her shoulder. She made a tiny sound, too overcome to move or speak as the butterfly slowly fanned its wings. Its legs tickled her skin.

"They like the water," Roan said softly. He captured it gently and placed it on her outstretched finger.

Tears rose to sting her eyes and clog her throat. *This is it. Happiness. This is how you find it. Not chasing after it recklessly, heedlessly. Standing still...letting it find you.*

All her life, it seemed, she'd been chasing that elusive butterfly, only to have it always dance away beyond her reach. And now, when she wasn't even trying, hadn't been looking for it, never expected it...happiness had come to sit on her shoulder.

The butterfly fluttered away, and Mary drew a happy, shivering sigh. Wondering if a day could be more perfect.

"You're gonna get burned," Roan said again, dropping a tender kiss onto her shoulder, just where the butterfly had been. "Better get your clothes on."

They dressed without urgency, helping each other, pausing to lean into lazy, intoxicated kisses. The breeze freshened, and the sun slipped behind a towering pile of clouds.

"Thunderheads," Roan said, squinting at the sky. "We'd better be heading on back— looks like it's gonna rain."

They walked back to the horses through the shade of the pines. Mary looked back over her shoulder for a last glimpse of the meadow, not sunlit now, but darkened by the cloud's shadow, and felt the shadow in her heart, too.

"It's such a beautiful place," she said wistfully. And then, though she didn't want to ask, the question forced its way past the ache in her throat. "Did you bring Erin here?"

There was only a slight pause while he bent to pick up a blanket and saddle and heave them onto the gray mare's back. Watching his hands settle the saddle and adjust the cinch, he said in a neutral voice, breathy and broken by the task he was doing, "Nope, never did…only found the place after Susie Grace was born…by that time she was home with the baby and I was busy being the sheriff… times of rambling through the wilderness like a couple of kids were over. Always meant to, though. Someday."

Mary cleared her throat and mumbled, "I'm sorry."

He threw her a look and a wry smile before he bent to pick up the second saddle. "I'm sure you've probably heard all about what happened. The fire, and all…"

She gave a shrug of apology. "It's a small town, Roan."

Roan gave the cinch one last tug and turned to look at her, one hand resting on the saddle. The sadness in his eyes and in his voice made her throat close. "Mary, Erin's always going to be here with me. I can't help that—

wouldn't be right if I tried. You don't stop loving somebody just because they die."

She nodded, aching, and whispered, "I wouldn't want you to." But she knew...her heart knew it was a lie.

After a moment, he gave an awkward little cough and his eyes narrowed with a frown. "Doesn't mean when a person loses someone, he can't ever love someone else again. If a man can't love, can't share his life with someone, he's only half-alive."

Mary didn't answer, only stared at him in silent agony while inside her battered heart was screaming at him. *What does that mean? Does it mean you think you might possibly... someday...love me? Don't talk in abstracts, dammit! Tell me what you* feel.

Thunder grumbled, not far off. Roan looked up at the sky and said, "Better get moving if we're gonna beat the rain home."

They made it to the barn by minutes— and not once during that wild ride home did Mary think to be afraid—though by the time she'd helped Roan unsaddle and rub down the horses and they'd made a mad dash for the house through the downpour, they were both soaking wet anyway.

* * *

On Monday morning, Roan went to his office early. He was planning on going back over
everything he had on Jason's murder, hoping
to find something—anything—that would
lead him to the real killer. In order to clear
Mary he knew he was going to have to go back
to the beginning, go over all the evidence,
photographs, autopsy reports, forensics—
everything. But even with the early start, with
Boomtown Days activities and aggravations
it was late evening before he got around to re-
interviewing witnesses.

Monday night of Boomtown week wasn't
the best time to be in Buster's Last Stand.
Roan expected it to be a madhouse and it was,
noisy and crowded with a whole lot of people dressed up like cowboys, a few of them
maybe even the real kind.

Buster had hired some temporary help to
handle the crowd, so when he saw Roan come
in he stopped what he was doing to come over
and talk to him. Roan asked if he had a minute, and the big man said "Sure," and flung
his bar towel over his shoulder and followed
him outside.

"Sorry to take you away from your Boomtown business," Roan said as soon as he didn't have to shout to make himself heard.

Buster shrugged. "Ah, hell, I'm glad to get away from the racket. What can I do for you, Sheriff?"

Roan told him what he was doing and why. "I know there must be someone else Jason pissed off besides Mary," he concluded. "I want you to think back a ways, try to recall if there was anything else Jason said or did that might have got him killed."

Buster looked at him sideways and rubbed a big meaty hand over the lower half of his face, fidgeting like a schoolboy. Roan's scalp began to prickle. "Come on, let's have it. You've obviously thought of something."

"Ah, hell. I been thinkin' about this— didn't want to tell you, didn't think it could have anything to do with Jase's murder, on account of…well, because the only person it might give a motive to is *you,* Sheriff."

Roan narrowed a stare at him and growled, "Tell me."

Buster held up a hand. "I…all right, look, don't shoot the messenger, okay?" He shifted, looked over his shoulder, then cleared his throat. "Happened awhile back. Jase was drunker than usual…got to bragging to a bunch of the regulars about how the law in this town couldn't touch him. He was hinting—more than hinting—about all the things he claimed he'd done and gotten away with. One of them—ah, Christ, Roan—he said he'd had the sheriff's wife."

Roan's world went cold and dark and scary. Somewhere in it he heard his voice quietly asking Buster why he'd never mentioned any of this. And Buster's voice, nervous and tinny, saying, "Shoot, I thought you already knew, Sheriff. Figured Boyd woulda told you."

For an instant everything stopped. Then the cold and the blackness began to whirl around him. "Boyd?" he croaked.

Buster nodded, looking miserable. "Yeah, he was in here that night. Couldn't help but hear what Jase was saying. Thought Boyd might go for him then and there, you know? But the old man just finished up his beer and walked out without sayin' a word.

"I never did think you had anything to do with killin' Jason," Buster called after him. Roan was already striding across the parking lot, the keys to his sheriff's-department SUV gripped in his ice-cold hand.

It was late. He knew he had to go home sometime. Knew he'd have to talk to Boyd...sometime. Instead he found himself driving aimlessly through the streets of the town he'd lived in all his life, streets as familiar to him as his own backyard. Right now it seemed like an alien planet. His world had blown apart, everything he'd trusted and believed in turned upside down.

He kept going over it in his mind—even though his mind cringed and rebelled against the images playing through it like some grim movie flickering on an old-fashioned screen.

The way Jason was with women. The way Erin had been acting, those few days before she died. She was upset about something. Worried. Or afraid. What Jason did to Mary. A fire deliberately set, started in the master-bedroom wing, on a night when I was working late.

Was it possible? Could Jason have tried to hit on Erin, the way he'd gone after Mary? What if she'd fought back, threatened to tell Roan...what would Jase have done then? If what had happened with Mary was any indication, could he have tried to rape her? Even succeeded? Then, scared, set the fire to cover up what he'd done?

With a screech of brakes, Roan pulled over to the side of the road. He barely got the door open in time before he was violently, wrenchingly sick.

* * *

Although Susie Grace had been grounded for a week for her horseback-riding escapade, the way Mary saw it, being grounded meant no TV or Internet or playing with friends—or in Susie Grace's case, kittens. It didn't include books. So that evening when Susie Grace pouted about missing her favorite TV shows, Mary offered to read to her instead. She'd found a well-thumbed copy of *Charlotte's Web* in a bookcase in Roan's bedroom, with a hand-written inscription on the flyleaf that read: To Erin Elizabeth on your ninth Birthday. Love, Mama and Pop.

She was sitting on Susie Grace's bed with the child snuggled up next to her, her small scarred chin nudging against Mary's arm. Susie Grace had her arm around Cat, who was curled up on the other side of her, softly snoring. They hadn't gotten far into the book—a frightened and bewildered Wilbur had just been banished to the barnyard—when Cat lifted his head and gave a low growl. For a moment he froze there, big yellow eyes staring intently at the dark windows, the growl rising in pitch and volume. Then he jumped off the bed, landed with a heavy *thump,* and vanished under it.

Mary felt herself go cold. She closed the book and put a finger to her lips to tell Susie Grace to be quiet, then reached to turn off the lamp. With her heart beating fast and hard, she crept to the window and looked out. At first she didn't see anything unusual. Then something caught her eye—the glint of moonlight on the hood of a car. Not the pale buff of Roan's SUV, but a dark sedan, coming slowly along the lane with its headlights off.

"Where are the dogs?" she whispered, and jumped when Susie Grace answered her from close behind.

"They're probably at Grampa's. He lets them come in the house sometimes before he goes to bed. To keep him company."

Mary put her hands on Susie Grace's shoulders and bent down so her face was close to hers in the darkness. "Susie Grace," she said, her voice low and urgent, but calm, "I have to ask you something. Do you know if your daddy keeps guns in the house?"

Susie Grace's head moved emphatically back and forth. "He only has guns at work. Grampa Boyd has guns, though. Lots of them. They're at his house."

"Okay...sweetheart, here's what I want you to do." Mary's fingers tightened on the little girl's shoulders. "I want you to run to your grampa's house as fast as you can. Tell Grampa Boyd somebody's here—tell him it's a car you don't know. Then you stay there, you understand? No matter what happens, *you stay there*. Got it?" She gave Susie Grace a tiny shake, and the little girl nodded. "Okay—off you go. Quickly—go through the kitchen. And don't turn on the lights."

Halfway out of the room, Susie Grace turned. Mary could see that her hands were on her hips and her head tilted with indignation. "I don't need lights, I know my way blindfolded."

Mary gave a little spurt of laughter, went to her and bent to gather her into a hug. She could feel the little girl's heart beating, a slightly lighter and faster cadence than her own. "Go now—scoot. *Hurry.*" She kissed her, and Susie Grace slipped into the dark hallway.

After a moment, Mary went back to the window.

Empty and clammy, Roan drove the SUV through the darkness while more images flickered across the movie screen of his mind. *Jason lying in the morning sunshine with a bullet hole in his head and another one in his heart, and no fear at all on his face. Bullets from a Colt 45...the Gun that Won the West. Frontier justice. Boyd's collection of Old West memorabilia. Boyd, marching with his gun club in past Boomtown Days parades.*

Boyd.

There was no doubt whatsoever in Roan's mind that if Boyd Stuart believed Jason Holbrook guilty of setting the fire that killed his daughter, with no way of proving it in the eyes of the law, he wouldn't hesitate to take matters into his own hands. *He'd consider it frontier justice. Justice...for Erin.*

Calm settled over Roan like a cold thick fog, insulating sensations, muffling feeling, letting him calmly key on his radio mike and sign out for the night the same way he did every night. *"SD Mobile one, Donna... I'm headin' for the barn.... Out."* Then he headed home to confront the man who'd all but raised him, the man who'd been, in every way that counted, a father to him. The only one he'd ever known.

The storms that had blown through the day before were gone. The night sky was clear. The moon wasn't full, but it had risen to shed enough light so Mary could see clearly, now her eyes had adjusted to the darkness.

The dark sedan had rolled to a silent stop in the shadow of one of the giant cottonwoods. She didn't know how long she watched, standing beside the window while her heart kept up its frantic pounding and sweat crawled down her back in icy tickles. Then…she saw something move out there in the darkness. The car door opened…then shut without a sound, with no flare of light from the interior. Whoever it was, he'd thought to turn it off.

She wondered if it would be the hitman who'd shot at her on Saturday…or if Diego would come for her himself this time.

One thing she knew—she wouldn't wait for him here. In the house she'd be trapped; there was no place to hide where he wouldn't find her. Now that Susie Grace was safe, she thought, it would be better to run. Outdoors, in the maze of corrals and sheds, stables and animals, she'd have a chance. But how to escape? If she picked the wrong door she could run right into the intruder's arms. And there were only two ways out of the house, not counting the boarded-up hallway—the front door, and right around the corner from there, the kitchen.

Susie Grace had gone out the kitchen door, so it would be unlocked. The intruder would probably come in that way. Which left the front door for her.

She crept out of the bedroom, down the hall and into the living room. When she heard the kitchen door creak softly, she wrenched open the front door, flew across the porch and down the steps, and *ran*. She ran instinctively, away from the sinister dark sedan, down the lane toward the old barn, bypassing the stables and the restlessly whickering horses. She ran without heed, praying her feet would find their own way in the darkness, praying she wouldn't trip on a hummock of grass, praying Susie Grace had done what she'd been told and stayed at Boyd's where she'd be safe. *Praying*.

Running as hard as she was, with her heart and breath loud in her ears, she didn't hear the pounding footsteps until they were almost upon her. When she did hear them she gave a high, frantic cry and tried to run faster, but cruel hands caught her just inside the barn's wide-open door. She struggled wildly, but the hands jerked her back against a hard, panting body. An arm clamped viciously across her throat, cutting off her breath.

A breathless laugh gusted through her hair. "What're you fighting me for, Yance? I'm your fiancé, remember?" The voice was softly accented...well known to her.

The arm across her throat eased enough for her to gasp it out. *"Diego?"*

"Yeah, *querida,* who did you think? You know how long I been looking for you? Nice of you to make the news broadcasts, so I know where to find you, eh?"

"Diego, please—"

"Are you surprised to see me? Ah—well, you see, after the man I sent to kill you missed, I got to thinking...shooting is too easy a way for you to die." His lips were close to her ear...his hot breath misted her cheek. "I think you should know what you did to me, sending me to prison. I want you to experience what I did...what was done to me, all those years. *Then* I kill you slowly...with my bare hands...while you look in my eyes—"

"Turn her loose." The voice rasped through the darkness, a sound like a rusty hinge.

Roan turned the SUV onto the ranch's gravel road, his fingers beating a restless tattoo on the steering wheel. Now that the moment of truth was here, his heart felt sore and heavy. How could this have happened? He'd have done just about anything—paid a high price in sweat, blood and tears, to set Mary free from the murder charge against her. Now he knew just how high that price was going to be. *Dammit, Boyd.*

Up ahead he could see the house was dark. Kind of early for everyone to be in bed, he thought, but maybe because Susie Grace wasn't allowed to watch TV...

Then he saw the dark sedan.

Diego spun toward the sound, jerking Mary around too, pressed against him, his arm tight against her throat again.

"I said, turn her loose." Boyd was a dark silhouette in the barn doorway, his bow-legged shape like something out of an old Western movie. Like something from a Western movie, too, was the old-fashioned weapon he held in his hand.

When Mary heard the clicking sound of the gun being cocked, she reacted out of instinct, perhaps helped by the self-defense classes she'd taken long ago. She stomped savagely on Diego's instep, then let her body go limp.

Diego DelRey wasn't a powerful man. In pain, and finding himself with Mary's full dead weight in his arms, he gave a bellow of rage and let her slip to the ground.

Roan was out of the SUV before the wheels had stopped turning. A quick check of the sedan told him it was empty. He was heading for the house at a dead run when he heard the shot.

It sounded like thunder, trapped in the confines of that old wooden building. As it died away, Mary could hear panic-stricken wings flapping somewhere up in the rafters. Somewhere behind her, Diego was a motionless dark shape in the straw. She lifted her head and saw Boyd standing in the barn doorway, his arm hanging limp at his side, the gun pointing at the floor. She gave a little whimpering cry and was scrambling over to him on her hands and knees when she saw Roan running toward her.

She tried to rise, but her legs wouldn't hold her. And then he was there, helping her up, folding her into his arms and holding her tightly. Whispering brokenly into her hair. "Oh God... Mary... Mary. Are you okay? Did he hurt you? Oh... God... Mary."

Roan held on to her shaking body and knew he didn't want to let go of her ever again. But when Boyd walked over to him, he knew he was going to have to, for a little while, at least. He peeled himself away from her and turned her into the curve of his arm to keep her close, and Boyd handed him his old Colt 45 revolver, butt-first.

"Want you both to know," the rancher said in his gruff and crusty voice, "I wouldn't'a let her go to jail." He hesitated, then touched the bill of his cap and gave a little nod. "You got things to finish up here. I'll be waitin' for you in the car."

His footsteps crunched away into the night.

Roan caught Mary's arms. "Susie Grace—"

"It's okay—she's okay. She's at Boyd's." Her voice broke and grew thick with tears. "Oh Roan… *Boyd?*"

"I'm afraid so." Aching with love and grief, he took her face between his hands and whispered as he kissed away her tears, "It's all over, Mary. The nightmare's over. You're free."

It was the wee hours of the morning before Mary got to sleep. Long after Roan had left to accompany Boyd and Diego DelRey's body back to town, after Susie Grace had fallen asleep with a placidly purring Cat tucked under her arm, she sat huddled in the middle of Roan's bed, hugging her drawn-up knees, with the words Roan had said to her echoing inside her head.

The nightmare's over. You're free.

Why, then, did she feel such desolation?

She must have fallen asleep at last, because she woke up when she heard Susie Grace in the kitchen, rattling cereal bowls and scolding Cat for jumping on the counter. She got up, sticky-eyed and fuzzy-headed, long enough to see Susie Grace off on the school bus, then crept back to bed, too dispirited to begin the task of packing. She knew she had to do it— Roan would be coming back, soon, to take her home. *Not home. To Queenie's house, not mine.* Boyd had been arrested for the murder of Jason Holbrook, who had killed his daughter... Roan's wife. The charges against Mary would be dropped. She could have her car back. Her life.

My life. But what is my life now?

Again, she must have slept. She woke with her throat parched and chest aching, having dreamed—Roan had been wrong about the nightmares—of being chased endlessly by something or someone terrifying she couldn't see. As she lay in groggy half-awareness, it came again—the sound that had awakened her—a wrenching metallic screech.

Scrambling out of bed, she rushed into the hallway. And saw Roan, with a crowbar in his hands, pulling nails out of the boards that held the plywood barricade in place.

"Roan?" she said in a wondering voice. Her stomach dropped and her legs weakened at the sight of him. He threw her a look of such endearing uncertainty, it grew hard for her to breathe.

"Sorry to wake you," he grunted as he attacked another nail, not sounding sorry at all.

"What are you doing?" She ventured closer, catching her hair with both hands and dragging it back from her forehead.

"Thought maybe it was time I finished this." He glanced at her, then quickly away to stare narrow-eyed at the last remaining board, just above his head. His voice was a muffled rumble. "Never know —might have need of it someday."

He lifted the crowbar, wedged it under the board and gave it a mighty yank. The board came away with another of those ear-splitting screeches. He tossed it aside and stretched his arms wide to grasp the edges of the plywood. His muscles bulged beneath the soft fabric of his shirt as he lifted it, turned it, and propped it against the wall.

Mary gave a little gasp as light poured into the dark hallway. Then she followed Roan as he stepped across the ragged threshold, into a forest of two-by-fours.

"Doesn't need all that much," he said, peering up at the underside of the roof. "Sheet-rock…a little paint. Bathroom's all plumbed." He looked at Mary, a longer look this time, and she saw the vulnerability he tried so hard to hide. "It'll be a nice big bathroom when it's done."

It came to her then, with a force and clarity that rocked her to the depths of her soul, what he hadn't been able to bring himself to say. *She knew.* "Roan," she said softly, "don't you think you should get back on the horse?"

For another long moment he glared at her, eyes narrowed and fierce, blue and bright as chips of sky. A great breath rushed from his chest. "Ah, hell, Mary, what do you want me to say? That I'd like it if you'd stay here with me? Maybe help me rebuild this place? Shoot, you know I would. But *I* know this ranch is a long ways away from the life that's waitin' for you out there. You're free to go back to it now. Pick up from where it got taken away from you ten years ago."

No—he wouldn't ask it of her. Wouldn't do that to her. The tears he could see shimmering in those green-gold eyes of hers were hard enough to bear. He was so busy denying himself happiness, denying it so vehemently, it was a moment before he realized what she was saying, in her husky, shaking whisper.

"Roan...don't you know? There's nothing of that life I want. Not anymore. That life... was my past. My future?" She hitched one shoulder, and a tear spilled over and ran down her cheek. She brushed it away with a little laughing sob. "I'd like to think that might be here...with you. And Susie Grace."

"Really?" He felt exhausted, suddenly... wracked with pain and a sort of dazed and wary hope, the way he imagined a marathon runner must feel when he staggers across the finish line...unable to grasp the fact that the long race is finally over, and that he's won. "I'm just a small-town sheriff, Mary, all I've got—"

The tears in her eyes seemed to sizzle, now. "Maybe a small-town sheriff is what I want."

He frowned down at her, still not ready to believe. "You'd really stay with me? Marry me?" She nodded, vigorously, touching her fingers to her tear-drenched lips. He let out an exasperated breath. "Then I've really got to ask you, *why?*"

"Because I *love* you," she burst out, laughing and crying again. *Fire and rain.* "I really love you. So much I'm willing to marry you in the hopes that someday you'll come to love me."

"Come to—" He stared at her, stunned, then reached for her with shaking hands. "My God, Mary," he whispered as he pulled her to him, "don't you know? I do already. Love you."

"I know," she murmured with a long sigh as she snuggled joyfully against him. "I just wanted to hear you say it."

On the day Boyd Stuart was arraigned on murder charges for the shooting of Jason Holbrook, and the charges against Mary Owen were formally dismissed, Roan paid a visit to the cemetery. He went there fairly regularly, especially in the spring and summertime, when there were fresh flowers to put on Erin's grave. On this particular day, though, he found he wasn't there alone. When he saw the tall figure standing beside his wife's tombstone, head bowed, hat in his hands, expensively cut Western-style jacket hanging loosely from stooped shoulders, he checked and hitched in a breath before he went on.

"Mornin', Cliff," he said as he joined him.

Senator Holbrook looked over at him, nodded, then shifted his hat to one hand. "Roan... Uh, listen, I'll be getting out of your way. I just..." He waved a hand, cleared his throat and said gruffly, "They set Jason's marker today. I wanted to stop by before I left town, you know...just to check—make sure everything was right." He paused...gestured with his hat toward the simple granite block that bore the words, Erin Elizabeth Stuart Harley—Beloved Wife and Mother—Beloved Daughter. "I hope you know how sorry I am."

The pain in the other man's voice made Roan look at him, much as he didn't want to. The man who was most likely his father looked haggard...a hundred years old. Roan tightened his jaw and nodded, knowing the senator wasn't asking for his sympathy, wouldn't want it if it was offered.

"Jason was my son," Holbrook said in a voice like tearing cloth. "But I never would have—" His voice broke, and he finished in a harsh whisper. "You have to believe—I didn't know."

"I know," Roan said, with a tightness in his own throat. He held out his hand. After a brief hesitation the senator took it in both of his, his politician's handshake.

"Son…" For a long moment the man's glittering blue eyes gazed back into Roan's. Then he squeezed his hand once more—hard—and went striding away across the grass.

Roan watched him go, then huffed out a breath and reached to lay the sprays of lilac he'd brought on top of the tombstone. A few minutes later Mary came to join him, holding Susie Grace by the hand—his two red-headed women. Tears misted his eyes as he lifted Susie Grace up so she could add her sprig of lilac to his, then took Mary's hand and held it while she put hers there, too. Then they all turned and walked back to the car together.

Something stirred through his hair like warm breath…caressed his cheek with loving fingers. The wind? Perhaps…it could have been. But Roan knew better; his Spirit Messenger's touch was familiar to him now.

This time, he had the strangest feeling she was saying goodbye.

Epilogue

Joy gave the bridal veil one last twitch, then leaned down to lay her cheek alongside Yancy's—*no, Mary*—she must remember to call her Mary from now on. "It's just perfect—you look absolutely beautiful, sweetie pie."

She straightened up to look out the windows, checking on the girls. She saw her daughter Carrie prancing across the Hartsville United Methodist Church lawn, showing Susie Grace exactly how she was supposed to scatter the rose petals in her basket. Susie Grace looked absolutely perfect, too, in her frothy yellow flower-girl dress and blue cowboy boots, a wreath of daisies in her red hair.

"Okay, now, stand up," Joy ordered, turning back to the bride. "Let me have a look at you…okay, no wrinkles…oops—you've got a smudge of lipstick…" She stood back, hands on her hips. "Darlin', have you been kissin' the groom ahead of time? Now, *shame* on you."

Mary gave a guilty giggle. "Guess I just couldn't help it. You should see him—he looks so adorable in his black Western-style suit—kind of like a riverboat gambler."

Joy reached for her hands and gave them a squeeze. Her throat was tight with emotion. "Oh, honey—you really have found it, haven't you? That rainbow you were chasing? The fairy tale…happiness."

A laugh burst from her dearest friend's lips, along with a sob. Her lovely green-gold eyes sparked fire…streamed rain.

"Yes," Mary whispered, and her smile was like the sun breaking through. "Oh, yes."

* * * * *

YES! Please send me **The Hometown Hearts Collection** in Larger Print. This collection begins with 3 FREE books and 2 FREE gifts in the first shipment. Along with my 3 free books, I'll also get the next 4 books from the Hometown Hearts Collection, in LARGER PRINT, which I may either return and owe nothing, or keep for the low price of $4.99 U.S./ $5.89 CDN each plus $2.99 for shipping and handling per shipment*. If I decide to continue, about once a month for 8 months I will get 6 or 7 more books, but will only need to pay for 4. That means 2 or 3 books in every shipment will be FREE! If I decide to keep the entire collection, I'll have paid for only 32 books because 19 books are FREE! I understand that accepting the 3 free books and gifts places me under no obligation to buy anything. I can always return a shipment and cancel at any time. My free books and gifts are mine to keep no matter what I decide.

262 HCN 3432 462 HCN 3432

Name _____ (PLEASE PRINT)

Address _____ Apt. #

City _____ State/Prov. _____ Zip/Postal Code

Signature (if under 18, a parent or guardian must sign)

Mail to the **Reader Service:**

IN U.S.A.: P.O. Box 1867, Buffalo, NY, 14240-1867
IN CANADA: P.O. Box 609, Fort Erie, Ontario L2A 5X3

Get 2 Free Books,
Plus 2 Free Gifts—
just for trying the Reader Service!

Get 2 Free Books,
Plus 2 Free Gifts—
just for trying the
Reader Service!

HARLEQUIN *super romance*

Get 2 Free Books,
Plus 2 Free Gifts—
just for trying the Reader Service!

HARLEQUIN
HEARTWARMING™

Get 2 Free Books,
Plus 2 Free Gifts –

just for trying the Reader Service!